Of Cats and Elfins

Also published by Handheld Press

Of Cats and Elfins

Short Tales and Fantasies

by Sylvia Townsend Warner
with an Introduction by Greer Gilman

Handheld Classic 13

This anthology was published in 2020 by Handheld Press.
72 Warminster Road, Bath BA2 6RU, United Kingdom.
www.handheldpress.co.uk

ISBN 978-1-912766-15-4

2 3 4 5 6 7 8 9 0

Series design by Nadja Guggi and typeset in Adobe Caslon Pro and Open Sans.

Printed and bound in Great Britain by Short Run Press, Exeter.

MIX
Paper from
responsible sources
FSC® C014540

Contents

Greer Gilman is the author of *Moonwise* and *Cloud & Ashes*, and two critically-acclaimed novellas about the poet Ben Jonson, as well as poetry and criticism. Her fantasy fiction, rooted in British myth and ritual, has won the Tiptree, World Fantasy, and Shirley Jackson Awards. Her essay 'The Languages of the Fantastic' appears in *The Cambridge Companion to Fantasy Literature*.

Introduction

BY GREER GILMAN

> 'So you speak cat.'
>
> 'A little,' I replied. 'I understand it better than I can speak it.' (87)

Sylvia Townsend Warner had an ear for languages:

> I have three cats, all so loving and insistent that they play cat's-cradle with every train of thought. They drove me distracted while I was having influenza, gazing at me with large eyes & saying: O Sylvia, you are so ill, you'll soon be dead. And who will feed us then? FEED US NOW![1]

Like Warner's ruthlessly exquisite Elfins, cats are pragmatic creatures – predatory, sleek, unsentimental in affection – going on with their quite other lives, aslant of us.

On reading her *Kingdoms of Elfin* stories, David Garnett wrote to her:

> They are magnificent. Unequal perhaps, but quite unlike anything written before. It is rather as though a child who was quite certain of the facts of its imagination had dictated them to – Voltaire perhaps – and imposed her vision on that skeptical creature.[2]

There is not a trace of romanticism in her fantasy: no smoke and sulphur hang about her witches, no 'tufts and vapour' glorify her Elfins.[3] Indeed, John Clute sees in her writing 'an almost impersonal joy'.[4] From the first – her witch-book *Lolly Willowes* (1926) – Warner's ethos is unique to her: an anarchic imagination bodied in a style of crystalline and formal beauty. Both artistry and anarchy are hers in grain. Even the kindergarten that expelled her for unruliness admitted grudgingly that 'Sylvia always sings in tune'.[5]

Of Cats and Elfins brings together Warner's uncollected short fantasy fiction, from the lovely, Ovidian 'Stay, Corydon, Thou Swain' (1929) to her magnificent last Elfin story, 'The Duke of Orkney's Leonardo' (1976). At its centre is *The Cat's Cradle Book* (1940), a collection of feline folktales, nimble and merciless. You will note the long intervals. Fantasy ran underground with Warner, flashing out like a hidden river, each time in a new landscape: witchlore; myth; folktale; invisible kingdoms. What they share is Warner's worldview, her inimitable voice.

I

In 1929, Warner wrote two Englished variations on the *Metamorphoses*. *The True Heart* tells a story of Sukey Bond, in love with Eric Seaborn on the Essex marshes; it retells the myth of Cupid and Psyche. In 'Stay, Corydon, Thou Swain', an unApollonian West Country draper pursues a nymph. As in *A Midsummer Night's Dream*, the trouble begins at a rehearsal:

> Moonshine had to be consulted, for many of the singers lived outside the town and would not venture from their homes at night unless they could see the ruts and puddles. Mr Mulready was independent of the moon. (71)

Or so he thinks: for at a line of a madrigal, he is bespelled. 'Thy nymph is light and shadow-like'. (220)

Mr Mulready 'had never to his knowledge given a thought to these strange beings before, and yet it now seemed to him that he had an idea of them both clear and pleasant – as though perhaps in childhood he had been taken to see one as a treat' (72). And at once, 'as though' is simple fact: 'He wished to see a nymph again' (72). Desire – or perhaps design? – calls her into being. 'His mind's nymph was Miss Edna Cave, the young lady who sold stay-laces and suchlike female oddments in a dark secluded corner of his shop' (74).

Riding into Merley Wood by moonlight, they lay down their bicycles beside a blackthorn hedge. 'It seemed ... as though light had rested upon the dead boughs and turned into blossom' (78). Blackthorn flowers are ill-starred. He knows that. But moon-meddled, possessed by his vision of the bright elusive other, he is not attending to the lyrics:

> Thy nymph is light and shadow-like;
> For if thou follow her, she'll fly from thee;
> But if thou fly from her, she'll follow thee. (220)

II

The Cat's Cradle Book

It begins with an enchantment:

> With trees all around it, with a deep mossy lawn in front of it, the house lay like a pear fallen from a tree – a pear beginning to grow sleepy. (85)

We are at the threshold of a dream – and its dissolution. For a 'sleepy' pear is one just over-ripe, and turning toward rot. The spell will not hold.

The introduction is itself a fable on the fraility of storytellers, the enduringness of story.

But for now, the passer-by is bidden into the walled garden by its startlingly handsome *genius loci*: the spirit-servant of his nineteen cats and their kittens. '"Three O'Toadies, Melusine's five ... I should have said twenty-seven cats," said the young man. "But I was reckoning them as a caterer."' (89)

He is the cats' Grimm, collecting the fables that cats tell their kittens.

> The milk flows, and the narrative flows with it [...] But what is remarkable [...] is the universality and unanimity of these stories, the fastidious feline memory which enables Mrs O'Toady in Norfolk and Haru from Siam to preserve an uncorrupted text. I have as many as five separate versions of some of these stories. I have taken them down in shorthand and collated them. And there is scarcely a variant. (96)

Like Aesop's, their tales are of us; or of creatures trying on our manners, teetering in our shoes, a-swish in vestments. Like ballads, they are ruthless.

There is the fox who decides to become a saint, 'taking with him a great bundle of lettuces and a cold chicken to eat on Sundays and saints' days' (137), but refuses to be Pope; the poor tiger who has a Buddhist's virtue thrust upon him; the wolf 'who yearned for popularity' but decides to 'be as wolfish as possible' (195). An owl was a baker's daughter. 'Odin's Birds' are what they are.

> 'Did you ever see worse fools, quarrelling amidst such plenty? Which eye will you take, right or left?' (114)

The marquises of Carabas live haunted by the image of a cat whose vast inquity they cannot quite recall. They swoon in horror at the living sight of one. Among the fiercest of the fables, in 'The Magpie Charity', a rook and a crow refuse a wretched cat relief: he's not yet absolutely destitute. He can sell his black skin.

Two stories are of not-quite humans, young women whose distrusted strangeness is liberating. Bluebeard's daughter's monstrous heritage is evident. 'Her hair was a deep butcher's blue ... the inside of her mouth and her tongue were dusky blue like a well-bred chow-dog's' (198). With her (equally inquisitive) husband, she turns her curiosity skyward: 'it was she who worked out the mathematical calculations which enabled him to prove that the lost Pleiad would reappear in the year 1963' (214).

The trumpeter's daughter is a changeling and a maker of songs. She was hatched of a chrysalis; but now that her newborn green has faded, she's remarkable only for her unscrewedupness, her immunity to mortal, moral ills. Her otherness comes out in her insouciance. The songs she makes are heard as treasonous, blasphemous – and irresistible. As she has no place in this world, she steps out of it: steps down from the scaffold, out through the city gates, and onto the heath, where she meets with a tall brown man.

> 'Who are you? Have you a place in this world?'
>
> 'I have a hundred places,' he replied. 'I am a gipsy, and go where I please. Last week I was in Denmark, and tomorrow I am going to Wales.'
>
> 'That sounds a life to suit me,' said the girl. And she went with him. (172)

III

Elfins

Warner's roads led elsewhere for some while. Her later, historical novels are fantastic only in their power of world-rebuilding, as if imagining the past were subcreation. Her 1967 biography of another great queer fantasist, T H White, is a masterpiece. From 1936 on, she wrote scores of stories, largely mimetic, and delectable light memoirs for her 'gentleman friend' *The New Yorker*,[6] though she found some of its editorial choices 'too familiar, or not quite strange enough to be real'.[7] The stories are wonderful, uncommonplace – I fell in love with her voice before I even knew that she wrote fantasy – but the strangeness is restrained, downshifted into eccentricity: a very civil disobedience.

Then came her glorious outburst: 'Bother the human heart, I'm tired of the human heart. I want to write about something entirely different.'[8] Nearly all of her astonishing fairy tales, written from 1973 to 1976, were collected as *Kingdoms of Elfin*, and reprinted by Handheld Press last year – but not all. We get dessert.

In a letter to David Garnett (3 : iv : 1976), Warner wrote:

> I have just painted a Leonardo – very convincingly. It was part of the cargo of a ship bound for the Duke of Orkney, diverted by the Elfins, of Elfwick in Caithness, who lived by wrecking and pillage. I have also laid a hedge, raised a storm by witchcraft, eaten wild strawberries after midnight when they are chilled with dew, and enjoyed myself very much. After I had sorted and tidied the earlier Elfins to come out this autumn I forswore Elfinity and settled to a respectable human story. It was a pleasure to break my vow and go back to Elfindom.[9]

You can get drunk on windfalls. It is an absolute dizzy delight to have these Elfin tales again, since they fell out of print from their first presentation to the world by Susanna Pinney in 1984.[10] Three, from the Kingdoms of Deuce and Elfhame, and in exile from Tishk and Dreiviertelstein, are slighter pleasures; but 'The Duke of Orkney's Leonardo' is a seventh wave of a story.

'The child, a boy, was born with a caul. Such children, said the midwife, never drown' (52). Trammelled at birth, the boy will live a more-than-mortal span of years in thraldom to the wants of others, their ambitions and desires, and to his own self-loathing: a captive of his beauty and disfigurement. His mother sees him as a market asset, to be kept unblemished by the sun:

> In winter a woollen veil was tied over his face. This was worse than the hat, for it blinded him to his finer pleasures: the snow crystal melted in his hand, the wind blew the

feathers away before he had properly admired them. Baffled by the woollen grating over his eyes, he came indoors, where sight was no pleasure. (53)

He has a value, but no identity.

'Are you young what's-his-name?' he asked. The boy said he thought so. Sir Glamie said he was old enough to know his name. The boy agreed, and added, 'It used to be Bonny.' Sir Glamie replied that Bonny was a girl's name, and wouldn't do. (53)

He dubs the boy Gentle, for 'the worms, small and smooth and white, that fishermen called gentles, and impale on the hook when the water is too cloudy to use a fly' (54). In their naked vulnerability, there is an unsettling hint of prepubescence, of a changeless larval state.

At the Court of Rings, he's called Gentil. And there, Lief, a princess of Elfwick in the howling north of Scotland, takes the bait like a pike. Her power of choice, her confidence, are lordly. 'She had the air of being assured of admiration, but there was nothing beautiful about her except the startling blue of her eyes: a glance that fell on one like a splash of ice-cold water' (55). But he cannot drown in her. Though Lief can bully him into submissiveness, she cannot make him love: he is 'cold like a sea mist and as ungraspable' (58). Undaunted, she bears him off to Caithness, where 'the first winter lasted into mid-May' (57).

Lief's unfemininity is implicit in her verbs – 'compelled', 'assaulted', 'snatched' – and in her clashes with her mother. Performance is distasteful, but 'schooling herself to be daughterly and beguiling, she ... put on the gold and silver beads, and asked if she could borrow them'. The trinkets are for Gentil, but Queen Gruach 'thought she might be returning to her right mind' (63). Even when she's explicitly gendered as feminine, the princess is rough stuff:

'Lief continued to love her bad bargain with the obsession of a bitch … If anyone showed her a vestige of sympathy, she turned and rent him' (58). The bitch, one feels, is a deerhound.

As for Gentil, 'Her love was the worst of his misfortunes. He submitted to it with a passive ill will, as he submitted to the inescapable noise of the sea, the exploitation of a harshly bracing climate' (57). Like Shakespeare's Adonis, he 'had to be wound up to pleasure like a toy' (58). And like Adonis he will meet his boar: 'a young man, a Caithness mortal' (59). An artist.

> He was repairing a tumbled sheepfold. … The lappet of hair, the light toss of the small head that shook it back, the strong body stooping so easily, the large, deft hands nestling the stones into place were as beautiful and fit and complete as the marvels he had seen in his childhood. (59)

And then his living Goldsworthy moves on to 'a battle of opposing forces' (60) with a thorn hedge. Gentil follows.

Love has not the grace to kill him outright. His metamorphosis is botched, his wound not flowerlike but fungoid. And it locks Gentil and Lief into their roles of patient-prisoner and keeper, melancholia and rage on his part, weariness on hers.

The sea has a gift for them: but fortune must be forced

> 'A wind from the east?' said the head witch. 'You should go to my sister in Lapland for that.' He [the Purveyor] answered that he was sure a Caithness witch could do as well or better. She threw in another toad and said he should have his will. Handing over the purse, he asked if there was anything else he could supply. A younger witch spoke up. 'A few cats … seven, maybe.' 'Alive?' 'Oh, aye.'

> He carried the hamper of squalling cats to the place they commanded, and fled in trust and terror.

> The storm which impaled the Duke of Orkney's ship on the

Elfwick Cow did so at a price. Hailstones battered down the stooks and froze the beehives. A month's washing was whirled away from the drying yard. Shutters were torn from their hinges, fruit trees were uprooted, pigs went mad, the kitchen chimney was struck by lightning, the Purveyor, clutching at his heart, fell dead. Lief stepped over him on her way out. (65)

Her spoil is miraculous. The Leonardo that the sea casts up is both a mirror, a reversal of what is and what has been; and a window, opening out on what will be: 'the landscape of a summer morning ... each tree in its own territory of air' (67). It enlarges them both.

The likeness was inescapable: Gentil was gazing at himself in his youth, at the Gentil who had come forward and asked if there was anything she wanted; she had said, 'Nothing,' and nothing was what she had got. Tears started to her eyes and ran slowly down her cheeks [...] He turned and looked at her [...] The glittering, sidling tears were beautiful, an extraneous beauty on an accustomed object [...] She heard him give a little gasp of pleasure, saw him looking at her with delight, as long ago he had looked at an insect's wing, a yellow snail shell. Cautiously, as though she might fly away, he touched her cheek. She did nothing, said nothing, stretched the moment for as long as it could possibly last. They rose from their knees together and stood looking at the picture, each with an arm round the other's waist. (68)

Nothing sliding into nothing, into touch: into possibility.

$$0=0$$
$$\infty$$

After crossing over, they go on together:

List of Sylvia Townsend Warner's publications

BY INGRID HOTZ-DAVIES

For the establishment of this list, I am indebted to Claire Harman's (2008) very detailed chronology and to Janet Montefiore's bibliography (2014).

1925: *The Espalier* (poems, Chatto and Windus)

1926: *Lolly Willowes* (novel, Chatto and Windus)

1927: *Mr Fortune's Maggot* (novel, Chatto and Windus)

1928: *Time Importuned* (poems, Chatto and Windus)

1929: *The True Heart* (novel, Chatto and Windus)

1931: *Opus 7* (poem, Chatto and Windus)

1931: *A Moral Ending and Other Stories* (short stories, Furnival Books)

1932: *The Salutation and Other Stories* (short stories, Chatto and Windus)

1933: *Whether a Dove or Seagull* (poems, with Valentine Ackland, Viking Press)

1934: *Whether a Dove or Seagull* (poems, with Valentine Ackland, Chatto and Windus)

1936: *More Joy in Heaven* (short stories, Cresset Press)

1936: *Summer Will Show* (novel, Chatto and Windus)

1938: *After the Death of Don Juan* (novel, Chatto and Windus)

1940: *The Cat's Cradle Book* (short stories, Chatto and Windus)

1943: *A Garland of Straw* (short stories, Chatto and Windus)

1947: *The Museum of Cheats* (short stories, Chatto and Windus)

1948: *The Corner that Held Them* (novel, Chatto and Windus)

1949: *Somerset* (non-fiction, Paul Elek)

1951: *Jane Austen* (criticism, The British Council)

1954: *The Flint Anchor* (novel, Chatto and Windus)

1955: *Winter in the Air* (short stories, Chatto and Windus)

1957: *Boxwood*, first edition (poems, Monotype Corporation)

1958: *By Way of Sainte-Beuve* (trans. of Marcel Proust, *Contre Sainte-Beuve*, Chatto and Windus)

1960: *Boxwood*, second enlarged edition (poems, Chatto and Windus)

1962: *A Place of Shipwreck* (trans. of Jean-René Huguenin, *La Côte Sauvage*, Chatto and Windus)

1962: *A Spirit Rises* (short stories, Chatto and Windus)

1966: *A Stranger With a Bag* (short stories, Chatto and Windus)

1967: *T. H White* (biography, Jonathan Cape)

1968: *King Duffus and Other Poems* (poems, privately printed)

1971: *The Innocent and the Guilty* (short stories, Chatto and Windus)

1977: *Kingdoms of Elfin* (short stories, Chatto and Windus)

Posthumous publications (excluding reprints)

1978: *Azrael*, intr. Peter Pears (poem, Libanus Books)

1980: *Twelve Poems*, pref. Peter Pears (Chatto and Windus)

1981: *Scenes of Childhood and Other Stories* (short stories, Chatto and Windus)

1982: *Collected Poems*, ed. Claire Harman (Carcanet)

1984: *One Thing Leading to Another*, ed. Susanna Pinney (short stories, Women's Press)

1985: *Selected Poems,* ed. Claire Harman (Carcanet)

1988: *Selected Short Stories*, ed. Susanna Pinney and William Maxwell (Chatto and Windus)

2001: *The Music at Long Verney: Twenty Stories*, ed. Michael Steinmann (Counterpoint Press)

2006: *Dorset Stories*, ed. Peter Tolhurst (Black Dog Books)

2008: *New Collected Poems*, ed. Claire Harman (Carcanet)

2008: *Journey from Winter: Selected Poems of Valentine Ackland*, ed. Frances Bingham (Carcanet). Contains full text of *Whether a Dove or a Seagull* (1934).

Elfin stories published in *The New Yorker*

January 22, 1972: 'Something Entirely Different', 28–33 (titled 'The One and the Other' in *Kingdoms of Elfin*).

June 23, 1973: 'The Five Black Swans', 36–39.

September 10, 1973: 'The Revolt at Brocéliande', 38–42.

Note on the text

The text of this edition was generated by non-destructively scanning earlier print copies of the stories in their first editions, or later editions where the first editions were unavailable. Obvious typographical errors have been corrected, but Warner's punctuation and deliberately archaic spellings have been retained. The stories are products of their period, and *The Cat's Cradle Book* in particular contains words now considered problematic but which at the time of publication – first published in the USA in 1940, in the UK in 1960 – were in common use.

1 The Kingdom of Elfin

No census has numbered them; no income-tax collector knocks on their green hills, or drops yellow forms into their hollow and holy trees; their children, except for a few changelings, do not attend the Board Schools, their criminals slip through the fingers of policemen, and their dead are buried without certificates. As regards this last point, indeed, there are some who hold that fairies do not die; yet one of our most reliable and accurate poets has confuted them. 'Did you ever see a fairy's funeral, madame?' Blake once said to a lady who happened to sit by him in company one night at dinner. 'Never, sir,' was the answer. 'I have,' said Blake, 'but not before last night. I was walking alone in my garden; there was great stillness among the branches and flowers, and more than common sweetness in the air; I heard a low and pleasant sound – I knew not whence it came. At last I saw the broad leaf of a flower move, and underneath I saw a procession of creatures of the size and colour of grey-green grasshoppers, bearing a body laid out on a rose-leaf which they buried with songs and then disappeared. It was a fairy's funeral!'

Blake was fortunate. It is not given to many humans to see the Little People so clearly, still less to assist at their ceremonies; a peaked face looking down for a moment from the dusk of an ash-tree, a sudden small fierce nip on one's arm, a vapoury streak across the snap-shot of a picnic-party ... that is as much as the commonalty have any reason to expect. It is sometimes said that we have but our own obtuseness to blame for not seeing fairies more often than we do; but this is to attach too much importance to our idiosyncrasies, even to such a well-established, long-standing idiosyncrasy as obtuseness; for if we fail to see the fairies it is not because we are too stupid to see them, but because they are too clever to allow themselves to be seen by us.

It is a sad fact, but undeniable; the Kingdom of Elfin has a very poor opinion of humankind. I suppose we must seem to them shocking boors, uncouth, noisy, ill-bred and disgustingly oversized. It is only the fairies with a taste for low company, like Puck and the Brownies – who are considered in Elfhame to have exchanged their birthright for a mess of pottage – that make a practice of familiarity. And it is to be observed that they, for choice, frequent the simple and rustic part of mankind, and avoid professors and students of folk-lore as witches avoid the herbs vervain and dill. For example, we may instance Robert Wace, who about the year 1155 made a journey to the forest of Broceliande, at that time a sort of Elfin Le Touquet. Not a wing, not a wand, not the least gleam of a fairy did he see; all that he got for his pains was a country holiday, healthy, no doubt, but severely shorn of the amenities that a well-educated poetical gentleman considers his due; and in his pique he summed up an account of his fool's errand in the following lines:

> La allai je merveilles querre;
> Vis la forêt et vis la terre,
> Merveilles quis, mais ne trovai;
> Fol m'en revins, fol y allai;
> Fol y allai, fol m'en revins;
> Folie quis, por fol me tins.

Which may be Englished something like this:

> Thither went I wonders to seek;
> The forest I saw and the pastures eke.
> Wonders I looked for but found none,
> And a Fool came home whence a Fool has gone.

Whence a Fool had gone a Fool came home;
What a Fool was I after Folly to roam!

Yet perhaps Robert Wace may be thought to have got off pretty lightly to have come home with nothing worse than a few scratches, some midge-bites, and a revised estimate of his wisdom; for many of those who have thrust themselves in upon the fairies have had good cause to rue their presumption.

'The useuall Method for a curious Person to get a transient sight of this otherwise invisible Crew of Subterraneans,' says Mr Robert Kirk, Minister of Aberfoil, a worthy cleric who found the fairies a great deal more congenial than his parishioners, 'is to put his left Foot under the Wizard's right Foot and the Seer's Hand is put on the Inquirer's Head, who is to look over the Wizard's right Shoulder … then will he see a Multitude of Wights, like furious hardie Men, flocking to him haistily from all Quarters, as thick as Atoms in the Air. These through Fear strike him breathless and speechless.'

Nor do the fairies always content themselves with giving these Peeping Toms the fright of their lives. Often they go further, causing them to fall into languishing sicknesses, harrying them with ignominious accidents, and even pursuing them to death. They commonly employ one or two methods: blasting, or shooting with an elf-bolt, a weapon preserved in great quantities in County Museums under the name of flint arrow-heads. Jonet Morisoune, accused in 1692 of witchcraft and consorting with evil spirits, being asked the difference between shooting and blasting, declared that: 'quhen they are shott ther is no recoverie for it and if the shott be in the heart they died presently (*i.e.,* immediately), bot if it be not at the heart they will die in a while with it yet will at last die with it and that blasting is a whirlwinde that the fayries raises about that persone quhich they intend to wrong quhich may be healed two wayes ether by herbs or by charming.'

To those who seek some scatheless method of scraping acquaintance with these proud and capricious 'little Puppet Spirits which they call Elves or Fairies' I would recommend one of the following expedients:

1. To be a country-woman with a new-born baby;
2. To be a young child;
3. To be a handsome man;

Fairy mothers are passionately attached to their children, but, as one might expect, they are not of a very domesticated temper, and the royal and noble fairies in particular have so many social engagements that it is essential for them to employ a nurse. As some human mothers believe that the most devoted nurses are to be found among the less sophisticated races – an ayah, an amah, or a Coal-black Mammy – so do the fairies think that the plodding and bovine nature of human-kind is peculiarly well-adapted to provide reliable old-fashioned nurses for fairy babes. So earnest are the fairies to get them that there is no sleight or boldness that they will stop at, sometimes wiling them from their homes with the show of a gold ring or cup bobbing upon the current of a stream, at other times actually entering the house of a lying-in woman and spiriting her away in a gust of wind or a sudden darkness.

It is not so clear why fairies should steal human children, putting a changeling in their place. One school of thought holds that the fairies are obliged to sacrifice one of their number every seven years to the Devil, and that they have hit upon the scheme of substituting a human tribute, one of them, perhaps, having peeped over the shoulder of a clergyman who was reading his Bible abroad in the fields and seen therein how Abraham substituted a ram for his own flesh and blood. Be this as it may, the accounts of changelings are numerous and well-authenticated. And to give the fairies their due it must be said that their parental solicitude appears very strongly in their behaviour to their foundlings. In Waldron's *Works* is a description of a changeling child whose human mother was a charwoman. Though this child 'were left ever so dirty, the woman, at her return, saw him with a clean face, and his hair combed with the utmost exactness and nicety'.

But undoubtedly the best way of getting to know a fairy is to marry one. This has frequently been done, though – humbling reflection for my sex! – it is only female fairies who enter into these marriages, for though there have been cases of fairy seducers no earthly woman's charms have been powerful enough to bind a fairy to her in honourable matrimony. The first authentic notice of the fairies is that of Pomponius Mela, the Roman Geographer; but on one count Pomponius would seem to have been misinformed; for he describes the nine fairy women who lived on the island of Sein, off the coast of Brittany, as being vowed to perpetual virginity; and from all that we know of fairies this must seem extremely improbable. Their amorousness is proverbial, and no doubt the fairies who married human mortal husbands were induced to this rash step by the violence of their passions, coupled with a romantic and high-flown notion that there is something very fine about defying convention. Once married, however, they make admirable wives. Scandal has never dared to breathe a word against the fair fame of the Lady Tiphaine, wife of Bertrand du Guesclin: 'Laquelle avoit environ vingt-quatre ans, ne oncques n'avoit esté mariée, et estoit bonne et sage, et moult experte aux arts d'astronomie.' Nor was the celebrated Melusine, wife of Guy de Lusignan, Count of Poitou, any less wise and virtuous. She built her husband a castle by her enchantments, and bore him numerous children; and though in the end she was obliged to leave him it has always been admitted that the fault was on his side, and that any other self-respecting woman, under similar circumstances, must have done as she did.

next year's broad beans. For a queen, she was knowledgeable about vegetables. They fell into conversation, and did not see the young man come into the Royal Glade.

He was short, five foot, perhaps, only a head taller than an Elfin, but active and well-knit. He had a book in his hand, and read as he walked, pausing now and then to read aloud some passage that pleased him. Then a flush of excitement swept over his face as though the blood had leaped into his cheeks; and waned as quickly. With his hand on the tum of a page he looked round him with a sort of unrecognizing delight, then turned the page and read on. At last he closed the book, kissed it passionately and thrust it into his pocket. From the other pocket he pulled a stout cord, climbed nimbly up a young aspen, straddled along a bough, tied one end of the cord to it and a running knot at the other, fitted on the noose impatiently – for it stuck at his ears – and jumped.

The bough gave a pettish creak. Ermine and Jessamy turned at the sound. Jessamy took wing and flew to the tree, grasping his pruning knife, and muttering 'The young fool!' as though he would attack the trespasser. He slashed at the cord. The jerked bough was tom from the tree. Bough and young man fell to the ground together.

When Ermine ran up Jessamy spoke to her from his heart.

'Here's a fine piece of work, your Majesty. Why couldn't he choose an apple tree? Apple wood's too tough to break, he could have hung himself from an apple tree and harmed nobody. But the young fool must needs pick on an aspen – and the best bough of it. Look how the leaves are trembling!'

The leaves were trembling, but silently. She picked at the knot of the noose and broke her fingernails before she could loosen it. Jessamy went off to get tar for the tree's wound. For a moment, sight came back into the young man's eyes. In that moment he saw a beautiful lady, richly dressed, bending over him. Behind her stooped head he saw the tremor of her wings. It was true.

On one of her impulses, Ermine had the young man carried into the palace and put to bed in a dressing-room where she could keep an eye on him. Moschatel, her mother's old bower-woman, would nurse anything from a privy counsellor to a hound: she took a mortal in her stride. He was a dull patient, for he gave her no trouble; he could give her no thanks either, for the jolt of the slashed cord had broken his larynx. When Ermine came in with a bunch of grapes or a flask of Hungary water he stared at her as though he would fill his eyes. She did not know what to make of him, and did not stay long.

Others knew exactly what to make of him. Jessamy had summed him up as a young fool. Lovers of nature, grieving for the young tree which would never be the same again, called him a typical vandal. Lovers of retirement saw him as the ultimate trespasser from whom not even the privacy of the Royal Glade was safe. The librarian who had examined the book in the young man's pocket said he had no taste: the book was vilely printed and the poems sentimental trash. As for his attempted suicide, it was universally condemned. The mortal span was contemptibly brief, anyhow; to shorten it, mere exhibitionism. Moschatel had never seen such bunions, and displayed them to Ermine.

'I wish I hadn't seen them,' Ermine confided to Sir Haggard. 'Do you think that's why he tried to hang himself?'

'To take the weight off his feet? No, my dear aunt. I can tell you all about that young man. His feet wouldn't carry him fast enough. He was a clerk at Tut Hill. He stole money, tried to falsify the accounts, spilt ink on the page, and ran away.'

'But how do you know all this? Moschatel says he can't speak a word.' Sir Haggard said he had heard it from Simpson.

'Simpson?'

'Simpson. Since nobody else would stir a finger to defend your property, I made it my business to introduce myself to Simpson, the fellow at Tut Hill, and remind him that he owed you rent for subterranean rights, and way-leaves. And that if he did not pay immediately we would blow the whole thing skyhigh – which as owners we are entitled to do.'

'But could we?'

'No need to. You never saw anyone more taken aback.'

'And he will pay?'

'Better than that. I am now on the board of directors. His conscience is in my hands.'

'But do people really have consciences? I thought they were a figure of speech!'

'We have no need of them. We have reason. But they are part of the mortal apparatus, as tails are to cats – and as sensitive. I admit, it took me some time to make Simpson acknowledge his conscience. You have a nose, I said. It tells you when an egg is bad. If you do not heed its warning, if you eat the egg, the badness of the egg infects your conscience. Proceeding from the analogy of his nose, I got him to agree that he was liable to fall into error and make incorrect decisions; and that when he did so, his conscience suffered, and revenged itself on him. He admitted that worry gave him dyspepsia. From that moment, I was sure of him. By process of correct analysis, I convinced him that his conscience was exasperated by his inattention, that hell has no fury like a conscience spurned, that it needed to be calmed and reassured; and that as he had lost control over it, he must entrust its welfare to an expert, who would guide him into discretion and inoffensiveness. And suddenly, as one who sees the light of reason, he asked me to join the board of directors. The other directors, I may say are quite useless – mere materialists, fettered to effects, incapable of deriving effects from causes. They thought pills would cure his dyspepsia.'

'What do they think about you?'

'They assume that I am just another director. Naturally, I remain visible, keep my wings well furled, and wear a cloak.'

Thinking all this over, Ermine wondered how Sir Haggard had directed Mr Simpson's conscience about the young man. In any case, the young man was dying. Jessamy had claimed the corpse for the kitchen garden, where he was preparing a new rhubarb bed; it wouldn't make up for the tree but was better than nothing. She hated rhubarb, but consented.

No money had come in from Tut Hill. However, no one expected it. Sir Haggard scorned the Managing Committee. Ermine was his only confidante, and sworn to secrecy.

'About those rents, Haggard. Are they any nearer?'

Sir Haggard explained that he was now entered on an extensive redirection of Mr Simpson's conscience, which was to be awakened to the undesirability of iron. If iron were desirable, the scheme of nature would have made it available, like water or herbage. It would not have to be dug out of the bowels of the earth, where the scheme of nature had wisely concealed it. Potatoes were in a different category. Reason buries them, reason knows where they lie and in due course digs them up; but in no case does it have to dig more than a foot below the surface, and never at random. Potatoes were demonstrably part of the scheme of nature; in some countries they form the staple diet of a population. Further, they have a secondary function as commodities and can be sold by the peck. Finally, they are labour-saving. The grower plants in spring, lifts in autumn, for the rest of the year he is free to enlarge his mind. Compare – Sir Haggard continued – the generous potato with iron. Unnaturally ripped from the depths where the scheme of nature has secreted it, even more unnatural – when dislodged by explosives, dragged through dark windings by women harnessed to trucks, it comes to the light of day unlicked as a bear cub, a confused lump which has to be smelted in a furnace. While all a potato needs is boiling, iron goes through a dozen processes, all of them noisy and laborious. And to what end? It can't be eaten, it is incapable of increase, its detritus smothers natural fertility.

'So you want him to grow potatoes?' said Ermine, again forgetting that he disliked being interrupted. 'They have pretty flowers – blue or lilac.'

'And grow them all over the Great Park with an easy conscience? No, dear aunt. My purpose is to make him dissatisfied with iron, then to repudiate it, then to go away.' Her interruption had disarranged him, and he went away himself.

She did not like being addressed as 'Dear Aunt'. But the fact remained, he was her nephew as well as her subject, she was consanguineously as well as constitutionally bound to see he didn't get into mischief. She sent a message to Lady Briony, announcing that she would visit her, without ceremony. Even if Briony, too, were sworn to secrecy, a little tact would unswear her.

'And how is Cato? As busy as ever?'

Lady Briony said Cato was busy as ever.

'And with the same interesting ideas? He can make the dullest subject quite enthralling. I envy you hearing so much of his conversation.'

Lady Briony's face grew red, and she stared at the carpet.

'Though I'm sometimes afraid he may overtax himself. Does he still talk in his sleep?'

'Yes, he still talks in his sleep. All night long. I don't know who he's talking to, but he's talking to somebody – arguing, cajoling, insisting, saying the same thing over and over again, wearing her down. I know it's a woman, some woman he's obsessed with. Of course, I don't mind. I've always said … But he has never been so frantic, so wrought up, before.'

'My dear Briony, I'm sure you're mistaken. You know how excited Cato gets when he's bent on something.'

'Yes. And she's what he's bent on now.' Lady Briony burst into tears.

'Come, come.'

'Some very stupid woman at that.'

'There, there.'

'I'm sure I wish him joy of her.'

'Briony, I can give you my word it's not a woman.'

'Then it's some boy! That's not much comfort.'

It was sufficient comfort for Lady Briony to dry her eyes and agree to Ermine's suggestion of a walk round the garden. The visit ended on a calm horticultural note.

Time went on. Rhubarb tart appeared on the menu. The plants grew splendidly, their stems were sturdy as walking-sticks and later in the year were made into rhubarb wine – for the water supply was still erratic. No rent money came from Tut Hill. Nothing was decided as to where the court should go when it left Deuce. The mine-workers had still to decide to revolt. The Managing Committee matured and perfected its plan for rehabilitation after the revolt had taken place. Rhubarb tart again appeared on the menu. Blackbirds and thrushes flocked to the Great Park, where they fed on the leftovers of picnic parties. At long last Jessamy's complaints precipitated Ermine into summoning her nephew.

'I don't wonder you are beginning to feel impatient. Simpson's mental progress would drive a tortoise to despair. But he's improving fast since I adopted a new method. I now combine strategy with reason. While I continue to work on his conscience with reason I appeal to his cupidity with strategy. I pointed out to him that the inherent property of iron is to sink. He saw the force of that quite readily – for him. Hidden underground by the scheme of nature, the inherent property persists. It goes on sinking. It can't do otherwise. Instead of rambling about horizontally, I said to him, follow it down, sink a perpendicular shaft. Persevere, I said. Blast your way. Think of that massy deposit awaiting you. My dear, he swelled like a bullfrog. It's really shocking, this mortal cupidity.'

'And will he find it?'

'That's neither here nor there. If he does he'll be so grateful, he'll eat off my hand. If he doesn't, he'll be so disheartened and out of pocket and probably bankrupt that his conscience will make mincemeat of him.'

❧

The door slammed, the light footsteps trotted down the passage. Mr Simpson said, 'Now we can get back to business.' Mr Simpson had grown grey, his forehead was deeply wrinkled, he stooped, he was a shadow of his former self.

'Who is that queer little packet?' asked Mr Utterthwaite, the new partner.

'He's what you might call a habituee. You'll get used to him.'

'He seems to talk a lot.'

'It's more than seems. He does. Not that there's any real harm in him. The men in the works call him the Tut Hill Mascot. The fact of it is, he's not all there. Delusions, and so on. One of those people with only one foot in the real world. There was a time when he used to right startle me, he seemed so positive – especially for a man of his size. Well, as I was saying, last year's profits—'

'Good Lord, what's that?'

There was a loud explosion.

The two men rushed to the window. Down in the hollow a cloud of thick yellowish smoke was wallowing out of the ground, wave after wave of it. A jet of water leaped up, pierced it, rose above it, wavered in a rainbow, frayed into descent. The jet continued to rise, the cloud of smoke was tinged with a watery sheen. As the jet slowly weakened, the watery sheen was transferred to the ground. Little jets of water rose everywhere, puddles were spreading, running together, beginning to form a shallow lake. A man was leaning over the pit-head, shouting 'Jack! Jack! Jack!' Suddenly a hundred voices were shouting. The man who had called for Jack had roped himself and been lowered down the shaft. When they pulled him up, he was drenched to his shoulders, his teeth chattered, his eyes stared out of his muddied face. By then, it was almost dusk. The cry, 'We've got him up,' sent the women surging to the pit-head. The hope that in a moment had grown sky-high was snapped short. They sat down to endure, and to gain the support of being huddled together, less wretchedly themselves in a common misery. Rumours flitted among them: that the jet of water had carried men in the deep shaft up to the surface, safe and alive; that the water had come from an upper layer and that at the bottom of the shaft it was dry; of what had been foretold by tea leaves, seen in a dream. Mr Simpson had hot drinks and food distributed among them; the parson came and exhorted them to trust in God, led them in prayer and got them hymn-singing. Because he was praying out of doors, he struck them as comical.

All night the water rose slowly and imperturbably, and as it rose an icy air came from it. By the first light they saw a lake with trees dabbling their branches, submerged islands of bushes, floating planks, drowned rabbits, and a bobbing bucket. The dawn wind rippled its surface.

The explosion had knocked Sir Haggard senseless. He came to, lying in a puddle. It was an uncomfortable repose, but better than the exertion of moving. He lay, and tried to account for it, and postponed that for later, preferring to watch a tiny fountain that twirled up among the grasses, and a couple of ants who had fastened on a pupa and were trying to carry it off in opposite directions. The insect world is dominated by instinct, he thought, which is why one so seldom sees an insect in a state of repose. He shifted his position. He saw concentric rings of water gliding away from him and realized the puddle had swelled to a wide pond. He struggled to his feet, fanned his wings to dry them, and flew to the palace to see how the Regulating Committee was managing.

They were holding a special meeting on the first floor, and had decided that the Queen must leave in the Royal Barge; working fairies had floated it out of its shed and moored it by the palace steps. They had also decided that there was no cause for alarm. Ermine was sitting in constitutional silence. Sir Haggard said that for himself he intended to be vulgar and fly. He kissed his aunt's hand and left.

It was the last he saw of her.

By midnight the Royal Barge had broken from its mooring and was knocking hollowly against the first floor balcony. In little more than an hour's time, the embarkation was in train. The youngest member of the Regulating Committee jumped aboard, the barge was steadied, the Queen was assisted into it, the rest of the Committee followed. It was then realized that there were no oars. Working fairies were sent to find them. After some time of searching in the darkness they returned with one oar and a hay-rake. The Chairman seized the hay-rake and pushed off – so vigorously that he almost fell overboard, and would have done if his fellow-members had not caught hold of his legs.

The Royal Barge was purely an Object of Parade. In the course of its long career as a symbol its timbers had shrunk. The heavy load and the scramble to save the Chairman forced them apart. Water poured in. It filled and sank. Other members of the court who were escaping on an extemporized raft saw the loss of the Royal Barge with horror. In order to get a full view they lined the side of the raft; it tilted and discarded them. All the working fairies survived, and so did Sir Haggard's minority party.

The flood subsided, leaving a thick layer of mud, strewn with corpses and the haunt of bluebottles. Those who returned recognized a few features, reclaimed some possessions, and withdrew to wait for better days. Sir Haggard did not return. Lady Briony had relations at the Court of Pomace in Herefordshire; he went as a visitor, was pleased to see Briony taking a more extrovert interest in life, liked the climate, and stayed on. It was there that he wrote his treatise, *On the Advantages of a Presidential System*. A copy of this, with Jefferson's marginal annotations, was in the library at Monticello, but has since been lost sight of.

3 Queen Mousie

As Elfins do not believe in survival after death they feel no obligation to placate the dead by post-obit tributes: monuments, animal sacrifices, shaving the head, wearing crape arm-bands, etc. Funeral pomps are reserved for monarchs. In the Northern Kingdoms of Thule and Blokula, the dead queen is sunk in a crevasse. At Broceliande she is cremated with fireworks. At Elfhame in Scotland queens are buried in air.

Before Queen Tiphaine had stiffened, the orifices of her body were plugged with spices, her corpse was dressed in scarlet and closely stitched into a scarlet shroud. Round the scarlet chrysalis was clasped a silver harness to which a couple of long silver chains were attached. To complete the rite, the chrysalis, attended by the court, would be carried to a remote and ancient pinewood on the heath, pulleyed onto a strong bough, and left to hang in the silver chains. The new Queen would set it swinging, and ride back to the palace where a banquet was served – distinguished from other banquets by the mort-breads (small buns with currant eyes and sugared teeth to represent skulls) laid in every place.

But the hanging and the banquet had to be postponed. Tiphaine had not named her successor. Till this was determined, she was put by in a cellar.

There she lay for some time. The season was quellingly cold, a freezing mist hung over the heath, the larks kept cover. Not till they mounted and a sufficiency of them had been netted and brought down to the Castle could the ceremony of Divination be carried out, for which the Court office-holders, accompanied by pages carrying flambeaux and caged larks, descend to the depth of the castle, where there is a well. Here the larks, which have had little weights wired to their feet, are cast one by one into the well. The name of each lark's lady is pronounced as it strikes the water and the Horologer with a stop-watch measures how long it struggles in her cause. It was beyond living memory when last a divination had been carried out but the Archivist had looked it up and compiled a list of Court ladies eligible for the succession. When at last the wind changed, the skies cleared, the larks mounted in skirl of song and the lark-catchers flew after them, all was in readiness. The list was in alphabetical order. 'Finula!' said the Archivist. The lark struggled and sank. The Horologer noted down the time. 'Nimue!' The lark struggled and sank. 'Parisina!' The lark struggled, the Horologer's eyebrows rose in amazement, but eventually the bird went under. 'Who is this Parisina?' asked the Bursar. 'I've never set eyes on her.' 'You have, you know,' answered the Archivist. 'But everyone calls her Mousie,' – and he hastened to call the next name. The final name – which if this had been a race-meeting one would call the favourite's – was 'Yolandine!' The lark barely flapped a wing before it sank. After a hurried conference the diviners agreed that it must be disqualified.

Fortunately, there were two larks left over for a retrial. To encourage a happy result, the larger was chosen for Yolandine. It struggled and sank. The diviners watched with embarrassment the Mousie lark making a brisk fight for its life. It seemed hours before it finally yielded. They climbed the long cold stairway to the Throne Room where everyone was assembled. Making their way into the back row they knelt before an inconspicuous middle-aged fairy and said with chattering teeth, 'Hail, Queen Mousie, Queen of Elfhame!' – for in the consternation of the moment, none of them could remember her right name. Mousie held out a trembling hand to be kissed, said, 'I am not worthy to follow such a queen,' and fainted.

It was the correct phrase of acceptance, and the thought darted through every mind that Mousie had been nursing ambitions ridiculously beyond her deserts. However, the larks had decided; the chopfallen expressions of the divining party showed there could be no possible handky-panky about it. Elfhame must submit to a Queen Mousie (the name uttered in the first loyal salutation is unalterable) and be the laughing-stock of Elfindom. Meanwhile, Mousie had recovered from her faint and was asking the Court Functionaries to retain their posts and guide her inexperience.

Two hours later, the mort-breads were in the oven and the hanging procession had set out. Queen Tiphaine was hoisted to her last resting place. Queen Mousie on horseback delivered the firm push which started her swinging, the court choir sang the traditional farewell of 'Rockaby, Lady, on the tree-top' (it still survives in a mutilated form as a Scottish lullaby), the mourners turned about and Queen Mousie led them back to Elfhame, where she presided at the banquet.

The worst was yet before her. She had to be undressed by her Ladies of Honour and laid to sleep in an unfamiliar bed.

Mousie was the child of a well-pedigreed house which was always meritorious and never rewarded – the kind of family which in Spain is called a *casa agraviada*, a slighted house. She was named Parisina, a family name; but as she was small and quiet and had a sharp nose, she was affectionately called Mousie, and by the time her parents were dead and Mousie no longer a pet name, it stuck to her as a nickname. As a nickname it was spoken without affection, but tolerantly. As the name of a Queen, it was spoken derisively.

She was not without her well-wishers. The functionaries, once they had got over the shock, built hopes on her simplicity and her willingness to be advised. Elfhame could do with a tractable constitutional monarch after the years of Tiphaine's headstrong charm and glittering insolvency. It was part of that insolvency that she died without naming a successor; but they might yet be glad of it, when they had formed Queen Mousie a little more and polished her natural diffidence, and provided her with a suitable Consort – a good-looking one, to compensate for her insignificance; but not showy.

Other well-wishers, good-looking and some even showy, were bringing themselves to consider bettering Queen Mousie's lot by marrying her. She was not really ill-looking; it was just that she lacked bloom. Nothing bestows bloom like a husband. The Bursar took alarm. He had watched with tenderness the Elfhame finances reacting to Mousie's constitutional compliance with his advice. She, and they, must be preserved at all costs from the depredations of love. Being, most fortunately, a widower, he proposed himself as a Consort. Without a flutter, she refused him, adding that she would say nothing about it. Afterwards it occurred to her that she should have garnished the refusal a little. But her mind had been differently occupied. She had just found an anonymous letter in her glove, telling her that Lady Yolandine intended to poison her that evening. The poison would be smeared on the rim of a loving-cup, and would be instant. She had been expecting something of this sort; but as her mind was essentially practical she had not expected Yolandine to act before making sure of the succession. Perhaps she had already made sure of it with tampered larks? Perhaps the anonymous letter was only another ill-natured hoax? – there had been several. The one thing she could be sure of was the concert. She had an ear for pitch, but not for music.

Punctual to the moment, she made her inconsiderable entrance to the saloon, sat down, signed to the company to be seated, signed to the players to begin. She had foreseen that the concert would open with a display-piece by the chief harpist. She had not foreseen that the second harpist also would shake back her flowing locks and take part in it. They played a piece referring to the cuckoo. The chief harpist sounded the interval with a twang, the second harpist replied with the same interval not so twangingly, since she represented a cuckoo at a distance. It was a beautiful May evening, warm and serene, and the real cuckoos were still at it, as they had been all day. The second harpist's cuckoos grew bolder, came nearer. In a climax of agreement, both harps twanged their interval in an approximate unison. A tremor of distress flickered over Queen Mousie's face, and Lady Yolandine, who till then had been watching her complacently, wondered if by any chance some fool had blabbed.

There were two more items, a melody with variations and fanfare for drums and trumpets, before the interval. During the fanfare Mousie saw Yolandine's current admirer hand her a silver loving-cup.

The interval was attained, people began to talk and move about. She sat and waited, Yolandine approached, walking with unhurried elegance – she was celebrated for her beautiful gait. She rose like a wave from her curtsey and held out the silver cup. Her hand was so steady that the wine was still as water in a well.

'Queen Mousie, I crave a boon. Drink with me to our eternal friendship.' She tilted the cup to Mousie's lip. There was nothing for it. Mousie drank, her eyes fixed on Yolandine's lovely face. She saw it transfigure with a look of intense delight. So this was revenge! She would not die without knowing this bewitching bliss. She gave a sudden twitch to the cup. 'Now you must drink,' she said, and turned the side where she had drunk towards Yolandine. 'Strike up!' she cried to the drummers. The drums beat, and Yolandine drank.

They remained face to face, holding the cup between them, each expecting the other to fall dead. Neither staggered, swelled, turned blue; it must be a slower poison than it was supposed to be. The concert went on, and after the concert there was dancing. The morning birds were chirping when everyone went off to bed, laughing and limping. Mousie beckoned to Yolandine and drew her into a corner.

'When we meet in the morning, remind me I must tell the Purveyor to buy fresh spices. They've lost their virtue, they've been kept too long. But you must remind me. By tomorrow I shall have forgotten all about it. I suppose he had better renew the poisons, too.'

Yolandine remarked that there was no commercial poison to equal the Blue Death Cap. But now was not the season for it. Perhaps in the late summer they might slip out before sunrise one morning, pretend to be hags, and gather it together?

Foiled in their murderous intentions by a blunted weapon, they thought better of each other. Friendship was out of the question. They felt a kind of brazen affinity.

Secure, at any rate for the time being, against being poisoned by Yolandine and sought in marriage by the Bursar, Mousie plucked up her spirits and re-addressed herself to the duties of a sovereign. The spice and poison cupboards were restocked, the Elfhame pearls were restrung, the Court officials given new uniforms, several ageing changelings dismissed and a programme of gaieties devised: this included a tournament to take the suitors off her hands. While the fine weather lasted, she was ignored. The weather changed, the tournament was held in a downpour, the court returned to its customary gibing and caballing; wherever she turned, she was impaled on looks of hatred. It occurred to her that if they could be got to hate each other instead of her, life would be pleasanter, and she summoned the Archivist to attend her in the Muniment Room. There, in an odour of dust and decaying parchment, she insinuated that his care of the Elfhame archives was not properly appreciated: one would expect people to be interested in their own family trees at least. The Archivist was conscious that several pedigrees had been impaired by mice, and agreed that Elfins nowadays had little respect for their ancestors. Her Majesty's family was a distinguished exception. He raised a creaking lid on a quantity of neatly rolled documents, where a gold-leaf crown and the date of her accession had been added to her birth certificate. When the news got round that Mousie's parchments filled an iron chest there was a general desire to prove a greater antiquity and grander connections. While her subjects bragged, disputed, made allegations, fought duels in defence of great-great-grandmothers, claimed dazzling bar sinisters and imputed discreditable ones, Mousie lived a quiet unmolested life, calm as a fish in the pool under the waterfall, and had the stables set to rights.

By following this strategy while varying her tactics, she became an accomplished schemer. If her life was comfortless, it was not without interest. Her skill was covert, she got no praise for it; but she kept a critical eye on her progress and never allowed herself to jeopardise the inconspicuousness which destiny had endowed her with. Just as in the coat of the most splendid tabby cat there is always one patch of dull second-rate fur, only noticeable to the hand that strokes the animal, Mousie was the dull patch in the court life of Elfhame, but, as no one stroked her, unremarked. She never employed a spy: the anonymous letters and the pasquinades pinned on the backs of screens and hangings did as well.

Of late the anonymous letters had taunted her with physical malformation, and the pasquinades insisted on the aloofness of a Virgin Queen. She saw that this was the moment to open a campaign which she had already given some thought to. Calling a Council, at which she wore her crown – a thing she did not commonly do for she had headaches enough without that – she waived her sovereign right to choose a consort, and requested that a Committee, whose member should be chosen by acclaim, would decide for her. Choosing the Committee took some months and engaged strong feelings. At the first sitting, the Chosen quarrelled till sunrise. The sittings continued. The Unchosen took turns to listen at the keyhole and report progress. They caught the word 'lobster' spoken with energy, and taken up by other voices. Subsequent listeners overheard mention of brooms, and bedroom candlesticks. Finally a page was concealed in the committee room, who reported that the Chosen talked about food, curling-matches, gallantries of past days, scandal about Queen Tiphaine; and constantly asked one another if he remembered Old So-and-So. They talked very innocently, he said.

Meanwhile Tomason, the Court Shoemaker, who had been journeying about Europe for skins, presented a sealed and scented letter to Queen Mousie, together with a list of travelling expenses. When she had checked the expenses, she opened the letter. It expressed Count Wolf's ardent willingness to become her Consort.

A Consort was a part of a Queen's equipage. Since marry she must, she intended to startle Elfhame, by importing a Consort from Europe. During the previous reign when an embassy from Dreiviertelstein in Styria visited Elfhame, a Count Wolf had been one of the party. He had well-turned legs, a dashing figure, china-blue eyes – so much she remembered; and was – so she had gathered – impecunious. Now he was hers. Tomason had carried the letter to Queen Aigle asking for his hand, and brought back the reply. Tomason was a natural genius, couldn't read, thought only of shoeleather; so he was a safe agent.

She allowed the Committee to deliberate a little longer and watched the Unchosen working up a loyal resentment at being kept waiting to know her fate. One unexpected morning she put on her crown, summoned her court to attend her and went to the Committee room. Her Chamberlain knocked three times on the locked door. It was opened, she went in and everyone thronged in after her. To their delight the Unchosen heard her say that she could not in conscience take up any more of the Committee's valuable time; that she was deeply obliged to them for their exertions, which she would reward by granting life pensions; and that as a mark of her confidence she had come to tell them that her choice had settled upon Count Wolf of Dreiviertelstein. She swept a curtesy and withdrew.

For once, for the first time, she was universally popular. She had supplied a rousing topic for conversation, the Unchosen had got the news hot, the Chosen had got their life pensions.

The swiftest flyer in Elfhame was sent to summon Count Wolf, and from the height of triumph Mousie fell into a pit of self-torment. Suppose he didn't come? Suppose she had kept him waiting too long, and all those adjectives had withered and dropped off and he had closed with a better offer? Why had she been so shortsightedly prudent, why had she wasted so much time nursing public opinion? The work of years might be undone in a night; she would be back again where she started – no, lower than that, even! Then, she was despicable. Now, she would be ludicrous.

But she was smiling and gracious and showed no ungainly surprise at being popular; and the swiftest flyer came back with the date of Count Wolf's arrival.

She had been through such turmoils of anxiety that the image of Count Wolf had become somewhat blurred. He was impecunious, with blue eyes and well turned legs ... When he arrived with a considerable retinue of cousins and no air of impecuniosity, she found that she had not remembered that his legs were bow-legs. But that, she remarked to Yolandine, was due to his horsemanship. The Dreiviertelstein nobility had a passion for riding. She did not want Yolandine to take against him.

Count Wolf's bow legs turned out to be positively advantageous. Male legs at Elfhame were long and straight. Their owners looked tolerantly at the waddling importee, a typical European, who had never played ice-hockey or a round of golf or run down a wild goat, and was so well fitted to be the consort of a Queen Mousie. As for his cousins, a good hard winter would see the end of them, as with cucumbers. Mousie also hoped to thin the ranks of the cousins. But this must wait till her plan for Count Wolf had come about. She owed Yolandine a debt of gratitude for not trying to poison her again; now she was in a position to repay it and please everyone concerned, not least her loyal court.

At suitable moments she directed her Consort's blue eyes toward Yolandine. He was slow to take the hint; but she persisted, as though she were teaching a child to walk; encouraging his first faltering steps, picking him up when he tumbled, re-directing him when he went astray. The smiling Yolandine watched, drew a little nearer, withdrew, held out an apple … Wolf's advance suddenly became tempestuous. He whirled Yolandine out of a cotillion, and while the last figure was being danced the music was drowned by a series of high-pitched warbles. It was Wolf yodelling.

Oddly enough, her loyal court took it upon themselves to be prudishly indignant. She ignored everything except the relief of being able to give an undistracted mind to the business of rule. There were expenses to recoup, schemes withering for lack of attention, the affair of the Chief Harpist to be wound up, a territorial dispute with the Northumbrian Kingdom of Catmere about some quite accidental sheep-stealing to be tapered into a trading agreement, the purveyor to be consulted about a harmless deterrent for the cousins.

She drew a decent veil of composure over her contentment. Once or twice it struck her that Wolf was aiming sheeps' eyes in her direction, but she put it down to his short sight. She had not been rid of him for a tranquil ten days before he was back, telling her that his heart had never strayed, that Yolandine was cynical and painted up to the eyes, that a cosy togetherness with his busy little wife was all he asked. It was not quite all that he asked; but she could never feel sure of his infidelity again. However, the cousins went.

It was not long before there were other riders – mortals, riding without elegance, their mounts plastered with mud, their boots the derision of Tomason; but they rode with purpose, pausing on the summit of every knoll to scrutinize the surroundings, poking their swords into heather-clumps, spurring across the moor to wherever they saw a whaup rising or goats take to their heels. For this was the period remembered in mortal history as the Killing Times, when perukes and high head-dresses were the mode, and troops of dragoons were hunting down the schismatics, whom some called Saints. The changelings knew all about it, or said they did. At any rate, they knew enough to take sides. Some were for Law and Episcopacy, others for the Covenant. The notion of a God is an inherent fever in mortals. No mortal constitution can escape it, and though the changelings had lived in Elfhame since they were stolen out of their cradles they took to the Killing Times as if they had been brought up in Oxford or Geneva.

Inside the castle, changelings squabbled. Round about it, fully-developed mortals killed and plundered. They hacked down young plantations to get firewood, fouled the streams by throwing dead bodies into them, left excrement everywhere, hung prisoners from any tree tall enough to carry them, and made a common gallows of the pinewood where the Queens of Elfhame were buried in air.

Mousie had a just and accurate mind: though courtiers, Functionaries and the upper working fairies pursued her with complaints about the changelings, she hated the mortals outside more than she hated the mortals within, not only because she had no control over them but flatly and without qualification. She hated the killers, she hated the killed. All were vile, and made each other worse. She in her castle was safe from them. But the smooth grassy hill which roofed and walled it was a landmark. The dragoons used it as a gathering-place, grazed their horses on it, sheltered with its bulk between them and the weather; she was never free from a sense of their proximity. And as people make sure of a tumour by fingering the place, she listened for sound of them, watched for sight of them.

Her cabinet had a slot window, extended from a rabbit-earth, through which she could look down on the outer world. A noise called her to it. A dragoon was galloping past with an old woman strapped to his saddle-bow. She was screaming curses at him, he was laughing like a jack-ass.

Yolandine had come into the room and was standing beside her with an expression of pursed-up amusement. She bobbed a reverence, graceful and limber in all she did, and asked permission to speak. Mousie looked at her wall-clock and gave permission.

'I think it my duty to tell you,' Yolandine began, 'that since early this morning you have been graciously harbouring a distressed mortal – an enormous distressed mortal, practically a monster – who is out of his senses.'

'A dragoon?'

'No. One of the other lot. A Saint. Shall I continue?'

'Pray continue.'

'It seems the dragoons had been chasing him, but lost him in the dark. The changelings heard him boo-hooing in the castle ditch and hauled him in through the back door – a tight fit, but they managed it.'

'Where is he now?'

'Locked in the old granary with some straw and bone. He can't get out and no one can get in, for they've kept the key. I heard all this from my dear Dandiprat. I can't understand why you don't make use of your changelings. They're invaluable creatures.'

'And how many people have you told?'

'My dear Majesty, how can you suppose I would tell anyone before telling you? But it's bound to get out.'

The silver trumpets blew, and they went downstairs for the meal. A distant gusty clamour filled the air. People stood in groups listening and saying nothing. Yolandine bestowed here and there a reassuring *sotto voce*, 'Her Majesty's monster.'

Mousie did nothing about the monster in the old granary, so no one else could. He remained the perquisite and Helen of Troy of the changelings. They quarrelled furiously as to whether he should be turned out to Law and Episcopacy or preserved for the Covenant; meanwhile, they were united in pride of ownership. A guard sat outside the granary door. Twice a day it was unlocked, and bread and water hastily thrust in. Favoured members of the kitchen staff were allowed to come and listen to his roars and ravings, his screams of terror, his prayers, his chattering teeth. The changelings were prepared to withstand any one in authority, but no one in authority came. Approached by Dandiprat, they consented to a visit from Yolandine, who, all agreed, was a sweet lady. Unfortunately, the madman was not at his best that evening. He heaved great sighs, and wept, but that was the extent of the performance. However, she seemed pleased, and ordered a distribution of heather ale to strengthen them for the nightwatch. On the following night, when the madman had been silent for many hours and the fun seemed over, Queen

Mousie, holding a lantern, came among them stilly as the moon, beckoned them to their feet and demanded the key. Keeping the key she went in and closed the door behind her.

It was quite true. He was an exceptionally large man, raw-boned and sinewy. His naked feet stuck out through the straw like rocks. He was awake, but did not stir at her entry, or blink when she shone her lantern on his high forehead and hollow cheeks. He was bald, except for a few grey hairs. Remembering what she had heard about his frenzy, his wolfish howls, the violence with which he fought an imagined enemy, remembering the gusty clamour which Yolandine had dismissed as 'Her Majesty's monster', she felt defrauded. She waited a little, playing her lantern light on the straw which tomorrow she would order to be renewed.

'I know that my Redeemer liveth.'

It was the voice of a good child repeating its lessons. He had turned his head and his small grey eyes, pale in their red rims and dark sockets, looked at her, looked at her shadow, looked at the wall, saw, and saw nothing. After a while, in the same gentle, confiding voice, he repeated, 'I know that my Redeemer liveth.'

But it was to himself that he confided it.

She locked him in with himself and went away, taking the key. Clean straw, a better diet ... So weakened and harmless, he must not be sent out into the world again. She would give the key to some responsible person who ... No! He must be given his liberty, and his due death at the hands of his enemies. All night she lay awake, listening to his silence.

She could not match his crass mortal confidence; and did not want to. Her life, so wretchedly spent in scheming, counterfeiting, suspecting, placating and despising, was not susceptible of redemption. She had never been brave, only sometimes desperate; or honest, except as a personal relieving bitterness. Where he was mad, she was sensible. And in the moment between one straw's rustle and the rustle of another straw his madness had overthrown her.

She rose knowing she must be very busy that day. She would call no council, no helpers, consult with no one. Just as usual, she would continue her scheme, carry it out inconspicuously, end it successfully. First, she must take that roll of cloth from the coffer; then supply herself with the cord; and find some pretext for wanting two large flat-irons. Then she must arrange the banquet, and somehow find time to snatch a couple of hours' sleep before it. The banquet was the captain-jewel of her scheme: it was to be an explosion of lavishness and ostentation, held in Wolf's honour and a total surprise. It must celebrate some anniversary or other: there are always anniversaries to hand; it was not the right time of year for his birthday, but it might well be the anniversary of the day the embassy from Dreiviertelstein first brought him to Elfhame – she could not remember the date, but neither would he. There would be speeches, music, drinking of healths. Only the Bursar would remain sober – he had a poor stomach and toadied it. 'About that fellow in the old granary,' she would say. 'The noise and riot is insupportable. Please see to it that he is turned out tomorrow morning. Let him have a good meal, and send him packing.' At midnight she would make a gracious withdrawal and go on with her private life.

The banquet went on long after midnight, long after her ladies had taken off her crown and undressed her and were safe gone. She had found time during the day to cut out the dress and tack it together. Now she began sewing, pleased with her neat firm stitches, amused to remember the dressmaking lessons which had been part of her prudent upbringing as the daughter of a well-bred penurious family, and came in so unexpectedly handy to a Queen. The noise of carousing assured her that her plan was going just as she intended, but it was the silence of the previous night which dwelt in her mind.

Listening to that hidden silence, she sewed on, smoothly and steadily, till the last stitch was taken, and the tackings pulled away. Smoothly and steadily, she wrote the letter which would lie alone and conspicuous on her desk, naming as her successor the Chamberlain's niece – a tall waxwork, with the best ceremonial appearance in Elfhame. With a steady hand, she tied staylaces to the flat-irons.

In the grey twilight she fastened on the scarlet dress, put the cord and the flat-irons in a bag and woke her page, telling him to saddle two riding-horses without rousing the grooms. While she waited, she flexed her wings – disuse had weakened them but they would serve her purpose – pulled on her gloves and had a last look at herself in the mirror. The scarlet dress was so striking that she omitted to look at its wearer.

They set out over the moor. The dragoons had shifted their hunt elsewhere, nothing molested the morning. With Elfhame behind her, the time before her seemed to Mousie as wide as a holiday. A thousand things flitted through her mind like a charm of goldfinches, things of the present, things of the past, a mound of raspberries in a cabbage-leaf, a silver locket, the hoarfrost tinselling a withered fem-frond, the smell of gingerbread, eating woodcock, the stream chafing a lip of ice, her first fan, the sun rising: all of them delightful and none of them her doing. Now she had nothing to do but to enjoy herself and ride on. The pinewood enlarged against the sky. The bright fragments of sound she heard were Tiphaine's silver chains, idly clanking. How silly she had been, not to demand a second mort-bread, when she was so hungry with the sharp morning!

A stink of corruption came from the dangling bodies. She must ride round the wood and choose a tree to the windward.

The page saw Queen Mousie, who was behaving so strangely, rein up her horse, snatch the bag she had given him, unfurl her wings and fly high into the tree. There she hovered, putting the cord round her neck, knotting its other end to the bough. She threw down the flat irons.

'When I drop,' she said, 'you are to fasten the weights to my feet. That will be all.' She made sure of the slip knot and the holding knot, closed her wings and fell. Out of some other existence she felt the weights tied to her feet, and heard him ride away, with her horse trotting after him. Faster and faster they went.

4 An Improbable Story

(Part of a letter from Lady Ulrica, Dame of Honour at the Elfin Court of Dreiviertelstein in Styria.)

Bad Nixenbach … The baths are not doing so much for me as they did last year but the company is resplendent. The latest arrivals are Count Bibski and Count Muffski – vast estates, and such diamonds! I asked them about the Kingdom of Tishk. They had never heard of it. So Tamarind was an imposter – as we all thought. As for his journey to England, *he was here*, bragging on about how he had flown the Volga. Of course I cut him dead. The moment Bibski and Muffski appeared, *he vanished*! (Don't tell the dear Queen.)

When Tamarind, a political exile from the Kingdom of Tishk in the Urals, quitted Dreiviertelstein he intended to go to England, where he would study political economy and *le phlegme anglais*. He had not expected to leave Dreiviertelstein so soon, or understood why he left under a cloud – a cloud which suddenly gathered when he choked on a chicken-bone and Queen Aigle became so excited; but his intention was firm and heartfelt. One of the factors in the revolution which exiled him was that political economy was not sufficiently studied in Tishk; and though he had always admired spontaneity, Queen Aigle's declaration of love while he was choking made him think there was something to be said for taciturnity and calm.

He had crossed the frontier and was lodging economically at a mortal inn near Augsburg when in his bedroom, insufficiently tidied after a previous occupant, he found a pamphlet titled *Grub's Exposition of the Limited: an Account of the Grubian Philosophy*. Tamarind had often wished to have time for philosophy. It was a wet evening; he had had supper; he began to read.

The pamphlet opened with an account of Grub's career. He was the ninth son of a respected pig-breeder in Westphalia. As the family needed no more useful sons it was decided to make a scholar of him, and he was deposited with the Remigian Brothers, a teaching order, whose Superior reported for six years running that Hans (his given name) showed application but could do better. On returning home, he went through a period of storm and stress, learned to swim and took to horse-racing. Rashly ambitious, he put his mount to a jump it was not accustomed to. It reared, he was thrown, the horse fell and rolled on him. When pitying hands dragged him from under the animal, it was found he had broken both legs. It was at this moment that he conceived his Theory of the Necessity of Limitations to the exposition of which he vowed the remainder of his days. Beginning with the At Hand (in his case the parlour of the family home) he established that without its enclosing walls a room cannot functionally be. Complying with the walls' necessary solidity, those who wish to leave or enter the room must do so by a door, which is in itself a compensatory limit to the solidity of the wall. Further analysis led him to his Laws of Property and Tenure: a field must have boundaries before it can exist as a field; it is also governed by the limiting factor of Time: at the owner's death, he can no longer own it. From this, Grub soared to the heavens. Stars and planets observe their limits, therefore do not collide: only comets spurn limitations and dash about through space regardless; the reprehensibility of this is admitted in the international consensus that comets upset the weather and bode no good.

When the paternal Grub died Hans Grub, consoled by this further demonstration of the Necessity of Limitations, took his legacy and left home; hence forward he devoted himself to enlarging, deepening, enriching and codifying the theory which had flashed on him while he was under the horse. A modest man, he thought only of pleasing himself; but by degrees his theory became known, and its all-embracing adequacy admitted. He was resorted to by troubled souls, and calmed them; he was questioned by searching minds, and silenced them; he was invited to give a course of lectures. Those who saw him limp unhurriedly onto the platform (for his legs had mended unsymmetrically and he still needed a crutch), who listened to his clear and ample statements, who marked his simple but decent garments and, above all, his air of cheerful self-sufficiency (*selbstgenugsamkeit*) were almost unanimously reminded of Socrates (Grub was not, however, married), compared him favourably with Descartes, and realized that fulfilment could only be found in accepting the Necessity of Limitations and not barking the spiritual shins (*geistliche Schienbein zu abrinden*) by trying to transcend the necessarily untranscendable.

The rest of the pamphlet had been torn away.

But Tamarind was already so convinced by Grub's reasoning that applying the Grubian method he saw the removal of the rest of the pamphlet as imposing a providential limit, since it obliged him to settle down with what he had got and make the most of it. Like a handful of concentrated manure, it only needed to be spread. His first impulse was to return to Tishk where, brought to realize the necessity of limits, the savage gentry, the simple blood-stained peasantry, would accommodate themselves to their respective lots and form a harmonious society. If he re-entered the Kingdom of Tishk, the upper party would have him beheaded as a political subverter, the peasantry would tear him in pieces as a traitor to their cause. Nothing would be bettered and he himself would be the worse. Besides, he was on his way to England. Meanwhile, he would visit Grub. Grub had visitors, the pamphlet said so. He would find out where Grub lived and sit at his feet. He must first buy a firmly tailored surtout to hide his wings: Grub might not take a fairy seriously. Next he must buy a German dictionary. He had picked up a good deal of German while travelling in Styria, but it was not philosophical German: several fine compound adverbs in the pamphlet had stumped him.

There was, for instance, that statement that Grub had altogether wholly removed himself from his birthplace. The act was made plain: but where to? Neither the inn people, the tailor or the bookseller could tell him where the great Grub lived. Remembering that the world knows nothing of its greatest men, Tamarind visited several universities – places, he judged, where unworldly men studied the recondite. The universities were economically advantageous, for the unworldly men left a great deal lying about, but the name of Grub was unknown among them. He remembered that no man is a prophet in his own country – and that the disagreeable Lady Ulrica had expatiated on the Elfin Spa of Bad Nixenbach, and the number of distinguished foreign hypochondriacs she had met there: one of these might have come from somewhere sufficiently remote to have heard of the great Grub. He flew to Bad Nixenbach, buttoned on his surtout, spruced himself up, and bought a ticket to the Pump Room. While sipping what appeared to be warmish cabbage-water he caught sight of Lady Ulrica, who was examining him through her lorgnettes. Markedly avoiding her, he conversed with other drinkers, telling them briefly of the complicated chain of events which led him to seek out Grub. Minions of fashion, they cared neither for liberty or philosophy and knew nothing about Grub. One, indeed, surmised he must be dead; but it turned out he was thinking of Euclid.

Bad Nixenbach's parasitic shopkeepers (many of whom were fairies) were equally unrewarding. He was shaking off the dust of a Delicatessen, where he had been foiled in an attempt on a smoked eel and enquired in vain for Grub, when a voice from the doorway said, 'Never heard of Grub? You'd deny the Lord Jesus. That's a Grub cheese on your counter. I'd know it anywhere by the smell.' The speaker was a middle-aged mortal with a shopping basket. Tamarind seized on her. 'You know Grub, Grub the philosopher? Where can I find him?' 'The Grub I know is Bertha Grub, I always get my cheese from her. She lives in Old Nixenbach – Magdalen Lane, on the yonder side of the town. You'll know her place by the goats. Or you'd find her in Market Square, Tuesdays and Fridays. But I don't know about a philosopher – unless you mean her old uncle with the game leg.'

'I do, I do!' said Tamarind passionately. 'How can I show my gratitude?' Rummaging in a pocket he found a cake of soap from the Gentlemen's Cloakroom at Bad Nixenbach, pressed it into her hand, and asked the way to Old Nixenbach.

It was a distance of six miles, by a winding road, mainly uphill. Respect obliged him to approach on foot. The profile of Old Nixenbach (two spires and a verdigrised copper dome) remained obdurately on the horizon. When at last it condescended to be nearer, and then suddenly so much nearer that the dome disappeared behind the town wall, he was too hot and tired to feel anything beyond a sad certainty that just as when he had alighted on the western bank of the Volga he was immediately arrested as a spy some such formality would blemish his arrival in Old Nixenbach. He entered unmolested under a frowning archway. Except for a few dogs no one showed the least interest in him, and the mention of Magdalen Lane made people look supercilious, and believe it might be in the suburbs. It took him a long time, many enquiries, many wrong turns down narrow twisting streets darkened by tall houses, before he found his way to Magdalen Lane, which in the course of enquiring for it, he learned was called Cow Lane. Cow Lane exactly described it. He was wishing he had not wasted the cake of soap on that misdirecting ignorant woman with the shopping basket when he smelled a reviving odour of goats. He quickened his steps, snuffing the air, and was imagining himself saying to Grub that goats have many classical associations when the door of a shed opened and a solidly constructed woman came out with a milk pail in either hand.

'Are you Miss Grub?' She set down the pails. 'I don't usually sell cheese at this hour.' 'But may I visit your honoured uncle?' As an afterthought, he asked if he might carry the milk pails. She preceded him across a muddy paddock to a one-story cottage with a lean-to, opened the lean-to door, signed to him to put down the pails. 'There!' she said. 'This is where I make my cheeses.' Tamarind looked round politely. The walls were bare and newly whitewashed. There were wide earthenware pans holding very white milk, several skimmers, wooden bats, drainers and other things; lengths of coarse wet muslin hung from a line and dripped; there was a pervading smell of sour milk. Tamarind disliked cheese, but he tried to sound appreciative as he said, 'How interesting!', and allowed a decent interval before saying, 'And now may I see your honoured uncle?' She opened a partition door into a low-ceilinged room, whose walls were also bare, and also whitewashed, though not so recently. Grub sat before the fire in a cushioned armchair. He was old, he was smoking a pipe, his feet were on a hassock, and a spittoon was beside him. The woman went back to her cheese room, Tamarind gazed with veneration at Grub. After a time, he said, 'Forgive me if I intrude …' At the same moment Grub took out his pipe and said, 'Well?' His voice was loud and gusty, he was probably deaf. Tamarind began again. 'I have come ...'

'Where from?'

'From the Urals.'

Though almost overwhelmed by the realization that he was addressing the great Grub, Tamarind sketched the circumstances which compelled his departure from Tishk, and recounted the events of the journey (modifying his crossing of the Volga by introducing a raft, and bowdlerizing Dreiviertelstein to a gipsy encampment, in order to avoid any mention of wings) which led him to the inn where The Exposition of the Limited burst on him like the summons of a trumpet; the subsequent fruitless searching of universities, the good, unlettered woman at the Delicatessen, the final ascent ... he broke off, leaving the rest to the eloquence of silence.

'Foolish to come all that way.'

It was the authentic voice of the Exponent of the Limited! Trembling, Tamarind waited for more.

'Brought anything with you?'

Tamarind searched in his pockets and pulled out a bag of pear-drops and a jar of caviare.

'A tribute – a pilgrim's poor tribute ...' He sensed it was not enough, searched another pocket, found a half bottle of schnapps.

'Little,' pronounced the authentic voice. 'Little and often.'

Drinking steadily, Grub finished the half bottle, smiled, and fell into the blameless sleep of old age. Tamarind put more wood on the fire. It blazed up, and showed the idyllic austerity of the room, its bare walls, low ceiling, tiled floor, its boxlike assertion of limits, its content of the sleeping philosopher. Grub snored commandingly; from behind the partition wall came sounds of slapping and squelching, bursts of vigorous colloquial song. This was how to end one's days! One's conclusions reached, one's conversation whittled to essentials, one's wisdom matured and compacted (as with cheese), one's fame resounding in the monosyllable, Grub: a simple pyramidal identity, with a niece.

Tamarind could hardly wait for his old age. Meanwhile, he looked round for something to sit on. There were two stools; one was ricketty, the other uncomfortable, so he sat on the floor. When the niece came in she saw her uncle sleeping in his armchair, as he did every night, and Tamarind asleep on the floor. She tied on her uncle's nightcap and after thought fetched a rug and bolster for Tamarind. She then picked up the pear-drops, the caviare, and the emptied bottle, and carried them away.

Tamarind continued to sleep on the floor. He had become part of the Grub household – not so much a guest, for he had not been invited, as a habit. Every morning he rolled the rug round the bolster, thus providing himself with something to sit on during the day. Every evening he re-adjusted them into a bed, and fell asleep, garnering recollections of the words of wisdom which had fallen from Grub's lips; or if none had happened to fall, then lulled by the silence of a conscience that had nothing to take exception to. The sufficingness of the rug and the bolster symbolized how right he had been in his convictions: his dislike of etiquette and formality, his trust in the simple goodheartedness of the poor and oppressed, his acceptance of the Limited.

Life with the Grubs was regulated by the goats. When Bertha had milked, and staked them in the paddock to graze, she came in to wash and comb her uncle. When she had washed and combed herself, they ate a breakfast of bread and milk. At breakfast Grub was conversational talking about the weather and telling his dreams. They were the dreams of an untroubled mind; he had been eating doughnuts; his nightcap had turned into a bishop's mitre. Afterwards, he lit his pipe and meditated. After the first day, when it was caviare, the mid-day meal was cheese. Supper was curds and whey, eaten early because by sundown the goats had to be milked and put back in their shed. Goats were as good as a clock and don't need winding, was a favourite observation of Grub's. Grub delighted in proverbs and proverbial comparisons. When Bertha had settled him for the night she habitually asked if he was comfortable to which he habitually replied, 'Happy as a maggot in a nut.' Tamarind admired the consistency with which the great Grub rejected worldly, even philosophic terms of speech: it was the Necessity of Limitations exemplified in an acceptance of a way of life. He practised the same acceptance of the actual in regard to Tamarind. After the first evening's enquiries and Tamarind's explanatory narrative he showed no curiosity about Tamarind's past till two mornings later, when taking out his pipe he asked, 'Did they roast hedgehogs?' Tamarind, who had forgotten how he had bowdlerized Dreiviertelstein into a gipsy encampment, was at a loss. 'Did they roast hedgehogs in clay jackets?' amplified Grub. Tamarind recovered his wits, said they did and that the hedgehogs tasted delicious (he had always understood it was so). Grub said, 'Ah!' and resumed his meditation. Clay jackets, thought Tamarind. Of course, a variety of limitation: it was remarkable how unflaggingly Grub dwelt on the limited. He wished he could go further into the subject. His knowledge of it had ended where the pages had been torn out of the pamphlet.

Fortunately, there was one way in which he could solidly express his veneration. One morning Bertha, unexpectedly early to be out of a wrapper with her hair up, told him he must get his own breakfast as she was taking her cheeses to the market. The cheeses, dozens of them, were heaped in a hand-barrow. He offered to wheel the barrow part of the way. He wheeled it the whole way, Bertha following in case a cheese should fall off. As they neared the market the sharp morning air grew lively with voices, smells of fish and cabbage, new bread and hot coffee. He parted from Bertha, put on invisibility and went in search of a breakfast. A fairy's invisibility covers whatever is in his possession. A glass of hot coffee disappeared from the stall and reappeared empty. Tamarind was insinuating himself towards a mound of doughnuts when he remembered that Grub had dreamed of doughnuts, and took two, one for the philosopher, one for himself. They were good plump doughnuts, so he took four more to share between them. So far, he had stolen as a child might. Now he applied himself seriously to his mission, considering what would be the best value, rejecting apple tarts because the pastry would crush, choosing the sturdiest sausages. The caviare had not been a success with Bertha (possibly cheese had blunted her palate) so he added some smoked sprats, and more pear-drops as a concession to her femininity. By now the shops were opening. The wine-shop provided three half bottles of schnapps.

He could feel his invisible pockets bulging, so he waited for a quiet moment in Cow Lane before he made himself apparent.

This was the first of many excursions. As a matter of prudence, he distributed his attentions among the stall-holders and patronized more than one wine-shop. His personal fastidiousness prevented him from making as free with the fish-stall as he would have wished: some crawfish from the Nixenbach left an unpleasant clamminess in his pocket, eels, though coiling very conveniently, were slimy. He thought to overcome this difficulty by thieving from a charitable establishment which sold baskets made by the blind. But invisibility does not absolutely include impalpability. The basket was angular, and roomy; adjacent mortal marketers complained of being dug in the ribs and improperly assaulted.

Quarrels arose. He had to give up the basket, and use plaited straw carriers instead.

None of this flawed his pleasure. Till now, he had never been responsible for others. A well-wisher to society, he had forwarded no interests but his own, expending his talents, his luck, his ingenuity, in looking after himself: he had lived in exile all his life. Now he was one of a household, and responsible for its well-being. The charm of being depended on was a thing he had never experienced, never imagined. It far excelled any satisfaction that could be sucked from the gratitude of the benefited (he had seen instances of that sort of thing and how poorly it worked out). Gratitude is conditional. Dependence, such dependence as that of the Grubs, is calm, implicit, inexhaustible. As Grub so often remarked, still waters run deep. Indeed, the surface of the Grub dependence was so unrippled by expressions of gratitude that the metaphor of running water was inappropriate; a pond would be nearer the mark. They received whatever he brought them, swallowed it, and were sure of more. Their calm trust in him touched Tamarind to the heart. It made him pleased with himself, and confident he could do better and be even more pleased. By nourishing the great Grub he had reached the end of six months' ambition. He had sought, he had found, he filled the Exponent of the Limited. And it had all come about quite naturally, a state of things to be taken for granted – a state of things taken for granted in mystic India where the disciple (he understood) is *ipso facto* also the purveyor.

If he could help it, there should never be another disciple.

Time went sweetly on. The goats were milked morning and evening, all day Bertha was busy making cheese. Tamarind had suggested that as the household was now not so dependent on cheese, she might crumble some and scatter it for the birds. She refused, saying it was wasteful to feed wild creatures who could fend for themselves. She had a womanly attachment to economy. If Tamarind came back with some unusual profusion she commented on it, though without censure. She took a peculiar pleasure in remainders. 'Look at all that pickled salmon left over! I can't use it for soup, we must finish it at breakfast.' Grub put by the schnapps bottle. 'The within is best. I will finish it now.' He did so, gravely and exactly, as if reverencing what he was about to contain. The salmon renewed his thirst. He took up the bottle. There was not much left in it, and there was not another bottle in the house.

Next morning Tamarind went to get more. Neither of the wine-shops had yet opened, so to pass the time he went for a stroll. It took him to the street by which he had first entered Old Nixenbach. He remembered the cobbles, the square beyond, where the dogs had snuffed him, the cart-rank with the chalked tariff for using it; it even seemed to him that he remembered some of the horses. Everything from the cobblestones to the verdigrized dome at the end of the square was endeared to him by the recollection of how dejected he had been – and how near his happiness. A procession came down a side street and entered the square. It was a funeral procession. The hearse had gilded skulls on its four corners, the coachman wore a gold-laced cocked hat, the horses were plumed. Mutes accompanied the hearse, and some black-scarfed mourners followed it. A few onlookers were gathered to watch it pass. Tamarind turned to one of them, and asked whose funeral it was.

'It's Doctor Grubenius. He came to give lectures, and honoured us by dying here. If he had been a citizen, the procession would have been larger.' Tamarind sighed. The procession reminded him that Grub was an old man, and mortal. His sigh was noticed.

'You knew Doctor Grubenius?'

The coffin was being carried into the church. He shook his head.

'Grubenius the Pragmatist. His grasp of the real renovated Moral Philosophy. In brief ...'

The onlooker repeated precisely what Tamarind had read in the pamphlet, and added what in the pamphlet had been torn away.

'You should read his treatise, *The Exposition of the Limited*. You would find it most interesting – revelatory.'

A hen whose head has been chopped off can still make a few steps. Tamarind said, 'Indeed,' and walked away. Grub-Grubenius was dead and about to be buried. Grub-Grub was sitting by the fire and waiting for his schnapps and the midday meal. Bertha was slapping cheese. They had done him no harm. They had taken him in, a stranger. He had slept at Grub's feet. They were a simple, trustful, good-hearted pair ... And they could go hang!

A yell, compounded of disillusionment, fury, woe, exasperation, burst from him. It was answered by a whinny. He turned on the mimic. The horse looked at him with a mild expression. It was harnessed to a two-wheeled cart. He leaped into the cart, gathered up the reins, lashed the startled beast into a gallop. They vanished under the archway, the noise of clattering hoofs died out on the Bad Nixenbach road.

5 The Duke of Orkney's Leonardo

The child, a boy, was born with a caul. Such children, said the midwife, never drown. Lady Ulpha was cold to the midwife's assurances; the same end, she said, could be reached by never going near water. She was equally indifferent to the midwife's statement that children born with a caul keep an unblemished complexion to their dying day. Lady Ulpha had long prided herself on her unblemished decorum. The violent act of giving birth, the ignominy of howling and squirming in labour and being encouraged by a vulgar person to let herself go, had affronted her. Seeing that encouragements were unwelcome, the midwife did not mention that cauls are so potent against drowning that mortals making a sea voyage will pay a great price for one. The child was washed and laid in the cradle, and a nurse given charge of it. As for the caul, by some mysterious negotiation it got to Glasgow. There it was bought by the captain of a whaler and subsequently lost at sea.

Sir Huon and Lady Ulpha were fairies with a great deal of pedigree, pride to match it, and small means for its upkeep. On the ground that it does not do to make oneself cheap, they seldom appeared at the Court of Rings, a modest Elfin kingdom in Galloway, preferring to live on their own estate, small and boggy, and make a merit of it. When the boy was of an age to be launched into the world, it would be different.

He was still spoken of as The Boy, because he had been named after so many possible legacy leavers that no one could fix a name on him, except his nurse, who called him Bonny – a vulgar dialect term which would get him nowhere. He was the most beautiful child in the world, she said, and would grow into the handsomest Elfin in all Scotland. Looking at her child more attentively, Lady Ulpha decided that though he was now an expense, he might become an asset.

His first recollection of his mother was of being lifted onto her high bed to have his nose pinched into a better shape, his ears flattened to the side of his head, and his eyebrows oiled. As time went on, other measures were imposed. He had to wear a bobbing straw hat to shield him from getting freckles, and was forbidden to hug his pet lamb in case he caught ticks. In winter a woollen veil was tied over his face. This was worse than the hat, for it blinded him to his finer pleasures: the snow crystal melted in his hand, the wind blew the feathers away before he had properly admired them. Bailed by the woollen grating over his eyes, he came indoors, where sight was no pleasure. The veil was pulled off and he was set to study an ungainly alphabet straddling across a dirty page.

It was in summer that he got a name of his own. A trout stream ran through the estate, and as he couldn't be drowned he was allowed to play in it, provided he kept his hat on. Sir Glamie, Chancellor of the Court of Rings and an ardent fly-fisher, had permission from Sir Huon – who knew he would otherwise poach – to fish there on Wednesdays, provided he threw back every alternate fish. Having scrupulously thrown back a small trout, Sir Glamie approached a pool where he knew there was a large one. A ripple travelled toward him, and another. He saw a straw hat, and advanced on the poacher. Under the hat was a naked boy, whose limbs trailed in the pool. The boy was not even poaching, merely wallowing, and scaring every trout within miles; but as Sir Glamie drew nearer he saw that the boy was winged. 'Are you young what's-his-name?' he asked. The boy said he thought so. Sir Glamie said he was old enough to know his name. The boy agreed, and added, 'It used to be Bonny.' Sir Glamie replied that Bonny was a girl's name, and wouldn't do. Overcome by the boy's remarkable beauty, he had a rush of benevolence, and casting round in his mind remembered the worms, small and smooth and white, that fishermen call gentles, and impale on the hook when the water is too cloudy to use a fly. 'I shall call you Gentle,' he declared. By force of association, he took a liking to the boy, extricated him from Lady Ulpha's clutches, and took him to Court, where he was made a pet of and called Gentil.

It was not the introduction his parents had intended: it was premature, since clothes had to be bought for him and he would outgrow them; it was also patronizing, and made their heir seem a nobody. But as none of the legacies they invoked had responded, they submitted, called him Gentil, made him learn his pedigree by heart, and loyally attended banquets.

Gentil was scarcely into his new clothes before he grew out of them. A fresh outfit was under consideration when the need for it was annulled: the Queen made him one of her pages, and a uniform went with the appointment. For the first time in his life he was aware of his beauty, and gazed at his image in the tailor's mirror as though it were a butterfly or a snow crystal – a snow crystal that would not melt. At intervals, he remembered to be grateful to his parents, but for whose providence he might still be admiring the veined underwater pebbles without noticing his reflected face. It needed no effort to be grateful to his new friends at Court: to the Queen, who stroked his cheek; to her ladies, who straightened his stockings; to his fellow-pages, who shared their toffees with him; to Sir Glamie, who chucked him under the chin with a fishy hand and asked what had become of the hat; to Lady Fenell, the Court Harpist, who sang for him

> I love all beauteous things,
> I seek and adore them

–an old-fashioned ditty composed for her by an admirer,

which exactly expressed his own feelings. For he, too, was a beauty lover, and loved himself with an untroubled and unselfish love.

Fenell's voice had grown quavering with age – she had actually heard Ossian – but her fingers were as nimble as ever, her attack as brilliant, and young persons of quality came from all over Elfindom to learn her method. The latest of these was the Princess Lief, Queen Gruach's daughter from the Kingdom of Elfwick, in Caithness. She had the air of being assured of admiration, but there was nothing beautiful about her except the startling blue of her eyes: a glance that fell on one like a splash of ice-cold water. During the reception held to celebrate her arrival, the glance fell on Gentil. It seemed like a command. He came forward politely and asked if there was anything she wanted. After a long scrutiny, she said, 'Nothing,' and turned away. He felt snubbed. Not knowing which way to look, he caught sight of Sir Huon and Lady Ulpha, whose faces expressed profound gratification. He knew they did not love him, but he had not realized they hated him.

If it had not been for Lady Ulpha's decorum, she would have nudged Sir Huon in the ribs. All that night they sat up telling each other that Gentil's fortune was made. There could be no mistaking such love at first sight. Gentil would be off their hands, sure of his future, sure of his indestructible good looks, with nothing to do but ingratiate himself with Queen Gruach and live up to his pedigree. And, as the castle of Elfwick stood on the edge of a cliff, the caul would not be wasted. The caul might count as an asset and be included in the marriage settlement.

It was just as they foresaw. Lief compelled Lady Fenell into saying she had nothing more to teach her (the formula for dismissing unteachable pupils), assaulted Gentil into compliance, and bore him off to Elfwick, where, after a violent set-to with Queen Gruach, she had him proclaimed her Consort and made a Freeman of Elfwick.

The ceremony was interrupted by the news that a ship was in the bay. Every male fairy rushed to the cliff's edge. Narrowing his eyes against the wind, Gentil was just able to distinguish a dark shape tossing on the black-and-white expanse of sea. He was at a loss to make out what the others were saying, except that they were talking excitedly, for they spoke in soft mewing voices, like the voices of birds of prey. Gulls exploded out of the dusk, flying so close that their screams jabbed his hearing. They, too, sounded wild with excitement. The sea kept up a continuous hollow booming, a noise without shape or dimension, unless some larger wave charged the cliff like an angry bull. Then, for a moment, there seemed to be silence, and a tower of spray rose and hung on the air, hissed, and was gone. Ducking to avoid a gull, Gentil lost sight of the ship. When he saw it again, it was closer inland. He saw it stagger, and a wave overwhelm it, emerge, and be swallowed by a second wave. There was a general groan. A voice said something about no pickings. A flurry of snow hid everything. He heard the others consulting, their voices dubious and discouraged. They had begun to move away, when a shriller voice yowled, 'There she is, there she is.' They gathered again, peering into the snow flurry. When it cleared, the ship was plainly visible, much smaller and farther out to sea. Everyone turned away and went back to the castle, where the ceremony was resumed, glumly.

When he said to Lief that he was glad to see the ship still afloat, and hoped no one on her was drowned, she said, embracing him, that he would never be drowned – that was all she cared for. He learned that Elfwick had rights over everything that came ashore – wreck, cargo, crew: the east wind blew meat and drink into Elfwick mouths. Next day she walked him along the cliffs, and showed him where the currents ran – oily streaks on the sea's face. A ship caught in a certain current would be carried, willy-nilly, onto a rock called the Elfwick Cow, which pastured at the entrance to the beach, lying so temptingly in the gap between the cliffs. She pointed to a swirl of water above the rock, and said that at low tide the Cow wore a lace veil – the trickle of spray left by each retreating wave. He clutched at his retreating hopes. 'But if a sailor gets to shore alive —' 'Knocked on the head like a seal,' she said, 'caul or no caul. Cauls have no power on land.' Seeing him shiver, she hurried him lovingly indoors.

Her love was the worst of his misfortunes. He submitted to it with a passive ill will, as he submitted to the inescapable noise of the sea, the exploitation of a harshly bracing climate. Wishing he were dead, he found himself at the mercy of a devouring healthiness, eating grossly, sleeping like a log. 'You'll soon get into our Elfwick ways,' Queen Gruach remarked, adding that the first winter was bound to be difficult for anyone from the south. She disliked her son-in-law, but she was trying to make the best of him. If Gentil had inherited his parents' eye for the main chance, he could have adapted himself to his advantages, and lived as thrivingly at Elfwick as he had lived at Rings – where everyone liked him, and he loved himself, and was happy. At Elfwick, he was loved by Lief, and was appalled.

The first winter lasted into mid-May, when the blackthorn hedges struggled into bloom and a three-day snowstorm buried them. The storm brought another ship to be battered to pieces on the Elfwick Cow. This time, the cold spared her plunderers the trouble of dispatching the crew. The ship was one of the Duke of Orkney's vessels, its cargo was rich and festive: casks of wine and brandy, a case of lutes (too sodden to be of any use), smoked hams (none the worse), bales of fine cloth. In a strong packing case and wadded in depths of wool was an oval mirror. Lief gave it to Gentil, saying that the frame – a wreath of carved ivory roses delicately tinted and entwined in blue glass ribbons – was almost lovely enough to hold his face. She was in triumph at having snatched it from Gruach, who had the right to it. He thanked her politely, glanced at his reflection, saw with indifference that he was as beautiful as ever, and commented that he was growing fat. The waiting woman who had carried the mirror stood by with a blank face and a smiling heart. To see the arrogant Princess fawning on an upstart from Galloway was a shocking spectacle but also an ointment to old sores.

Baffled and eluded, Lief continued to love her bad bargain with the obsession of a bitch. She beset him with gifts, tried to impress him by brags, wooed him with bribes. She watched him with incessant hope, never lost patience with him, or with herself; she was so loyal she did not even privately make excuses for him. If anyone showed her a vestige of sympathy, she turned and rent him. This and quarrelling with her mother were the only satisfactions she could rely on.

At first, she hoped it was winter that made him cold. Summer came, and Gentil was cold still – cold like a sea mist and as ungraspable. If she had believed in witches, she would have believed he was under a spell; but Caithness was full of witches – mortals all, derided by rational Elfins. He was healthy, could swim like a fish, leap like a grasshopper – and none of this was any good to him, for he was without initiative, and had to be wound up to pleasure like a toy. The only thing he did of his own accord was sneak out and be away all day. Sometimes he brought back mushrooms, neatly bagged in a handkerchief. Otherwise, he returned empty-handed and empty-headed, for if she asked him what he had seen, he replied, 'Nothing in particular.'

And it was true. He could no longer see anything in its particularity – not the sharp outline of a leaf, not the polish on a bird's plumage. It was as though the woollen veil had been tied over his face again, the woollen grating that had barred him from delight. He saw his old loves with a listless recognition. Another magpie. Another rainbow. More daisies. They were the same as they had been last summer and would be next summer and the summers after that.

❧

It was another April, and Gentil, wandering through the fields, was conscious only that a cold wind was blowing, when he heard a whistling – too long-breathed for a thrush, too thoughtful for a blackbird. The whistler was a young man, a Caithness mortal. He was repairing a tumbled sheepfold. Each time he stooped to pick up a stone, a lappet of black hair slid forward and dangled over one eye. Gentil was accustomed to mortals, took them for granted, and never gave them a thought. At the sight of the young man he was suddenly pierced with delight. The lappet of hair, the light toss of the small head that shook it back, the strong body stooping so easily, the large, deft hands nestling the stones into place were as beautiful and fit and complete as the marvels he had seen in his childhood. Weakened by love, he sat down on the impoverished grass to watch.

He went back the next day, and the morning after that he got up early and was at the sheepfold in time to collect some suitably sized stones and lay them in a neat heap at the foot of the wall. Love is beyond reason, and when the young man took stones from the heap as though they had been there all the time, Gentil was overjoyed. Civility obliged him to attend the celebrations on Gruach's birthday, telling himself furiously that no one would notice if he was there or not. On the morrow, he woke with such a release into joy and confidence that he even dawdled on his way to the sheepfold. It was finished, the young man was gone. Gentil took to his wings and flew in wide circles, quartering the landscape. A flash of steel signalled him to where the young man was laying a hedge.

This task had none of the scholarly precision of mending a dry stone wall. It was a battle of opposing forces, the one armed with a billhook, the other armoured in thorns. It was an old hedge, standing as tall as its adversary; some of the main stems were thick as a wrist, and branched at all angles with intricate lesser growths. Here and there it was tufted with blossoms, for the sap was already running. The young man, working from left to right, chose the next stem to attack, seized it with his left hand, bent it back, and half severed it with a glancing blow of the billhook. The flowing sap darkened the wound; petals fell. Still holding the upper part of the stem, he pressed it down, and secured it in a plaited entanglement of side branches, lesser growths, and brambles. Then he lopped the whole into shapeliness with quick slashes of his billhook. The change from dealing with stone to dealing with living wood changed his expression: it was stern and critical – there was none of the contented calculation which had gone with rebuilding the sheepfold.

It changed Gentil too – from a worshipper to a partisan. He hovered above the hedge, watching each stroke, studying the young man's face – how he drew down his black eyebrows in a frown, bit his lip. Secure in his invisibility, Gentil hovered closer and closer. They were moving on from a completed length of hedge when a twig jerked up from the subdued bulk. 'Look! Here!' – the words were almost spoken when the young man saw the twig and slashed at it. The bright billhook caught Gentil in its sweep and lopped off half his ear. Feeling Gentil's blood stiffening on his hand, the young man licked the scratch he had got from a thorn and went on working. Another length of hedge had been laid before Gentil left off being sick, and crept away.

Several times he trustingly lay down to die. The trust was misplaced; the cold shock and loss of blood forced him to rise from the ground into the clasp of the sunny air and walk on. When he tried to fly, he found he could not: the loss of half an ear upset his balance. He walked on and on, vaguely taking his way back to Elfwick and wondering how he could put an end to his shamed existence. He could not drown, but he remembered a place where a ledge of rock lay at the foot of the cliff, and if he could get that far he could let himself drop and be dashed to pieces. But he must make a detour, so that no one from the castle would see him.

Lief, impelled by her bitch's instinct, was there before him, not knowing why but knowing she must be. In any case, it never came amiss to look seaward: there might be another ship. He went past without seeing her. She grabbed him. As they struggled on the cliff's edge, she saw the bloody stump of his ear but held him fast.

As time went on Lief sometimes wondered whether it would not have been better to let him have his way. But she had caught hold of him before she saw what had happened, and her will to keep him was stronger than her horror at his disfigurement. So she fought him to a finish, and marched him back to the castle.

The return from the cliff's edge was perhaps the worst thing she had to endure. There were no more people about than usual but it seemed to her that every Court Elfin was there, gathering like blowflies to Gentil's raw wound, turning away in abhorrence. It was natural, she accepted it. Elfwick had never lost the energy of its origin as an isolated settlement, embattled against harsh natural conditions: cold and scarcity, wind and tempest. Its savagery was practical, its violence law-abiding. Though it had grown comfort-loving, it had never become infected with that most un-Elfin weakness, pity.

She herself nursed Gentil through his long illness without a tremor of pity traversing her implacable concern. She risked her reason to save him, exactly as the wreckers risked their limbs to snatch back a cask from the undertow, and she recognized the rationality and loyal traditionalism of the public opinion she defied. The mildest expression of it was Gruach's. 'He must be sent back to Rings.' While he was thought to be past saving (for the stump festered and his face and neck swelled hideously) there was hope. But the swelling went down and Gruach visited the sickbed to remonstrate in a motherly way against Lief's devotion. 'I chose him. I shall save him,' said Lief.

'But have you considered the future? It's not as though you were saving a favourite hound. He is your Consort, remember. How can you appear with such an object beside you? How could you put up with the indignity, the scandal, of his mutilation?' Lief replied, 'You'll see.' She put a bold front on it, but at times she despaired, thinking that if Gentil once left her keeping, public opinion would soon do away with him.

As it happened, this problem did not arise. No one was more horrified by his deformity than Gentil himself. He refused to be seen, he would have no one but Lief come near him. If she had to make an appearance at Court, he insisted that she lock him in and keep the key between her breasts. She still did not know what had happened. When she questioned him he burst into tears. She did not ask him again, for by then she was as exhausted by his illness as he, and only wanted to sit still and say nothing. They sat together, hour after hour, saying nothing, she with her hands in her lap, he fingering his ear.

The oncome of winter was stormy; two profitable ships were driven onto the Cow, the castle resounded with boasts and banquetings. Then for months nothing happened. A deadly calm frost clamped the snow, waves crept to the strand and immediately froze, the gulls flew like scimitars through the still air. Gentil sat by the fire, fingering his wound.

❧

The smell of spring was breathing through the opened casement when he suddenly raised his head, looked round the room and on Lief, and said passionately, 'Everything is so ugly, so ugly!' Casting about for something to please him, Lief remembered her mother's gold and silver beads, which the Duke of Orkney had thought to hang round a younger neck. Schooling herself to be daughterly and beguiling, she persuaded Gruach to unlock her treasure chest, questioned, admired, put on the gold and silver beads, and asked if she could borrow them. And though Lief had never shown the least interest in the Duke of Orkney's importations, except when she carried off the oval mirror, Gruach thought she might be returning to her right mind, and handed over the beads and some other trifles. Gentil tired of running the beads through his fingers; a jewelled bird trembling on a fine wire above a malachite leaf and a massive gold sunflower with a crystal eye were more durable pleasures. Later, he was spellbound by a branching spray of coral. At the first sight of the coral, which to Lief was nothing to marvel at, since there was no workmanship about it, he gave a cry of joy that seemed to light up the room.

But this, too, eventually went the way of the sunflower and the bird. And when she brought fresh rarities to replace it, he thanked her politely and ignored them. Except for sudden fits of rage, when he screamed at her, he was always polite. The fits of rage she rather welcomed; they promised something she could get to grips with. It never came. He sat by the fire; he sat by the window; the maimed ear had thickened into an accumulation of flaps, one fast to another, like the mushrooms, hard as leather, that grow on the trunks of ageing trees and are called Jew's-ears. A scar extended down his cheek. The rest of him was lovely and youthful as ever.

Nothing deflects the routine of a court custom. The Freemen of Elfwick had no particular obligations except to wear a badge and have precedence in drinking loyal toasts at banquets; but in times of emergency they were expected to rally and attend committee meetings. Gentil was now summoned to such a meeting. Naturally, he did not attend. The emergency was still in the future, but it was inevitable, and must be faced with measures of economy, tightening of belts, and finding alternative sources of supply. For the Duke of Orkney was mortal, and over sixty – an age at which mortals begin to fall to bits. His heir was a miserly ascetic, always keeping Lents; there would be no more casks of wine and brandy, no more of those delicious smoked hams, no more candied apricots from Provence, fine cloth from Flanders, spices to redeem home-killed mutton from the aroma of decay; the Cow would advance her horns to no purpose, the Elfwick standard of living would fall catastrophically. The meeting closed with a unanimous recommendation to make sure of the Duke of Orkney's next consignment.

It could be expected before the autumnal equinox. Spies were sent out for hearsay of it, watchers were stationed along the cliffs, where they lolled in the sun, chewing wild thyme. It had been an exceptionally early harvest; rye and oats were already in stooks, rustling in the wind. It was a lulling sound, but not so to the Court Purveyor. For it was a west wind, and though it was gentle it was steady. Of all the quarters the wind could blow from he prayed for any but the west. With a west wind keeping her well out to sea, the Duke's ship would be safe from those serviceable currents that nourished the Cow. Elfwick would get nothing.

Subduing his principles, consulting nobody, the Purveyor put on a respectable visibility and sought out the nearest coven of witches. They were throwing toads and toenails into a simmering cauldron; the smell was intolerable, but he got out his request, and at the same time got out a purse and clinked it. 'A wind from the east?' said the head witch. 'You should go to my sister in Lapland for that.' He answered that he was sure a Caithness witch could do as well or better. She threw in another toad and said he should have his will. Handing over the purse, he asked if there was anything else he could supply. A younger witch spoke up. 'A few cats ... seven, maybe.' 'Alive?' 'Oh, aye.' He carried the hamper of squalling cats to the place they commanded, and fled in trust and terror.

The storm which impaled the Duke of Orkney's ship on the Elfwick Cow did so at a price. Hailstones battered down the stooks and froze the beehives. A month's washing was whirled away from the drying yard. Shutters were torn from their hinges, fruit trees were uprooted, pigs went mad, the kitchen chimney was struck by lightning, the Purveyor, clutching at his heart, fell dead. Lief stepped over him on her way out. The clamour of wind and voices, the reports of a superb cargo, of a cargo still at hazard, had been more than she could withstand. Settling Gentil with a picture book, she locked him in, put the key in her bosom, and ran to the cliff's edge. Bursts of spray made it difficult to see what was going on. She caught sight of a Negro, fighting his way to shore against the suck of the undertow. He was down, he was up again, still grasping an encumbering package. It was wrenched from him by the undertow; he turned back. When she could see him again, he had retrieved it. Curious to know what it was he guarded so jealously, she descended the path. By the time she reached the strand, he had been dispatched, and lay sprawled over his package – an oblong wooden box, latticed with strips of iron – as though he would still protect it. She tried to pull it from under him, but it was too heavy for her to shift. More and more plunder was being fetched ashore. She stood unnoticed in the jostle till one of the Freemen tripped over the Negro. He started at seeing Lief there, and panted out felicitations: never had the Cow done better for Elfwick. She told him that the Negro's box was hers, under the old law of Finders Keepers; he must call off one of the wreckers to carry it after her to the castle.

On the cliff's summit she stopped to look back. Twitches of lightning played incessantly over the sea. Remade by wind and tempest, she felt a lifetime away from Gentil; when the grunting porter asked what to do with the box, she had forgotten it existed.

Yet in the morning the box was the first thing in her mind. Gentil had a cat's pleasure in anything being unpacked: had a crate been large enough, he would have jumped in and curled up in it. The box was brought to her apartment, the castle's handyman called in. Practised in such duties, he made short work of it. The iron bands were eased and tapped off, screw after screw withdrawn. At intervals he remarked on the change in the weather. The wind had fallen as suddenly as it had come up, and when he had finished the box he would see to the shutters and then the pigsties, which the pigs in their frenzy had torn through like cannonballs. This box, though, was a different matter. Made of solid mahogany, it would baffle the strongest pig in Scotland. He laid the screws aside and raised the lid. Whatever lay within was held in place by bands of strong twine and wrapped in fold on fold of waxed linen. The handyman cut the twine, bowed, and went away. Gentil came out of hiding. Kneeling by the box, Lief lifted the oblong shape and held it while Gentil unwound the interminable wrappings. The oblong turned into a frame, the frame held a padding of lamb's wool. Gentil folded the linen and smoothed it affectionately. Pulling away the lamb's wool, he was the first to see the picture.

It was the half-length portrait of a young man, full face and looking directly before him. Behind him was the landscape of a summer morning. Wreaths of morning mist, shining in the sun, wandered over it. Out of the mist rose sharp pinnacles of mountain, blue with distance yet with every rocky detail exactly delineated. A glittering river coiled through a perspective of bronzed marshes and meadows enclosed by trees planted in single file, each tree in its own territory of air. It was as though a moment before they had been stirring in a light wind which now had fallen. Everything lay in a trance of sunlight, distinct, unmoving, and completed. Only the young man, turning his back on this landscape, sat in shadow – the shadow of a cloud, perhaps, or of a canopy. He was not darkened by it; but it substantiated him, as though he and the landscape belonged to different realities. He sat easily erect, with his smooth, long-fingered young hands clasped like the hands of an old man round a stick. His hair hung in docile curls and ringlets, framing the oval of his face. He had grey eyes. In the shadow which substantiated him, they were bright as glass, and stared out of the canvas as though he were questioning what he saw, as smilingly indifferent to the answer as he was to the lovely landscape he had turned his back on.

Lief tired under the effort of holding up the picture. She propped it against a chair, and went round to kneel beside the kneeling Gentil and discover what it was he found so compelling. The likeness was inescapable: Gentil was gazing at himself in his youth, at the Gentil who had come forward and asked if there was anything she wanted; she had said, 'Nothing,' and nothing was what she had got. Tears started to her eyes and ran slowly down her cheeks. She shook her hand impatiently, as if to dismiss them. He turned and looked at her. The sun shone full on her face. He had never seen her cry. The glittering, sidling tears were beautiful, an extraneous beauty on an accustomed object. He shuffled nearer and stared more closely, entranced by the fine network of wrinkles round her eyes. She heard him give a little gasp of pleasure, saw him looking at her with delight, as long ago he had looked at an insect's wing, a yellow snail shell. Cautiously, as though she might fly away, he touched her cheek. She did nothing, said nothing, stretched the moment for as long as it could possibly last. They rose from their knees together and stood looking at the picture, each with an arm round the other's waist.

Love – romantic love, such as Lief had felt for Gentil, Gentil for the young man at the sheepfold – was not possible for them. In any case, Elfins find such love burdensome and mistrust it. But they grew increasingly attached to each other's company, and being Elfins and untrammelled by that petted plague of mortals, conscience, they never reproached or regretted, entered into explanations or lied. This state of things carried them contentedly through the winter. With the spring, Gentil astonishingly proclaimed a wish to go out-of-doors, provided he went unseen. Slinking out after midnight, they listened to owls and lambs, smelled honeysuckle, and ate primroses chilled with dew.

After the sweetness of early morning it was painful to return to the stuffiness of the castle, its oppressive silence shaken by snores. Gentil planned stratagems for escaping into daylight: he could wear a sunbonnet; they could dig an underground passage. But the underground passage would only deliver him up to the common gaze, the sunbonnet expose him to a charge of transvestism – more abhorrent to Elfwick than any disfigurement, and certain to be more sternly dealt with. Seeing him again fingering his ear and staring at the morning landscape behind the young man in the painting, Lief racked her brains for some indoor expedient which might release him from those four walls. Build on an aviary? Add a turret? The answer swam into her mind, smooth as a fish. The court library! It was reputed to be a good one, famous for its books of travel. And was totally unvisited. She had heard that some of the books of travel were illustrated. Gentil enjoyed a picture book. The midsummer mornings which had curtailed their secret expeditions now showed a different face: no one would be about at those unfrequented hours of dawn.

No one was. The snores became a reassurance and even a blessing, since they could be timed to smother the squeaks of the library door. Gentil sat looking at the travel books and Lief sat listening to the birds and looking at Gentil. One morning, he gave a cry of delight, and beckoned her to come and see what he had found. It was a woodcut in a book about the Crusades – a battle scene with rearing horses and visored warriors. It was unlike Gentil to be so pleased with a battle scene, but he was certainly in a blaze of joy. He pointed to a warrior who was not visored, whose villainous dark face was muffled in a wimplelike drapery, whose eyes rolled from beneath a turban. 'That ... that ... that's what I need, that's what I must have!' She said it would be ready that same evening.

Having embraced Islam, Gentil found a new life stretching before him. Turbaned and wimpled, he appeared at Court, kissed the Queen's hand, sat among his fellow-Freemen, studied sea anemones. This was only an opening on wider ambitions. It seemed excessive to go to Mecca, and Lief did not wish to visit his parents. But they went to Aberdeen, travelling visibly and using the alias of Lord and Lady Bonny. From Aberdeen they took ship to Esbjerg and inspected the Northern capitals. As travellers do, they bought quaint local artefacts, patronized curiosity shops, attended auctions. One has to buy freely in order to discover the run of one's taste. They discovered that what they most liked was naturalistic paintings. They concentrated on the Dutch School, Lief buying seascapes, Gentil flower pieces, and by selling those which palled on them they made money to buy more. In course of time, they acquired a number of distinguished canvases, but never another Leonardo.

6 Stay, Corydon, Thou Swain

The moon was at her full, and the choral society of Wells in Somerset was holding a practice. Moonshine had to be consulted, for many of the singers lived outside the town and would not venture from their homes by night unless they could see the ruts and puddles. Mr Mulready, however, was independent of the moon; he lived in the market place, and a gas lamp shone in at his bedroom window until 10.30 pm, when all the street lamps gave a little jump and died.

Mr Mulready was a draper. He lived above his shop, though he was sufficiently well-to-do to live, had he wished to do so, in a villa near the station; and this evidence of proper feeling made him much esteemed by the local gentry. He was a small, bald-headed, puggy man, and could sing both bass and alto. What was more, he could read music at sight. These good gifts he employed weekly at the Bethel Chapel, and it was said that Mr Bulmer, a vicar-choral, had fervently attempted Mr Mulready's conversion, in order that he might sing in the Cathedral, especially that alto solo in an anthem by Samuel Sebastian Wesley which declares that, 'as for the gods of the heathen, they are, are, are but idols' – a sneering chromatic phrase which would ring finely under the stone arches if delivered by the rescued Dissenter, but which that bleating old Philpot could never sing in tune.

But Mr Mulready was faithful to Bethel, as much from social as from religious convictions; for, as he said, he was a Baptist born and dipped, and it never did for people to pretend to be what their neighbours knew full well they were not. The Choral Society was another matter: he had been a member of it for nearly twenty years, and he knew most of its repertory by heart.

The piece they practised this evening was a madrigal by John Wilbye: 'Stay, Corydon, Thou Swain'. He had sung in it many times before; he knew every note of it; but this did not lessen his pleasure – indeed, it increased it; for he was able to enjoy its beauty undistracted by the sheet of music that Mr Fair, his neighbour bass, jerked up and down before him in time to the music.

Yet tonight he was destined to hear the old favourite with new ears.

'Thy nymph is light and shadowlike,' sang the first sopranos, coming in on high G, and the second sopranos took up the phrase a fifth lower. All of a sudden Mr Mulready found himself wondering about nymphs, and wondering, too, in a very serious and pertinacious way. He had never to his knowledge given a thought to these strange beings before, and yet it now seemed to him that he had an idea of them both clear and pleasant as though perhaps in childhood he had been taken to see one as a treat.

He wished to see a nymph again: not from motives of curiosity, not because he thought a nymph would be a pretty sight to gaze at, not for any reasonable, pleasure-seeking reason – for how could anyone entertain a rational wish about a mythological fancy? What he felt was more than a whim; it was an earnest desire, a mental craving somehow to recreate a bright image that Time had once timelessly given, and then by course of time effaced.

Even as he sang he looked round on the lady members of the Choral Society to see if they could afford him any clue as to the looks of a nymph. One by one he rejected them. Miss Fair was as pretty a girl as you could wish to see, young Mrs Buckley had a complexion as red and white as the rosebud chintz in his shop, little Jenny Davy was as light as a feather and as ruthless as a kitten – yet none of these answered to his idea of a nymph. She would be quieter, somehow – more ladylike.

So next he studied the ladies, the real ladies who came from the Cathedral Close or from the country houses round about. They were no more helpful. The Reverend Miss Perceval (so he thought of her) had something rather promising about her small pale ears; but, poor young lady, how she did stoop! And as for Mrs Hamlyn, whom there had been all that talk about, she was a high-flier, sure enough, but nothing like a nymph. Her nose was too large.

Not like any member of the Choral Society, not like his dead wife, not like his two daughters, not like any woman he had ever seen – how did it happen, then, that in his mind's eye there should be image of a nymph which he was now trying to confirm by looks of flesh and blood? A picture? On an almanac, perhaps; some of the wholesale firms sent out very handsome ones to the trade. But a picture was flat, a picture was dead: no picture could have become so living to him as this projection of a nymph which he couldn't quite see, but which was none the less present in his thought; for otherwise how could he reject so certainly all these un-nymph-like ladies?

'Thy nymph is light and shadowlike.'

The words haunted him as he walked home, and he hummed the phrase over and over as he sat at supper, with a kind daughter on either hand. As he kissed Sophy goodnight, he thought how cool a nymph's forehead would be. 'Light'. Lightfooted, that must mean, not light-complexioned; for his nymph was dark – at any rate, she had dark hair. The words ran into a new order: 'Light-and-shadowlike' – wavering, rippling as the light bubbles through the shadow of a bough that sways in a spring breeze. As one has a word on the tip of one's tongue, so Mr Mulready had a nymph on the tip of his imagination. And for one moment, just as he blew out the candle and resigned his senses to the bed, he thought he had caught her. Alas, she was gone again in a flash, and he was left with a new perplexity; for now it seemed to him that instead of having seen her long ago he had seen her quite recently, so that her image was indistinct and elusive not because Time had effaced it, but because Time had not yet enforced it, leaving it still a faint pencilling, a sketch.

❧

In the morning he had forgotten these thoughts; but he was soon to remember them again, for when he walked into the shop, there, behind the polished counter and laying out rolls of flannel and sarcenet, was his nymph. He recognised her as one recognises a melody; her looks, her gestures, fulfilled everything he had sought for overnight, as though a tune that he had tried unavailingly to recall had come back into his head complete. With the recognition came the identification; his mind's nymph was Miss Edna Cave, the young lady who sold stay-laces and suchlike female oddments in a dark secluded corner of his shop that in high-flown moments he referred to as the 'haberdashery department'. There she was, and, what was even stranger to him, there she had been for a couple of months. She was a very respectable, quiet-spoken girl, and a good worker, though she had somehow a rather languid air. He remembered wondering when he engaged her if she were anaemic, and if she would be strong enough to lift down the heavy boxes from the shelves. And from then till this moment he had scarcely given her a thought, perhaps because of her very merits as a satisfactory worker and respectable young person.

He wanted to think of her now, to examine her in this new and exciting aspect of a discovery. But it was market day, and the shop soon filled with customers. He was kept busy and could scarcely steal a glance at his nymph until the moment came for him to put up the shutters and for her to put on her hat and gloves.

'You look a little tired, Miss Cave. It's been a busy day, I'm sure. There's more than twenty pounds in the till.'

'I'm not tired, really,' replied the nymph. 'Only a little sleepy. It's the spring, I expect. These first warm days often make me feel a little queer.'

'You should go out more,' said Mr Mulready. 'Have you a bicycle?'

'Yes, I've got a bicycle.'

'I'll tell you what you should do. Tomorrow is early closing. Now, will you come out for a ride?'

'I must say that Annie will come too,' he thought; but before he could utter the words the nymph had answered, 'Thank you, Mr Mulready. I should like to very much.'

Even so, he fully intended to ask Annie, or, if not Annie, then Sophy. It would be nice for her to have the company of girls her own age – bright, friendly girls like his two. But on the morrow he learned from their talk at breakfast that they proposed to go off early in the forenoon to shop in Bath, and would not be back till late. Apparently it had all been settled long ago, even to the hats they were going to buy: a pink chip for Annie, and for Sophy a leghorn with a wreath of white roses.

'You won't mind, will you, Pa? Mrs Creak will see to your tea.'

'I don't know whether I shall want tea, my dear. I was thinking of going out for a ride with –'

The shop bell rang. A little boy had been sent in a great hurry for some narrow black elastic, and Mr Mulready did not have another chance of a word with his daughters. It seemed as though Fate had taken the affair in hand. It would be a pity to disappoint the poor thing, and on such a lovely day, too. But would it be right to ride with her alone? He tried to quiet his scruples by remembering the innocence of his intentions and the number of years that he had been a respectable widower. Yet in a small town one cannot be too careful; and he would be sorry to compromise a nymph. Besides, it would be dull work for her, riding through the spring lanes with such an old fogey as he; she would enjoy herself more when the girls could come too.

Just before closing time Miss Cave approached him.

'Would it be as convenient, Mr Mulready, if we don't start till about five? Mother wants me to help with the ironing.'

He would have spoken then, but suddenly she raised her eyes, and said, 'I am looking forward to it so much.'

No, he could not make difficulties now. After that stint of ironing, the hot room, the heavy sheets to handle and fold, a bicycle ride would be just what she needed.

It was after five when they set out.

'Where shall we go, Miss Cave? Is there anywhere you specially fancy?'

'I should like to go —' she had a low voice and spoke with a curious slight lisp, her speech seeming as it were to rustle 'I should like to go by Glastonbury to that wood called Merley Wood.'

'It's rather a rough road, you know. Have you been there before?'

'No. But I've heard of it; and I have often wanted to go there.'

He knew the wood she spoke of; that is, he had often passed below it, had heard it murmuring aloofly to itself, had seen the long shadow it stretched down to the road. He was not a fearful man; yet for some reason he did not much care to pass Merley Wood towards dusk. It gave him an uneasy feeling in his back and he had once declared in the safety of jest that he wouldn't walk through it – no, not for a five-pound note. But if Miss Cave wanted to go there, that was another matter. When one has a nymph vouchsafed one for a whole evening one does not boggle over details. He was extremely happy and excited at the thought of such a shy and rare being becoming his companion. Now he would really be able to watch, to discover, to make sure of her – or, rather, of the nymph-idea she represented for him. Whatever she did or said would be, he felt sure, the right, the revealing thing. He had already a general idea how a nymph would behave: she would be rather quiet, and take a great interest in flowers.

Yet when Miss Cave, riding ahead of him, suddenly jumped off her bicycle, he cried out, 'Is it a puncture?'

She did not answer. It seemed that she had not heard him. She stood looking into the hedge and smiling at whatever it was she saw there.

'White violets,' she said softly. And then she smiled again, and gently nodded her head, as though between them and her there were some especial understanding. Mr Mulready also nodded – nodded in approval. Yes, it was just as it should be; a nymph would certainly behave thus. It was a pretty sight, and he hoped she would do it again.

She did, jumping off her bicycle, as other people jump off when they see a friend, to greet a flicker of windflowers in an ash coppice, a new growth of Queen Anne's lace – very light and feathery, yet eminently vigorous with the thrusting strength of its sappy green stems – a handful of wild white hyacinths that some child must have gathered and then thrown down in the road to die. But these she took up without any word at all, and for a moment she looked almost severe as she considered them, drooping limply and exhaling their heavy smell of sweetness and untimely death, before she laid them among the grasses at the side of the road.

'It's a thing I don't like at all,' said Mr Mulready, 'picking flowers just to throw down.'

'No more don't I!'

He was surprised at the passion in her voice. He had never heard her speak so vehemently – nor, it occurred to him, in such a rustic way. But in a moment she was her ordinary self again, had mounted her bicycle and was pedalling on before him with her white thread gloves on the handlebars. She rode very fast for a girl of her build. He had quite an ado to keep up with her, and by the time they reached Merley Wood he was hot, and glad of a respite.

❧

They ran their machines into the field below the wood and laid them down under a group of blossoming thorns. A blackthorn hedge straggled up the slope towards the wood; the blossom was beginning to go over, and drifts of tarnished snow lay under the bushes. But in the shadow of the wood, where the sun had not penetrated, the thorn trees were at the perfection of their bloom. They were very old trees, gnarled, and tufted with greenish-grey moss, dry and dead-coloured. It did not seem possible that those angular boughs should have put out the lacework of milky blossoms, each a blunt star, each with its little pointed pink star within it. It seemed rather as though light had rested upon the dead boughs and turned into blossom.

Behind this flowery rampart the wood rose up – sycamore, and sad spruce, and larches sighing and swaying their young green overhead. It was certainly a mournful wood, but Mr Mulready could not now imagine why he had thought it to be a frightening one. Now that he was within it, walking about with Miss Cave, he thought of it as a gentle place. Presently they sat down side by side, and, having sat a little while, lay back, as everyone does, sooner or later, in a wood, to stare up at the treetops waving so high above them.

Mr Mulready watched till he began to feel a trifle sick. He sat up again, and as he did so it occurred to him that he had come out this evening to watch, not larches, but a nymph. And this was a good moment to begin; for she lay staring upward as though she had forgotten his presence – he could look as much as he pleased without being ill-mannered.

First, then, how slender she was, and how supple; for she lay among the wood sorrel as though lying on the ground could never make her stiff, could never give her rheumatism. And next? What struck him next? Her pallor – she was as white as the thorn blossom. But down here at the foot of the trees the light was dim and watery, as if it floated down to them through still, shadowed water. That was why she looked so pale. No real woman had naturally such a moonlight look.

And then? Her hair, which he now saw was not black, as he had believed, but the colour of very dark earth? Her eyes, which were a bright, spangled hazel? Her wide, thin mouth; the line of her jaw, travelling from the small chin to an ear that was quite as fine as Miss Perceval's? He noticed all these things, but he knew that there was something else, something more significant than any of these. Of course. Her silence. For, except for that one outburst over the wild hyacinths, she had scarcely put two words together during the whole evening. Yet you wouldn't call her uncompanionable. When he had spoken she had answered him, though not in words, now he came to think of it, but assenting with sighs of contentment, and acquiescent murmurs, and even little grunts – matching her speech, as it were, to that of the whispering and faintly creaking trees around them.

How still she lay! He could hear her light breathing among the sounds of the breathing wood. Had it not been for her eyes, still open and fixed upon the treetops, he would have said she slept.

Outside the woods, among the thorns, a blackbird had begun his vespers; and the rays of the sun slanted in and turned the larch stems pink. Time was getting on; they should soon be thinking of the ride home. When she woke, when she came out of her waking dream, he would take out his watch tactfully.

But suddenly she turned to him, saying, 'I am so happy here.'

One couldn't answer that by taking out one's watch: it wouldn't be manners.

He made a nice reply – hoped they might have another ride soon. A second blackbird was answering the first from the farther side of the wood. Their voices travelled through the solitary still dusk where these two sat, unguessed-at and secluded as though they lay at the bottom of a shadowy pool.

'Listen to those two chaps,' said Mr Mulready. 'There's singing for you! Are you fond of music?'

'I'm afraid not. At least, I don't care for the piano.'

He wondered if he should tell her how a phrase from a piece of music had brought them here together. But perhaps she wouldn't understand, for he was a poor hand at explanations; and perhaps it might wound her feelings if it came out that he had invited her for such a queer reason.

'Thy nymph is light and shadowlike.' He began to hum to himself, softly and strayingly. Music has a different meaning, a different beauty, out of doors.

❧

The sun had faded out of the wood, the stems of the larches were grown silvery, the wood sorrel they lay upon lost all earthly colour, became grey, became almost black. The smell of the thorn blossom drifted into the wood. Every moment it became more intense and more searching, as though it were the smell of the moonlight.

The nymph sat up and looked about her. She put her hands to her forehead as though to wipe away a dream. Then, shaking her head, she rose and began to walk out of the wood.

Mr Mulready picked up her hat and gloves and followed her. When he came to the edge of the wood he caught his breath and started. The thorn blossom shone so in the moonlight that it looked unearthly. The landscape lay before him, undulating to the horizon in swaths of grey and silver like the swaths of mown hay. Down in the field he could see the two bicycles. Their spokes glittered in the moonlight. The dew was falling, and they would be rusted.

He began to descend the slope, but stopped again; for the nymph delayed. She had turned back towards the thorn trees at the edge of the wood. She stood beside them, quite still, gazing at them as she had gazed at the white violets, earlier in the day – gazing as though, rather than seeing them, she were listening to them. Now she began to walk towards them, very slowly. She put out her hands. He thought that she was going to break off a spray, and, remembering the country belief that whoever takes home blackthorn blossom carries death into the house, he had a confused idea that he must call to her, warn her, tell her not to. And then in a moment she had disappeared.

He saw it happened but he could not believe his eyes. He told himself that she must have slipped round to the other side of the brake, and as he ran back across the dewy grass he kept on saying, 'Oh no, oh no! It can't be! It can't!'

But though he called, and searched, and fought his way into the strong mass of the thorn thicket, frantically believing that she had got in somehow and fallen there in a faint, there was no sign of her. She was gone. With his own eyes he had seen her vanish.

Breathless, and scratched all over, and trembling, at last he sat down on the grass; and, covering his eyes with his bleeding hands, he began to whimper like a lost child. But it was she – she who was lost! And as he abandoned his mind to an acceptance of what had happened he began to forecast in a confused terror all the things that would happen next: a scandal, nobody believing him; Edna's mother weeping and wailing, and perhaps bringing an action; his customers leaving him; his daughters disgraced and turning from him; misery, shame, ruin! The scent from the thorn trees flowed out over him. He caught hold of a branch and clasped it in his arms, awkwardly, as though he would embrace it. The thorns ran into his flesh and the petals slipped floating down on to the ground. 'Oh, come back, come back!' he implored. But there was no answer, no sound except the nightingales singing in the wood.

The Cat's Cradle Book

To
Ludwig Renn

7 Introduction

I had never seen a handsomer young man.

The house was handsome too, its good looks sobered by age and usage – a seventeenth-century house with a long façade and a reed-thatch roof. It gave an impression of slenderness, of being worn smooth and thin like an old spoon. The doorway was narrow and severe, the mullions and transoms of the windows remarkably delicate. Their white paint was worn to a dandelion-clock silver. The house was of brick, it had been coated with a yellowish limewash, and this too was worn thin and the colour of the brick showed dimly through, so the general tint of the house was that of a ripening pear with streaks of vague rose and pale madder flushing its sallow skin.

With trees all around it, with a deep mossy lawn in front of it, the house lay like a pear fallen from a tree – a pear beginning to grow sleepy, I thought. It was mid-May, the birds were singing at the top of their voices, their clamour around the completely silent house made it seem if not lifeless at any rate fast asleep; so there was no incivility in leaning over the wide gate and having a good look at it. Unless I leaned over the gate I could not see it at all, for the straggling hedge was reinforced by a belt of trees and a shrubbery – American currant, I remember, and lilac, syringa, and gipsy rose.

The first cat walked out from under the American currant, and I thought how befitting this was, since the smell of American currant flower is very close to the smell of cats. She was a light tortoiseshell, she looked rather as though nature had coloured her to tone with the house; and she came towards me yawning and stretching her hind legs, and marched up to the gate and began to rub herself against the bars. Presently two grey cats came from under a lilac and joined her. They were pewter-grey, short-furred and cobbily built, with strong shoulders, round heads, and short legs. To show that she had got me first the tortoiseshell cat climbed to the top rail of the gate, and began to rub against my elbow, caress my cheek with her tail, and purr. The two grey cats sat down and looked on.

After a while a fourth cat joined the group. She was older than the others and obviously of a lower social standing; for though she was long-furred she was shabby and down-at-heels, a half-Persian who had chosen to descend in the social scale, preferring the neighbourhood of rubbish heaps and stables to the parlour. Her manners, too, lacked polish. She came running, whereas the others had strolled; she mewed as she ran; and when she jumped on the rail and thrust herself against me I noticed that her jaws were stained with yellow, and that a little piece of egg-shell was stuck to her chops.

'You've been robbing a linnet's nest,' I remarked.

With artful inconsequentiality she said:

'You should see my kittens! They're wonderful – and what appetites! But praise be, all my kittens are fine feeders.'

'And no doubt you will bring them forward on birds' eggs,' I replied.

Meanwhile the tortoiseshell cat in an ecstacy was turning around on the rail, alternately rubbing her left side and her right side against me, as though she could not make up her mind on which side the sensation was most pleasurable.

'That's another of mine,' said the bird's-nesting cat. A black kitten came skidding down the trunk of a Spanish chestnut, a minute dauntless adventurer on the great girth of the tree. It uttered a wild mew (as though it were a hysterical train) and hurled itself at the gate-post. There it settled, washing its face with dignified industry.

It was then that I heard a human voice, saying: 'So you speak Cat?'

'A little,' I replied. 'I understand it better than I can speak it.'

My tone was apologetic. The voice that addressed me was slightly severe, and such beauty as this young man's has in itself the quality of a rebuke, being so immeasurably finer than the run of one's thoughts.

'You should study it properly. Why be so lazy?' he continued, fastening upon my mood of guilt and submission. 'It is just a matter of taking pains and of daily practice. If you speak Cat at all there is no reason why you should not speak it fluently. It is simply a matter of application.'

Speaking as one, the grey cats observed: 'She doesn't look as though she had much application.'

'But she's got a kind heart,' said the long-furred cat. The tortoiseshell cat added that I had a nice smell.

Hypnotized by all this Alice-in-Wonderland candour I continued to lean on the gate, thinking that I had never seen a handsomer young man, and wondering where he had fallen from. For I had not seen him approach. He might have come down a tree, he might have come out from under a lilac or a syringa: no hunting cat could have arrived more stealthily, more disconcertingly. Like a hunting cat, he was on his guard, and concealing it under an appearance of being there more or less by accident and on his way to somewhere else. But there was ownership in every inch of him – ownership of house, and trees, and cats, and privacy, and solitude. He was holding a rake, and a lock of hair fell over one eye.

Meanwhile, in a voice that was slightly haughty, slightly distant, he continued to urge on me the necessity for application, while the long-furred cat continued to demand that I should come and see her kittens. I enjoyed looking at him, and at his house, and I liked his cats; but after a while I began to ask myself why I should submit to being lectured by a strange young man, and said:

'You certainly have every opportunity to keep in practice. How many cats *have* you got?'

'The number varies. At the moment it is nineteen. But don't run away with the idea that I keep them. They live here, which is somewhat different. Indeed, Mrs O'Toady was here before I bought the house. That black kitten is an O'Toady, too.'

'So she told me.'

'An Irish family, settled in Norfolk. Yes, O'Toady, presently. Don't be so impatient, dear. He's one of four. Caspar, Owly, Henrietta, and London O'Toady.'

'Why London?'

'He is a fog-coloured tabby. They were an autumn litter; I found them in a disused pigsty, soon after I arrived. They were eating chestnuts and acorns, like wild cats.'

'And these others?'

'Tom and Martha, the grey pair, are related to Caspar on the father's side. He is a black poaching cat, he lives in the woods. I wish I knew him better, he is an admirable character. The tortoiseshell came with me from Greece. Basilissa. But her friends here call her Queenie.'

We were interrupted by a rattle of wheels, a clip-clop of hoofs. A tradesman's cart drew up at the gate. Simultaneously a great many more cats appeared.

'Excuse me.'

He opened the gate and the cart drove through. Painted on the tail-board were the words: *Craske. Fishmonger*. It drove on and the cats streamed after it.

The young man and I followed the cart round to a yard at the back of the house.

'Three dozen whiting, sir. Five pounds of saithe.'

Holding the clammy newspaper parcel the young man

gestured to me to walk in. A caressing flood of cats came with us.

It was a large old-fashioned kitchen with a wavy brick floor and a tall dresser. The window opened on a nuttery, and a green sunlight filled the room. On the range stood a fish-kettle in which the water was already boiling. Into this the young man emptied the three dozen whiting and the five pounds of saithe.

'China or Indian?' said he, filling a kettle.

'China – that is, if you are asking me to tea.'

He bowed, and began to put china on a tray.

'While the kettle boils I think Mrs O'Toady would like to show you her family.'

We went down a long stone-flagged passage. At the end of it a great door with heavy bars and a key Iike St Peter's stood open. Crossing the yard we entered the stables. These were four loose-boxes. Two of them were heaped with chestnut logs, and a mallet and wedges lay in a corner. The third loose-box contained a sawing-cradle and a bicycle. Mrs O'Toady, leaping onto the half-wall, squirming through the bars, had preceded us into the fourth. When we stepped in she was already lying on her side, her belly extended to the three morsels of smudgy fluff, her eyes gazing upwards in a vacant ecstacy.

'Three O'Toadies, Melusine's five ... I should have said twenty-seven cats,' said the young man. 'But I was reckoning them as a caterer.'

We stood for some minutes silently admiring Mrs O'Toady's motherhood, the look of ineffable contentment on her small mean face, the dignity of her abandoned attitude. At length she rolled over, dragged the three kittens into her embrace, and began to lick them. As we left the stable she was saying in a drowsy voice:

'Once upon a time there was a dog who had thieved a bone ...'

The young man turned, and gave me a searching glance.

'Æsop?' said I.

'That is what I shall talk to you about during tea.'

But he did not fulfil the promise. A sudden reserve had invaded him. Tea was made, and carried into a sitting room where a tarnished mirror reflected the mossy lawn, the patron trees; and I was introduced to some more cats, an affable young golden tabby and a silver tabby, not so affable, and a white cat, deaf and stately; and for the rest we exchanged only a few conventional remarks, while I looked out of the window, and thought how less than an hour ago I had stopped my car in order to look over the gate at a house like a sleepy pear in which I was now drinking China tea from a pink teacup; and the young man, while I looked out of the window, looked at me. Looked, indeed, is too mild a word. He stared: intently, unswervingly, as the explorer stares at the map or the mineralogist at the rock or the cat at the mousehole.

We had finished tea, we had come to the end of our remarks, when he got up, and said:

'Please come upstairs.'

I rose obediently, and followed him to a room filled with books, whose window reiterated the same view of lawn and trees with only the variation of being seen from ten foot higher.

'Sit down,' he commanded. He gave me one final violent stare, and then, seating himself at the further end of the room, said in a voice intensely controlled:

'Have you ever thought about the culture of cats?'

'No,' I said humbly.

'I have. I have given the subject a great deal of thought. During the last eight months I have studied it intensively. Perhaps it will be best if I begin by giving you a short account of how I came to take up the subject.'

'Please do,' said I.

'When I left Oxford I went into the diplomatic service. There was really no reason why I should, but I happen to be good at languages, and I suppose my father thought that my total lack of interest in the British Empire might not be so apparent if expressed in Portuguese or Hungarian. I disliked the life intensely. I was bored and I was homesick. Foreigners annoy me and I am the prey of regional diseases. Then, while I was in Turkey, I fell in love. The wife of the naval attaché had bought a Siamese cat. She was beautiful, sensitive, unappreciated. The formality and tedium of embassy life were as alien to her as they were to me. Though we were both egoists, we were both unhappy. Our unhappiness transcended our egoism, and by degrees, by a complicated process of advances and withdrawals, exchange of looks, fusion of silences, we fell deeply in love with each other. One night as I lay awake, listening to the incessant uproar of the city, the cries of the tourists being conducted from one night-club to another, and those tedious muezzins, I saw her spring into my balcony. There she stood in the first light of dawn, poised, rocking lightly like a soap-bubble. Then with a cry of joy, raucous and passionate, she sprang on to my bed.

'After that she lived with me. Naturally, there was a good deal of talk about it – embassies always gossip – and the naval attaché's wife made a fuss, and tried to reclaim her. But after Haru had scratched her to the bone and destroyed a coffee-service she recognized the inevitable and gave way.

'I had been so unhappy, and now my whole life was transfigured, full of entertainment and delight. Though, with my characteristic idiocy, I developed fever a few weeks later, Haru's devotion made sickness a pleasure. She used to lie on my chest, licking Brand's Essence of Chicken from my lips. One afternoon, during the long leisure of convalescence, she said she would tell me a story. It was the Scandinavian story of the Cat on the Dovrefell. I asked her where she had learned it. Amused by my curiosity, gently mocking, she replied that it was one of the stories that every kitten learns at its mother's tail.

'She was an exquisite story-teller, in the purest, most classical tradition of narrative. Never a word too much, never a point overstressed. It was as though she were dictating to Perrault. Thanks to her, every day I increased my knowledge of cat; and with every increase of knowledge I appreciated new beauties in her phrasing and choice of language.

'A month later we were in agonies. She came on heat. She howled incessantly, she howled the roof off. All her command of language was devoted to the filthiest eroticisms. She sulked, she made herself hideous, she destroyed my books and tore up my pyjamas. She refused to eat, and made her messes everywhere but in her tray of cedar chips. As for me, I behaved quite as badly as she, and quite as naturally. I refused to let her out. I called her every lewd name I could lay my tongue to, I beat her, I emptied the water-jug over her. Drenched and trembling she lay in my arms, staring with red eyes at the veins in my neck, alternately imploring me to release her and taunting me with my inability to console her lust.

'"I have only to hold out for another couple of days," I said to myself. And two days later she became suddenly gentle, melancholy, and abashed. I did l not know it, but even then she was dying. She began to cough, her fur grew harsh, she lost her beautiful smell of sandalwood and gave out the stink of fever. In her delirium she forgot our life together, and thought she was back at the naval attaché's. Almost her last words were a muttered plot to rip off his gold braid.

'Whether she died from the strain of thwarted passion or from pneumonia because I emptied the water-jug over her I don't know. In either case I was the cause of her death.'

I could find no words that would be suitable. After a pause he said: 'You had better stay for dinner.'

I said (hoping that my acceptance might sound sufficiently docile, sufficiently unobtrusive) that I would like to very much.

'Love,' he resumed, 'makes one sensitive, but it also makes one obtuse. The whole power of one's attention is focused like the beam of an electric torch on the loved person. Beyond that narrow circle is an unspeculated darkness. I was a perfect example of this. I don't mean merely that while I loved Haru I became perfectly stupid and useless as a member of the embassy staff: that goes without saying. But while I loved Haru I was stupid even where she was concerned. I knew that she was highly cultured, highly civilized; but it never occurred to me to speculate about the culture and civilization she represented. She was Haru, my Siamese cat; and other cats remained for me what they had always been: sharp-witted animals that it is a flattering pleasure to handle. After her death (for I was determined not to mutilate her memory by any sentimental faithfulness) I took another cat – a male neuter, a charming guttersnipe. As a kitten, I suppose, he must have been considered sufficiently well-bred to be robbed of his sex – but by the time he reached me he was perfectly *déclassé*. One day he too began to tell me a story. And his story was quite recognizably the same as one of Haru's stories – the story she called Bluebeard's Daughter. What was my conclusion? – that he must have learned it from her. I barely listened to him, all my thoughts flowing towards my lost Scheherazade. No wonder he left me the same night.

'Meanwhile I was becoming more and more disgusted with my profession – and my profession was becoming more and more disgusted with me. The wife of the naval attaché had never forgiven me for "stealing her funny little cat" – and she teased, and everything became very unpleasant and skittish, and I neglected my work, and wouldn't play tennis, and the air of the embassy became charged with a moral implication that it would be much better if I kept a terrier. Finally it came to a solemn official reproach; and remembering that if I abandoned any notion of a career I should have enough to live on, I gave in a chivalrous resignation, and came back to England, and found this house, and liked it, and rented it.

'I met Basilissa on my way back, and she settled in with me; and for a week or so I supposed we were alone here. It rained, and I was busy arranging my books and didn't go out much. One evening I went out to shoot rats. I was lying near the rubbish heap, waiting for them, when I heard a scream and knew that one rat, at any rate, had gone to another hunter. Then I saw her – Mrs O'Toady – looking an absolute rag-bag, slinking along on her belly and hauling her kill. She jumped into an old pigsty, and I heard her kittens.

'I didn't want to shoot and frighten them. But it was a lovely evening, and I went on lying by the rubbish heap, looking at the trees, and feeling the dew fall on me, and every now and then hearing an acorn drop. And then I suppose I fell asleep, for it seemed to me that Haru was sitting there telling me her story of the Hermit and the Tiger. Another acorn dropped, and I knew there was no Haru. But the story was there, and went on, and was being told in the pigsty.

'It was the identical story. Every detail, every turn of the narrative – even the same phrases, phrases which had seemed to me the fine flower of Haru's artistry. Yes, here, in a disused pigsty in Norfolk, a poor unlettered tabby was repeating to her kittens a story of Indian life which I had first heard from the lips of my Siamese cat in Ankara.

'Everything else fell into place – Haru's first narrative of the Cat on the Dovrefell, a story known to me since my childhood, when an aunt gave me Dasent's *Tales from the Norse*; and poor

Bubu's version of Bluebeard's Daughter; and Basilissa's vague babblings about Centaurs and a Fox-Pope; and Haru's own words about the stories kittens learned at their mother's tail. All these fragments of a whole dazzled in front of me, and like quicksilver ran into each other and lay still.

'I had vowed to myself that I would live only in the present, only for the present. I should not have vowed so hard if in my secret heart I had not suspected how listless it is to live without a future. Now my future was determined. It should be given up to studying the cultural heritage of cats.

'I have been studying it,' he concluded, 'ever since. For the last eight months.'

'With the collaboration of your cats? Or are they raw material rather than collaborators?'

'Primarily, they are sources. I am in the position of anyone collecting folklore, or traditional songs and dances. I have to get my material from them without making them self-conscious. Cats become self-conscious very easily; they dislike anything approaching investigation. In one respect, however, they are much better than humans. They don't turn into folk artists and invent.'

'And who is your best source?'

'Mrs O'Toady, by far. She has the widest repertory, the finest versions. She is inexhaustible.'

'A shanachie.'

'And a mother. This is her third litter since we met. You see, these stories are not merely works of art; they are nursery tales and education. No literary commissar in Soviet Russia (a fine country. I like it) could have a clearer notion of the social function of literature than a cat has. Just as the little Soviet citizens are reared on Marshak or simple histories of the development of the internal combustion engine, just, for that matter, as little Christian imperialists of a century ago in this country were taught how to manage subject races by reading *Little Henry and His Bearer*, kittens are trained up in a catly frame of mind by these stories learned at their mothers' tails. The milk flows, and the narrative flows with it. That is nothing remarkable, of course. Bend the twig and shape the tree. Train up a child in the way he should go and afterwards he will not depart from it. But what is remarkable,' he cried, waving a paper-knife, 'is the universality and unanimity of these stories, the fastidious feline memory which enables Mrs O'Toady in Norfolk and Haru from Siam to preserve an uncorrupted text. I have as many as five separate versions of some of these stories. I have taken them down in shorthand and collated them. And there is scarcely a variant.

'People write to the newspapers,' he went on, 'about the phenomenal memories of cats. Some cat is carried in a closed hamper from Land's End to John o' Groats; and six months later it is back at Land's End once more. Then some other newspaper busybody will write prating of instinct. Instinct, instinct! Pooh! It is memory. Memory as scrupulous, as unremitting, as the integrity with which they keep themselves clean.'

'But what are these stones like? They are instructive, you say. Are they like fables? Mrs O'Toady, I think, remembers Æsop.'

'We shall come to Æsop later. Meanwhile, don't run away with the idea that these stories have anything in common with the ordinary moral tales, the ordinary web-footed propaganda.'

'I don't,' said I.

'Good! Excellent! But really, I think you had better judge for yourself.'

He opened a drawer, pulled out a folder, and handed me some pages of typescript.

'The text comes from Meep – another excellent mother and narrator, though I saw you didn't hit it off with her, nor she with you, when you met at tea. I bought her from a level-crossing on the local railway. For having discovered, you see, that for the richest sources one has to go to nursing mothers, I went round collecting as many females as I could. Meep's *urtext* is collated with two other versions, me from Basilissa, whom you have met, the other from Noisette, a little tabby from the Channel Islands, whom I got off a fishing boat. Greek, Norman-French, East Anglian. You will see the variants, how few, how unimportant they are.'

On the title-page was written *Odin's Birds*. The story was typed with wide margins on very expensive, thin, tough paper. The annotations were typed with the red half of the ribbon. Corrections were added in a fine fidgety hand.

When I had laid it down he said:

'What do you think of it? Does anything strike you especially?'

'That it's so very objective.'

'Of course. Cats are objective. But did you notice nothing else?'

'The Scandinavian element, of course. But isn't it also the ballad of The Twa Corbies? And then the question of distribution ... East Anglia, Channel Islands, Greece. At first they seem far enough apart, but not too far for a Viking ship to have carried them the story. The Varangians went to Byzantium.'

'Go on.'

'To Vinlandia, too, perhaps. Have you been able to get a female cat from North America? – though I can see you might become embroiled with emigrants, cats that sailed in the *Mayflower*, Bay Settlements, and what not. Still, I think you should examine the cats of the New World. A cat from Yucatan, for instance. Even in Greenwich Village you would find representative cats of almost every nation, remarkably fine ones, too –'

I thought it would be nice to do a little talking myself, but he interrupted me, frowning behind his dangling forelock.

'As far as I am concerned, all this is rather beside the point. I am not interested in this humanistic approach, and I think, too, you are attaching far too much importance to nationalities. If my theory is correct – and I am more and more convinced that it is correct – the culture of cats transcends mere racial accidents; and as for trying to fasten it all on whether the Vikings went to Vinlandia, I have a strong notion that you are putting the cart before the horse. For as I see it –'

The doorbell rang. He got up and looked out of the window.

'Good evening, Mr Thurtle.'

'Good evening, sir. Mrs Thurtle, she ask me to call round for a kitten.'

'I'll get you a kitten immediately.'

My heresies – for the moment at least – were overlooked.

'You'll help me round up some kittens?'

'With pleasure.'

We went to and fro through outhouses and garden, gathering a kitten here and a kitten there. When we had half a dozen squirming in a deep hamper we carried them to the man standing by the door.

'Here you are, Mr Thurtle. Take your choice of these.'

The man made a careful choice, holding up each kitten in turn by the scruff of the neck.

'I'll take this here. Two and six, sir?'

'Two and six. Thank you, Mr Thurtle. I hope it will prove a good mouser. By the way, how's that golden cypress doing that you got for your sister-in-law?'

'He do all right.'

The man went off with his kitten. The various elder cats who had arrived to watch the transaction went their ways.

'I keep them thinned out like this. Only after their mothers have done with them, though, and only to good plain homes.

Quite a lot of my cats have gone to sea. Fortunately most people want toms, and for my purposes females are best. I always charge the same price. One week I made twelve and six.'

Talking, he had conveyed me down a narrow shadowy path into a square kitchen garden where there was a broken glasshouse with vine shoots ramping out of it, and several sentimental wire arches toppling under their burden of climbing roses.

'I thought we'd pick some asparagus for dinner.'

For one young man – and certainly he lived here alone – there was an inordinately ample extent of asparagus bed.

'It's nice to have enough asparagus. Enough for myself and for the cats. There's Dinah. She prefers it raw … Dinah, your black and white kitten has gone to live with Mrs Isaac Thurtle.'

She cast herself down and rolled at his feet, gulping down a mouthful of asparagus tips in order to say that she had done her best for the boy and now he must find his own way in the world. We cut a great deal of asparagus, and carried it into the kitchen. While I trimmed it and tied it in bunches he prepared nineteen fish dinners, and stood in the yard calling:

'The cats, the cats! The little cats!'

Besides the asparagus there was some cold pigeon pie, and a plateful of sugar biscuits. And there was a bottle of *vin d'Anjou*. Several cats sat in the dining room, some on chairs, some on the window-sill, some on the large rosewood table. When, with the sugar biscuits, coffee and brandy were served, one of these, a massive marmalade cat, rose up and began to sip delicately from the wide glass.

'I've never seen a cat drink brandy.'

'No?'

'Indeed, I've been told that a teaspoonful of brandy will kill a cat.'

'So it may – some cats. Havelock Ellis tells of a woman who for her own pleasure was enjoyed twenty-five times in a night. But he doesn't lay it down as a general law. One must not make these hard and fast rules.

'Which brings me back,' he said, 'to what I was saying when Mr Thurtle interrupted us. In my opinion you put the cart before the horse.'

'Exactly how?'

'By taking it for granted that when my cats tell a story that we know as a story from Scandinavia they must needs have learned it originally from a Viking; by trudging after your ridiculous Varangians, and supposing that Mrs O'Toady's ancestress must have sat by Æsop's inkpot. Why not be simple, why not be objective ... Why not suppose that our stories came to us from the cats? Try to clear your mind of humanism, and consider the evidence. Where do we find the stories most constant, most uncontaminated? Among the cats. It is among the misunderstanding forgetful humans that they become corrupt and prejudiced. What is the prevailing mood of these stories we call folk stories? Is it heated and sentimental like the undoubted products of the human imagination – or is it cool and dispassionate – what you like to call objective – and catlike? What are the qualities these stories praise – whenever they unbend sufficiently to praise anything – chivalry and daring, or sensibility and reserve? Think what a pother these ethnologists have got into, trying to account for the African and the Eskimo knowing the same tales, and linking them up, as you did, with Varangians and Phœnicians, or deciding that the peoples of the world were all and severally inspired to the same complicated narrative by observing the solstice. And under their noses the Eskimo and the African are repeating an identical creed carried among them by missionaries. Good heavens, what trouble people will put themselves to in order to avoid a simple conclusion! Do try to be reasonable! For ages the languages of men have kept them apart. For ages the Cat language has been catholic, explicit, unvarying. I understand it, you understand it, every child picks up an inkling of it. When cats creep into children's cradles, and the old women say they are sucking the child's breath, what do you suppose they are doing? Keeping them quiet with a story – and better than their mothers can. Let me fill up your glass.

'You may object that these stories do not deal exclusively with cats, that they are stories of mankind as much – or more – as stories of catkind. But why not? Cats have chosen to live among us, they have to reckon with us, analyse our motives, trace our weaknesses and peculiarities. The proper study of catkind is man. The results of this study they have embodied in narratives, which they tell to their children, and by superflux to our children. No highly cultured race keeps its culture to itself.'

'I can't object to anything,' said I, 'on the strength of one example. What you say is extremely interesting and I expect I shall believe it. But so far you have only shown me *Odin's Birds.*'

'I wanted you to read the others in a proper spirit,' he replied. 'Now, I hope and believe you will. You know where they are and I suppose you know how to light an oil-lamp. Take the brandy with you and I'll join you when I've washed up.'

We had sat late. I went upstairs through a house drowning in dusk. Through the open casements the moths came in, and the residual scent of a summer day. Very happy, I settled myself and began to read. Presently I heard a soft scrambling in the climbing white rose whose boughs festooned the window; and a young cat climbed in and looked at me, and then jumped into my lap and fell asleep.

When the young man returned from washing up he came over to my chair and began caressing the cat on my knee.

'I'm so fond of London. And I don't often get the chance to stroke him, for he is exceedingly shy and reserved. Do you like the stories?' he added; and for the first time that evening his voice lost its haughty quality and acknowledged a desire to please and be pleased.

'Very much. As much as I like cats. Is this one, *Bluebeard's Daughter*, the story Haru told you?'

'Yes and No. It's a farrago I constructed from her material – educated oaf that I was, thinking I could improve on perfection! And I have never found it again, which serves me right. If I had listened to my poor guttersnipe I might have got some sort of text. But because I was thinking of Haru I did not attend to him; and so all was smudged and mismanaged. One wastes so much – mislays so many felicities …' He carried his glass to the window and stood looking out.

'What make is your car?'

'Riley. The very word is like a knell.'

'No, no! Why? I don't suppose anyone's waiting for you. I want to ask you something. What am I to do about these stories?'

'About publishing them, you mean?'

'I suppose so –'

The Clarendon Press, the Pitt Press, the Rationalist Press, the Nonesuch, Random House … for each I pressed a dubious finger into the ribs of the young cat sleeping on my knee, and to each pressure he responded with a faint purr, ripples of pleasure breaking softly on the strand of consciousness. It pleased him, but it did not help me towards the fitting publisher.

'You would have a preface, I suppose, and give your sources, and variant readings as footnotes?'

'I suppose so. Yes, certainly. I intend to do the thing properly.'

Even should he find the publisher, what sort of reception

could he look for? And my mind's eye began to foresee the notices in the press, the accumulating ejaculations that the publisher would print on the jackets of the third and fourth editions. *A tour de force of delicacy. A fragrant new talent. Certainly the book of the week. An epoch in fantasy. Ideal for cat-lovers.* If it sold, that is. Otherwise, my mind's eye looked into a blank.

'The difficulty, so it seems to me, would be establishing its claim as a serious work of scholarship. Cat is not a recognized language. How are you to convince people that what is roughly a vocabulary of mew and guttural can convey such fine shades of meaning? Scholars of Chinese, accustomed to a tonal language, might understand. But for the rest, I doubt how they'd take it. Could you leave out the preface and the annotations?'

'The preface is essential. If it can't be done properly, then why should it be done at all? I can't have it coming out like a story-book for children.'

'But actually, that is what it is. These *are* stories for children.'

He sat considering. Out of the silence his voice exclaimed:

'But they'll say I wrote them! That I made them up.'

'Maybe. But then, however you publish them you will make them yours. You will hold the copyright, you will be paid a royalty, you will accept responsibility for anything that is libellous or offensive. If the Home Office –'

'How ridiculous!'

'Yes, indeed. But the law cannot move except against a defendant. The Home Office could not prosecute an indefinite host of cats. Or even one cat, now I come to think of it. Mrs O'Toady is *extra judice*. If she published a libel the law would have to proceed against you, as her owner or next friend. To proceed directly against the race of cats would need an act of Parliament. Then the language question would be a further difficulty. Experts in translating Cat would have to make their affidavits that Mrs O'Toady –'

'Now you are just being silly.'

'Yes, I am. If one goes even a little way into legality and constitution one inevitably becomes silly. But at least I hope I've made it clear to you that however you publish these stories you will be held to have a hand in them.'

'An editorial committee?'

'Would be considerably more convenient. Bear ye one another's burdens. Best of all if you could include in it a sprinkling of retired Viceroys, Fellows of the Zoological Society, big-game hunters, and an authority on vitamins.'

'There's no getting any sense out of you this evening. The *vin d'Anjou* must have gone to your head. Perhaps you'll be better if I take you out of doors.'

We wandered about the dusky garden; we went to lock up the toolshed; we stood in the echoing stable; we leaned on a gate opening into a small paddock; we trailed through the wet swishing grass of an orchard – still debating how best to publish the stories, and then if they should be published at all. What would the cats feel about it? If the thousandth chance were hit, if the book were seriously received, cats all over Europe would be interrogated, publicity impresarios would exploit and misrepresent them, their cultural heritage, guarded so long and so scrupulously, would be laid open to commerce and prettification, incalculable harm and misery might be the end of our beginning. Possibly the best plan would be to give a copy of the full text to the British Museum with a Joanna Southcott-like stipulation that the seal should not be broken until the coming of a more rational age. But who could tell, who should decide, when that age had come? – and in the interim the bequest might be forgotten. And at any moment a declaration of war, an airraid …

Now we stood by the drive gate, and I leaned on it, but

staring outwards this time, staring at the car and the line of oak trees beckoning the road away and away.

'We are powerless!' I exclaimed.

'We must rely on the cats,' said he. 'It is their business, and no doubt they know how to manage it.'

He took my arm and led me to the lawn. There we stood side by side looking at the house with its one window alight, the wavy line of the roof-tree, the heavy-headed trees beyond. Deftly he knocked me over, and with a sigh began to make love to me. The mossy grass was deep and cool, and in an interval of love I praised it.

'It has never been cut,' said he, 'except with a scythe. While I am here it never will be.'

A cuckoo woke me. I was lying on the lawn alone, and it was green now, and the sun flashed on the dew; the whole garden seemed to be vibrating with the sharp chime of the spectrum. I looked at it a little, and saw Caspar picking his way over the grass, shaking flashes of dew from his paws, and fell asleep again.

On my second waking the young man was kneeling beside me.

'Here is your coffee.'

He had made coffee but he had not shaved. It was like breakfasting on a journey, *café au lait* in thick cups, thick slices of bread and butter. The two grey cats, still taciturn, joined us, and Noisette, the cat from the Channel Islands, wreathed herself about the coffee-pot. He was as beautiful, as elegant, as grandmannered as yesterday. Only the fine stubble blurring the outline of cheek and chin assured me that it was now today.

I asked him to send me a carbon copy of the stories, and gave him my address.

'For it is safer not to keep both copies under the same roof. I will not show them.'

Having finished their milk the grey cats walked off.

'You must make my adieux to the cats.'

'I love you a great deal,' he said. 'Now I think you must be going.'

By the door grew a cistus bush, its blotched fourpetalled flowers widely, blindly, staring at the sun. As I moved I saw that Meep, the silver tabby, was sitting in its shelter. Her sharp face was expressionless as with delight she watched me go.

After a while the carbon copies arrived. Accompanying them was a brief letter telling me that a new female was a marvellous story-teller. *Her variants are particularly interesting. They seem to have a personal quality, to express a personal artistry. This is very strange and somewhat disconcerting. I shall soon be sending you another batch.*

In November I got a telegram:

They are all dying. Please come at once. London died at 5:30 this morning.

As I drove I heard myself reiterating desperately: 'While it is still daylight. While it is still daylight.' But darkness fell early from the low clouds, and where the oak trees hooded his lane I had to turn on my lights.

After staring for so long through the muddied wind-screen and the shuffling movement of the wiper the severe grey dusk seemed too pure for my eyes to assimilate. With the feeling that I was approaching something that was not really there I walked towards the house. A light, glaring and meretricious in this world of glimmering grey, shone through a window and disappeared again, and I knew he was carrying a lamp along the kitchen passage.

The front door stood open. I could hear dead leaves wandering about the hall. I went in, and a moment later he came in by another door.

'Thank God you've come! Do you know anything about the diseases of cats?'

While he spoke he was putting down the lamp on the table, placing it in the exact centre with the sleep-walking accuracy of someone half-dazed with shock or fatigue.

'Only that they are very difficult to cure.'

'You had better come and see them at once. Now let me see, which lot shall I show you first? I find it difficult to remember who's dead and who's alive. You'd better come and see Caspar and Melusine. They're upstairs.'

The house smelt of sickness, death, and disinfectant. In front of the fire was a nest of blankets, and Melusine lay there, draggled and heavy.

'Where's Caspar? He oughtn't to wander off like this, it's essential to keep them warm. This house is so damnably draughty! Caspar, Caspar!'

He knelt down and began peering under the furniture. From under a bureau he pulled out something basically black but smothered in dust and cobwebs. It struggled, and yowled suddenly, and with a look of despair he put it in my hands. I began to stroke it, to smooth off some of the cobwebs that had stuck to the fur that was matted with vomit.

'They're dying, aren't they? They're all like this, except for those that are dead. All the vet can tell me is that it's not distemper. He had Noisette for a post-mortem, to see if it was poisoning. But there was no sign of poison. They're just dying. The baker says it's a murrain. They were too many, too thick on the ground, he says.'

I told him we must try to save some of the kittens, that a breeding cat will sometimes go through an epidemic untouched. I said all the usual vain things that sensible people say in face of disaster. I made him drink a brandy and soda. Then we went the round of the house. It was desolately tidy, and everywhere were cats being sick, cats crouching in corners or stretched by draughty doors, cats dying. Basilissa, he said, had been the first to sicken. In broad midday the pupils of her eyes had distended, swamping the whole iris, and had not contracted again. She had complained of a headache, had become profoundly melancholy. That was five days ago. But Noisette, who sickened later, had been the first to die. Both the grey cats were dead, Meep was dead, and the old white cat who had been so stately, and London. As he talked he contradicted himself, miscalled them, killed a cat and brought it alive again in one sentence.

'Mrs O'Toady?' I asked.

'I don't know. She was alive the day before yesterday, for I saw her in the garden. I haven't seen her since. I expect she's dead by now. Half of them are out in the garden. They crawl under bushes and die. Noisette and Mince both left litters of kittens. I've been trying to keep them alive with sops of milk; they are too young to lap. There they are.'

He took me into the kitchen. There was a feeble mosquito wailing that seemed to come from the air itself like the wailing of lost souls. He pointed to a covered basket that was hanging from a hook in the ceiling.

'I have to keep them up there because of the rats.'

He pulled down the basket and unfastened the lid and we looked in. They were half starved, blind, and sneezing. The stronger trampled over the weaker. Though I did not suppose there was a chance of saving them I began to dribble milk and water into their jaws.

'What a charnel-house I've brought you to!'

Now we looked at each other, and I thought that already I must be looking as hopeless, as exhausted, as panic-stricken as he.

'We must try for the kittens.'

But early the next morning, having watched four cats die during the turn of the night, when I unhooked the basket and examined the kittens, feebly scuffling, feebly complaining, terror overwhelmed me. Two were dead, their bellies swollen, their paws thin and rigid like rat's paws. But it was the living I feared. Why should they live, what was I doing to keep them alive? The curse would drive on till death ended it, and it would be better to leave these living ones unsuccoured, since I had not the courage to end them. And even while I fetched the milk, and warmed it, a hand of iron seemed to lie on my shoulder; and when they swallowed and were immediately shaken with hiccups, I loathed them and loathed myself.

That afternoon, when three kittens were the only animals left alive in the house, we went out into the garden.

A washy sunlight had straggled through the morning's cloud. Pools of rain-water lay on the paths and in the furrows of the dug beds, palely reflecting the sky. The rain had brought down the last of the leaves; a good thing, I thought, for that matting of fallen leaves would hide the outdoor dead. We walked up and down through the kitchen garden, talking of Kinglake's *Eothen*. Waddling, and low to the ground, a tabby cat hurried towards us. For a moment I thought it was Mrs O'Toady. But it was Owly, who was very like her mother.

She rubbed her head on the earth and tried to roll, but her legs gave way under her. Then she sat down on her haunches and looked at us. She opened her mouth to mew, but no sound came.

I picked her up. For the moment when I thought she was Mrs O'Toady I had felt a piercing sense of victory. But it was only Owly, a foolish, almost witless creature; and though I held her and talked to her my feelings were of anticlimax and embarrassment.

She was skin and bone. Her feet were stone-cold, her thick

fur was shabby and sodden, and she had lost her voice. But she was alive; and leaning out of my arms she began to rub herself against his sleeve. He looked at her stomach.

'She's full of milk,' he said. 'I suppose she's had her kittens. But she's got it like the rest of them. Look at her eyes.'

Weak and sentimental, she laid her head against his shoulder and stared at the sky. Gradually her pupils contracted, narrowed to fine slits, the peaceful green iris smoothly subduing them.

'She's had it,' I said, 'and got over it.'

'Owly, where are your kittens?'

She lolled against him, looking foolish. I said it would be more to the point if we fed her. Having eaten, she would be ready to go back to them. He fetched milk and beef-tea from the house, and she ate ravenously. Then she trotted off, cunningly swerving this way and that.

'She's gone into the vinery. Go and get those other kittens. She'll adopt them. She'll adopt anything she can lay her hands on, she's made that way. And then we shall be rid of them,' he added, lowering his voice.

I fetched them, and gave them to him in silence, and in silence he carried them off. I knew well enough what was in his mind: the house standing empty again, the garden going back to ruin, the rough cats slinking through the undergrowth, eating birds and birds' eggs, acorns and chestnuts. I heard the vinery door grate on its hinges, and walked slowly back to the house, and turned on a bath. For if I were driving back to London I should be the better for washing off the last twelve hours. I did not think he would suppose me heartless for leaving immediately, since all was at an end.

8 Odin's Birds

Two ravens sat on a bough and talked of old times. Said the raven called Gret to the raven called Knob:

'The bodies were frozen so hard that my beak ached for days after. It was really a very disappointing slaughter. Showy, of course; but quite unrewarding.'

'I remember it well,' said Knob. 'I was there too. Odin was delighted. He said he had never gathered so many hero-souls in the course of a day's fighting.'

'Just what he would say. I have never known a more egotistic deity. Hero-souls! That's all he thought of. Never a moment's consideration for his poor faithful birds, hopping around the battle-field, worn out with a hard day's flying, and tantalized with the sight of a thousand corpses frozen too hard to be edible. Yet where would he have been without us? Who would have noticed Odin if it had not been for his ravens?'

'It must be a great many years since he died,' said Knob. 'He thought he was immortal. We have never claimed more than longevity, yet we have outlived him.'

'Haw-haw-haw!' laughed Gret.

'Yet he was not such a bad old god. After all, Gret, there were spring and summer battles too. Then we fed well.'

'A mere vulgar surfeit. Heaps of bodies rotting in the sun, when one-tenth of the number would have sufficed to feed us. It used to make my heart bleed to see such wastefulness.'

'Nevertheless, I wouldn't object to seeing a little of that wastefulness now,' said Knob, looking wistfully over the quiet moors. 'It is a very long time since I've had a good square meal of hero.'

'My worthy Knob, you are no better than the Israelites, who sighed for the fleshpots of Egypt. Believe me, it is both healthier and more agreeable to live as free ravens. A light varied diet — sometimes a lamb, sometimes a hare, little kickshaws of blackcock or stoat or badger, and maybe a dead baby dropped by the gipsies — such a diet is really more to my taste than Odin's monotonous table of heroes. Besides, think what an appetite sauces the food found by one's own initiative.'

Knob made no reply. For some time the birds sat silently on the bough. Then Knob began to turn his head to the wind.

'Tell me, Gret, do you not smell something? Perhaps it does not interest you. Your ideas are so progressive. But to me it smells like man.'

They took wing together, and flew upwind.

The smell grew stronger, and was undoubtedly the smell of man-flesh. They traced it to a scrubby and stony little oak-copse. There lay the carcass of a handsome man, large and in fine condition. But they were not the first to arrive. A young woman with dishevelled hair and a great belly was kneeling beside the dead man as though she owned him.

The two ravens flew low, and squawked, and flapped their wings, hoping to scare her. They mentioned repeatedly that they were Odin's ravens. But either the girl did not understand them or she felt no reverence for Odin, for she did not attempt to make way.

'I don't know what's coming to the world,' said Gret. 'Young people nowadays have lost every vestige of religious feeling. We're Odin's birds!' he screamed in her face.

She beat him off inattentively, and began kissing the dead mouth again.

'Look at that, look at that!' groaned Knob. 'Have you ever seen such selfishness? You don't think — you don't think she means to eat him herself?'

'She'll do what's as bad. She'll bury him. The minx! Yes, that's what she's up to.'

For now the girl, sighing and shuddering, had begun to drag the body towards a shallow grave newly scratched in the turf. The two ravens looked on despairingly. Then their fortune turned. Spurring her horse over the moor came another woman, who was older, and whose hair was neatly braided, and whose belly was flat. She dismounted, and ran towards the girl, exclaiming:

'So you think you'll have him, do you?'

'Think I'll have him? I know I've had him! And that's more to the point, and something you can never undo.'

'And now you propose to bury him out here as though he were some worthless tinker? You may like an outdoor bed yourself. But let me tell you that my husband will lie in the family vault, where in due course I shall lie beside him.'

'That will be a change for you.'

'Strumpet!' cried the older woman.

'Wife!' retorted the girl.

Leaping over the body, the wife threw herself upon the leman, and boxed her ears. She was the bigger-built, but the leman was the fiercer fighter. Presently the wife turned and ran, and the leman pursued her, screaming and throwing stones.

'Good riddance to bad rubbish,' said Gret to Knob. 'Did you ever see worse fools, quarrelling amidst such plenty? Which eye will you take, right or left?'

They settled down contentedly to their meal.

9 The Castle of Carabas

For five generations the heirs to the marquisate of Carabas had come into the world with a peculiar birth-mark, like the imprint of a cat's paw, and with a horror of cats.

The birth-mark was, under the circumstances, comprehensible; for the castle of Carabas, though situated on one of the healthiest mountains in Navarre, is remote from any society, and thus five marchionesses of Carabas had spent the most sensitive year of married life with little or nothing to look at except the armorial bearings of the marquisate, of which by far the most striking feature is the crest: *a cat rampant, booted and tached proper.*

The horror of cats was more gloriously accounted for. The crest records the exploit of the first marquis, who overcame a cat in single combat — but a cat of such gigantic size and hellish cunning and malevolence that the deed was considerably grander than it sounds at first hearing.

This cat, in all the grimness of heraldry, dominated the castle. Carved in stone it guarded the park gates and the main doorway, and ranged along the battlements, alternately with small cannon, was silhouetted against the sky. Engraved on silver its rampings were fixed on every spoon, tureen, and porringer. Carved in wood or modelled in plaster it supported fireplaces, buffets, and beds, and confronted one at each turning of the staircase. It was embroidered on the linen, painted on the coach, carved in halfrelief on the backs of the dining-room chairs (which made them very uncomfortable to lean back on), inlaid on floors, painted in windows, embossed on ceilings. It was also a conspicuous motive in the decorative scheme of the chapel.

There was, too, a large and curious oil-painting which was put out as a hatchment at the death of any of the family. It represented the first marquis just before the combat began. Serene and confident, he measures the strength of the animal, which is standing on its hind-legs and menacing him with its paw. In the distance is a mill. The canvas is said to be by Velazquez.

There were, of course, no living cats in or about the establishment. The mice were kept down by specially trained monkeys.

Anything hereditary becomes with course of time creditable; and the Carabas birth-mark, though unbecoming, and the Carabas swooning-fits, though inconvenient, were inseparably part of the family honours. When, in the sixth generation, a son was born there was a quiet satisfaction but no surprise that the cat's paw birth-mark was strongly impressed on his cheek. The boy (he was the only child to survive infancy) was named Ildefonso, after the first marquis, and brought up in the usual manner — that is to say, entirely within the castle boundaries, where no cats could cross his path.

He was a sickly child, and inclined to be intelligent. From his infancy he showed a particular reverence for the family crest, and almost the first word he uttered was *gato*. His father, Don Salvador, used to draw little cats on paper to please him, copying with a shaky hand the heraldic animal, all boots and whiskers, and giving it a tremendous tail that curled like a dragon's and was forked at the tip.

One day Doña Claridad said:

'You know, my dear, that is not in the least like a real cat.'

'No?' said the marquis. 'I have never seen one.'

'What is a real cat?' asked the child.

Doña Claridad gave a little mew.

'*Mon amie*,' said the marquis reprovingly, '*pas devant l'enfant.*

Now, Ildefonso, we will draw an archbishop.'

'No, no! Draw me the marquises.'

'The marquis, child. Your great-great-great-greatgrand-father, Ildefonso *el combatidor*. The other figure is the wicked cat.'

They walked to the end of the long gallery, the sickly child and the grave weakly man, and stood before the canvas.

'Why did he kill the cat?'

'Because it was a wicked cat, my child. A traitor, a Judas.'

'What did it do, Father?'

'That story can never be told. It is so terrible that it has to be forgotten.'

All over the castle the child went with his question. What did the cat do? In the stables they told him that it rode the horses into a lather. In the kitchen they said it was a thief. In the linen-room they said that it had dirty habits. His tutor, who was also the chaplain, said that the cat was an embodiment of evil, and perhaps a symbol of heresy and the Albigenses. Then he told the child about the Albigenses, the Cathari, and the Manichees.

Though the child listened attentively, in the end he walked away hanging his head and saying sorrowfully:

'But they were not real cats, either.'

One morning, a little before the child's eighth birthday, Doña Claridad heard a great outcry coming from the courtyard. She opened the shutters and looked down. Below was a circle of men-servants and maid-servants, all screaming and shouting, some wringing their hands, some brandishing brooms, rakes, and horsewhips, some beating on frying-pans, and others clutching their rosaries. Words detached themselves from the hubbub, and rebounded echoing from the castle wall.

'The cat! The monkey! The cat! The cat! The Virgin! The monkey! The devil! The saints! The monkey! The cat!'

In the centre of the ring, one of the castle monkeys was bounding to and fro, holding something in its jaws. What it held was a kitten.

The uproar increased.

'The cat! The monkey! The monkey! The child! The cat! The Virgin! The smelling-salts! The child! *The child!*'

Bruising her hands on the iron lattice, Doña Claridad saw from her window the child Ildefonso squirm through the crowd and step into the centre of the ring, and cuff the monkey. It chattered at him, and he cuffed it again, and it dropped the kitten. One of the gardeners ran forward swinging his spade; but before he could batter the kitten to death Ildefonso had picked it up.

He held it close to his face and gently rubbed his cheek against it. It was breathless, and almost dead; its tongue lolled out like a rose petal that is ready to fall. In the horrified silence that encompassed the two young creatures Doña Claridad could hear the kitten panting and the child's voice murmuring:

'Pussy, poor pussy! Don't die, dear pussy, now that I've found you at last.'

Walking slowly, not looking to right or left, and holding the kitten as the priest holds the pyx, he made his way through the crowd, and disappeared. Doña Claridad fell on her knees and prayed to the Mother of Sorrows.

She was still on her knees when the child came in. He was pale, and his hands were bloodstained.

'The cat is dead,' he said, speaking slowly and looking at the floor. 'I've killed the monkey.'

Later in the day, when Don Salvador was up (for he lay late a bed, having a poor constitution and little energy), Doña Claridad told him all that had happened. Speaking slowly, as Ildefonso had done, and looking at the floor, she assured him that the child had shown no horror at all, only compassion and a natural childish affection for so small and furry an animal.

'This is extraordinary! This is appalling!' sighed her husband.

'It is extraordinary. But is it appalling? Is it not perhaps a grace from heaven? The child is delicate. Fits would be very bad for him.'

'I cannot think it a grace from heaven that a family tradition should be set aside.'

'Then is it not the grace of a reproof from heaven — a token that in the sight of God we are equal, all of us alike His sinners and His children? God is no respecter of persons. In the court of heaven the grandees of Spain must uncover like any poor peasant.'

He was silent, looking at her with unhappy brows.

'You have never seen a cat, Don Salvador?'

'Never.'

'It is borne in on me that you should put this grace — or this rebuke — to the test. Perhaps you too can look at a cat without trembling.'

He crossed himself.

'I can deny nothing to such virtue as yours. You are my angel. I ask only one thing. Let the child be with me to give me courage.'

Ildefonso was sent for. A footman carried in the dead kitten in a pair of tongs. Ildefonso looked at it silently. Don Salvador fell down in a fit.

The kitten's body was thrown on the rubbish heap, and so was the monkey's. The chaplain, in a sermon to the household, uttered a warning against giving way to gossip and vain speculation. The remaining monkeys went on catching mice, and others were trained to take the place of those that died in service. Don Salvador began to play the bass-viol and Doña Claridad continued to educate orphans, and the castle of Carabas, with its cats brandishing their paws against the sky and sometimes being grazed by lightning, enclosed the same peaceful routine, the same ways that had been current since the horn was sounded in Roncesvalles. If Don Ildefonso thought of other cats than those of the castle, he kept his thoughts to himself. He studied the Latin authors, and the laws of Spain, and wrote poetry. When he was fifteen his mother died. The old man and the young kept house together, somewhat pestered by Doña Claridad's aunt, who came to guide the household.

One day, having looked long and fixedly at Don Ildefonso's birth-mark, Don Salvador said:

'Do you remember the kitten?'

Don Ildefonso replied that he remembered it very well.

'And you felt no horror? Strange! No horror at all, after a continuance through five generations. My son, perhaps you will think me foolish, but I cannot help feeling guilty towards you — as though I had denied or defrauded you of part of your inheritance. An inconvenient part, no doubt, yet still a family possession. When you were begotten the force of my blood was already abated. Perhaps I was too feeble to give you the whole of your inheritance. Or perhaps that part of it had already gone astray. As a young man I was no saint, unfortunately. Sometimes I ask myself whether there may not be, somewhere in Spain, somewhere even in France or Sicily, a bastard elder brother of yours who, when he sees a cat, falls down insensible.'

'In five generations something may be mislaid,' replied Don Ildefonso. 'And you have given me the birthmark.' Then, thinking that the old man seemed melancholy, he led the conversation to family traditions and to Don Ildefonso *el combatidor*. Don Salvador listened with a peaceful smile, then suddenly exclaimed with energy:

'You know, those boots had spurs on them! The cat's boots, I mean. Little spurs, such as to fit one of those animals. I saw them when I was a boy. I have not seen them, though, for a long time. I wonder where they are? In the garret, perhaps. As prayers mount to heaven, rubbish mounts to the garret.'

He mused, and fell asleep.

Don Ildefonso decided he would look for the spurs.

He looked in the first garret, and in the second. There was nothing there he had not known as a child. Thinking that after all the spurs were probably in the muniment room, he was about to go downstairs when he was touched by a slender ray of sunlight in which the motes danced. It was small, no more than a needle of light, and slanted from the wall. He looked closer, and saw that it came through a key-hole and that the key-hole was in a narrow door. He pressed, and the door opened, and he found himself in a third garret that he had forgotten. It had a lancet window facing west, and the sun struck in like a blow on the eyes and dazzled him. Something sat on the window-sill between him and the sun. It was a large speckled cat that sat basking and did not move.

He was so much used to seeing carved cats that he thought that this, too, was a cat carved from wood and painted with speckles — but more naturalistic than the others, for it wore no boots and its expression was cold and calm.

'So there you are at last,' it observed, not turning its head. He could understand its language perfectly.

'Have you been here long?'

'Personally, for about seven years. Long enough to know all about you. You are Don Ildefonso, the sixth in descent from Don Ildefonso *el traidor*. I have no name. But I am the seventy-seventh in the male line from the cat he betrayed and murdered.'

It turned and looked at him. It asked sharply:

'Why aren't you in a fit?'

'I am not like my ancestor. I — I like cats.'

'You like cats, do you? That's a change of heart.' It spoke

with assumed flippancy, but its voice was extraordinarily bitter. 'You like cats. *But I hate men!*'

Now it turned on him with bristling fur and blazing eyes. He thought it was about to spring at his throat; but after a moment it sat down again and stared at a fly in the window.

'Do you wonder?'

'Señor Don Cat, I feel I do not understand you. I am curious to know why you hate men.'

'You have never heard the story, then?'

'The story of our ancestors, Señor?'

'The story of our ancestors, Señor.'

With his heart thumping against his ribs, the young man explained how he had known there was a story, and had inquired after it many times, but always to no purpose.

'It is a story of human conceit and human ingratitude. Nothing very remarkable about that.'

Don Ildefonso felt himself beginning to turn crimson. The birth-mark on his cheek throbbed like a heart.

'It is a story of treachery and the vilest inhospitality. It is a story that has been handed down through almost fourscore generations of my family; and each one of us in turn has taken an oath to avenge our ancestor in single combat, if and when the opportunity came. We are alone in this garret. You have your sword and I have my claws. Shall we fight it out?'

Don Ildefonso looked at the cat's furry belly. He was no coward, but he remembered the kitten and the monkey, and knew he could not fight a cat. He drew his sword from the scabbard and threw it on the floor.

The cat quivered a little as it fell clanging down. Recovering its self-control, it said:

'I might also avenge my ancestor by telling you the whole story. That would be quite as effective, I think — and would entail less exertion. Listen!'

He settled himself on the window-sill, tucked his paws

under his bosom, curled his tail round, passed his tongue across his lips, and began.

The story was long and he told it minutely and composedly. There was now no malice in his voice, and presently no shade of irony, even. There was no need for such adventitious aids. As the narrative flowed onwards like a black river, its narrator seemed almost to vanish, to be no longer a personality, but instead a cloud of witnesses, a shadowy sum of seventy-seven generations, still vibrating with indignation at an intolerable piece of caddishness. Yet the recital eased him, for when he had finished he sat up and shook his ears once or twice, and then sprang lightly off the window-sill and began to mountaineer about the contents of the garret.

Don Ildefonso stood waiting. It seemed to him that he must wait until the birth-mark in his cheek ceased throbbing, until he could be sure that he would not weep like a shamed child, until he could grow hardened enough to carry out his next purpose without bungling.

'I offer my apology. I can offer no reparation.'

'None, none!' replied the cat briskly.

Don Ildefonso turned away.

'You've left your sword!' cried the cat, who did not resist this last scratch.

The young man walked through the outer garrets, and downstairs. Compassion for an innocent old man who was his father made it impossible for him to repeat the cat's story to Don Salvador. Instead, he merely told him that he had made up his mind to leave the world and enter the order of Trappists. The old man sighed, vaguely as a wind in summer, and said that Doña Claridad would have approved.

A few weeks after Don Ildefonso's going Don Salvador died. For a little while the castle stood empty, then it was bought by a community of nuns. They began to scrub and clean, and soon they reached the garrets. There they found the sword, and made small jokes about it, saying that it would serve to defend them against robbers. They did not find the cat, for he had retired to an outhouse. From there he observed them until he knew them thoroughly, and felt pretty sure of them. He decided that they were clean, quiet, and of regular habits. So he began to woo them, and before winter was established among them and living very comfortably with the past behind him.

10 Virtue and the Tiger

There was once a hermit called Avadavanda who was a man of great beauty, learning, elegance of thought, presence of mind, and holiness. He lived in the jungle, though in his youth he had lived in a court.

One morning while washing his feet in a brook and composing a *Hymn to Vegetable Being* he noticed the thicket rustle and the reeds begin to bulge. A tiger came out. Its head drooped, its jaws were stained with blood, and coming to the pool it drank long and greedily.

'Blood is so salt,' murmured Avadavanda.

'Men don't value it the less,' replied the tiger bitterly.

Avadavanda spoke soothingly to the tiger, and condoled with him on his hard carnivorous lot. Tears of self-pity began to stream down the tiger's cheeks, and Avadavanda spoke of fortitude. Ashamed of having betrayed his weakness, the tiger slunk off. Then Avadavanda returned to his meditations and completed another strophe of the hymn.

Extremes meet, opposites complement each other, and tigers, it is well known, are irresistibly drawn to the company of hermits. Avadavanda and the tiger now met frequently and became tolerably intimate. They had much in common: both loved nature, solitude, and sleep. Often they would lie down in some grassy glade, Avadavanda pillowing his head upon the tiger's flank, and together drowse away the afternoon. The tiger, who had a simple character, asked no more of their intimacy than this; but the subtle and high-minded Avadavanda was conscious of an inequality in their friendship. He could not hide from himself that it was always the tiger who kissed and he who offered the cheek.

And it seemed to him that he should do more, that it was discourteous to accept such generous affection and make so slight a return. One afternoon he said:

'Would you not like to eat me?'

The tiger looked at him with pained astonishment, and replied, shortly:

'No.'

Avadavanda begged his pardon with winning grace, but the tiger was grumpy for quite a while after.

'He showed his discernment,' thought Avadavanda. 'For, after all, what was such an offer worth? To me, it was but my life, a valueless illusion, a temporal wrapping that sooner or later I shall discard and renew as the snake sloughs its skin. And to him I proffered at best but a fleeting sensuous gratification, and at worst a further link in the chain that fetters him to carnality.' Yet still he felt an obligation to make some return for the tiger's affection; and it occurred to him that as he had amassed a great deal of virtue, and was in a way of life to amass even more, he might well bestow the present accumulation on the tiger. So one day he began to speak of virtue, tickling the tiger's stomach as he did so with a little wand. The tiger lay all loosened with pleasure, purring, extending and retracting his claws, and dribbling slightly. His eyes were pale and serene as the evening sky, and rolling at Avadavanda's feet he said:

'Oh, thank you, oh, delicious, oh, thank you! How delightful to hear you speaking so eloquently about virtue. I do like to hear about virtue.'

'You shall enjoy more than the hearsay,' replied Avadavanda. 'You shall experience it. Dear friend, receive, such as it is, my present stock of virtue. I give it to you with pleasure, and wish it were more.'

The tiger sat up as though a flea had bitten him. He stared

around him and twitched his ears. 'You will soon grow accustomed to it,' said Avadavanda.

In a faint, awestruck voice the tiger said:

'Excuse me.'

He rose to his feet and walked unsteadily away. He did not return.

Avadavanda was not surprised. He remembered how, when first acquiring virtue himself, he had felt a profound dissatisfaction with all his former life, and had quitted the court in consequence. No doubt the tiger was experiencing much the same emotions. Wishing him well, the hermit settled himself to a quiet attainment of further merit and holiness; and soon the tiger was wiped from his thoughts.

Meanwhile the tiger was feeling very oddly. At first it seemed to him that he had been overtaken by some mysterious illness, and this surmise was borne out by the fact that he had completely lost the impulse to kill. It was not that he was not hungry. As the days went by he grew famished with hunger; but at the sight of a live meal his desire suddenly failed him. Sometimes he managed to choke down a little carrion, and for the rest a morbid craving drove him to nibble grass and dig up sweet potatoes.

The face of nature was changed for him. He was continually struck by the deceitfulness of nature, the deceitfulness, that is to say, of flowers, that bloomed only to allure and fade, of birds who sang as though they had something worth singing about but in reality expressed only the most trivial and self-regarding sentiments, of monkeys whose energies ran all to waste. Only in thunderstorms, rocks, and serpents could he find truth; and those, only dismal truths. The face of tiger too was changed for him. He was no longer at home with his fellows; he did not even wish to fight them. He hated their company and at the same time he felt an obligation to serve them, to tame their passions and cultivate their minds. They would be better like that, he knew. And when he found a little tiger he tried to allure it away from its family and teach it modesty and sadness.

At times he wondered if he should revisit Avadavanda. But the thought of Avadavanda was no longer delightful. Avadavanda now seemed a quite uninteresting person, conceited, and surely rather selfish, and not good-looking. As for the gift of virtue he had bestowed, that gift, thought the tiger, did not amount to much. It was a negligible quantity, a mere pennyworth of virtue, and wholly unsatisfying.

Thus the tiger wandered about, disconcerted and listless, and yet at the same time deeply interested in himself. And one day as he went slouching through the jungle, not looking where he was going, a net fell round him, and he was a prisoner.

For the first time since Avadavanda's virtue had been bestowed on him the tiger began to feel comfortable and at ease. He sat down and waited for the worse things which, he had no doubt, would follow. Presently appeared a band of men who were collecting animals for a menagerie. When they saw that their net had trapped a tiger they hung back, and debated amongst themselves the high price of tigers and the danger of handling them. The tiger sat quietly under the net.

At last the bravest and most agile of the men came up with ropes, muzzles, red-hot pokers, and other apparatus for securing tigers. The tiger made no resistance, and when he had been well roped, and muzzled, and a collar fastened about his neck, they led him away, and sold him to a menagerie, where he was put in a cage.

The cage was small and dirty and stinking, and one in a row of cages all containing tigers. All day visitors shuffled past, staring and commenting and prodding their sticks between the bars. All day the other tigers growled and roared, paced to and fro, or snatched at the sticks. But our tiger sat tranquilly in a corner, upheld by virtue. In consequence he soon became accustomed to hearing the visitors say, as they walked past:

'Oh, there's that stick-in-the-mud animal! Don't bother to stop, he's no fun.' Or: 'Come on, Betty, don't let's waste time on him!' Or: 'Mummy, Mummy, I don't like that one. I want to throw my bun to a real roaring tiger.'

And so it became clear to him that virtue is a thing of no value among worldlings. Though it be rare as the phœnix, difficult as the ascent of Mount Ararat, agonizing as the nip of scorpions, and beautiful as the lotus, virtue is of no account compared to vulgar roarings and snatchings.

This fact was made even clearer in a few months' time, when the proprietor of the menagerie, pausing before the cage, remarked:

'As for that one, he's not worth his keep. Mark him down, and get rid of him.'

The tiger was sold to a travelling circus, where he was even more uncomfortable than in the menagerie, and where, under a cruel discipline, he learned to sit on a high stool and jump through a hoop. His virtue became even more apparent, and finally caused an indignant lady to protest that the wretched animal was drugged.

The circus-manager came forward to refute this accusation. 'Show the lady if he's drugged or not, boy,' he said.

The tamer lashed at the tiger with the whip. The tiger fell off his stool, and quietly reseated himself on the floor. Instantly the tent was filled with a clamour of hooting, whistling, and cat-calling. Some were hooting at the tamer's brutality, and others were jeering at the tiger's lack of spirit. But to the tiger all this uproar betokened one thing only: a general scorn of virtue.

On a sudden impulse of disillusionment he leaped the barrier, walked morosely through the screaming crowd, and left the tent.

Outside the tent was a little ragged girl, who had been too poor to buy a ticket. Seeing the tiger she screamed, and threw an orange at him.

'So you, too, hate virtue, do you?' groaned the tiger, and struck her a heavy blow, and left her a bloodied heap of torn flesh and shredded muslin. Filled with apostolic wrath and apostolic disillusionment, the tiger stalked through the village, smiting and tearing at anything that crossed his path. All night he travelled, howling with rage, and in the early morning came to the jungle, where the birds were singing and the monkeys playing, just as of old. Seeing him so angry and so shabby, the monkeys scolded and pelted him with nuts. Furiously he tried to climb the trees after them, for they too were scorners and mockers of virtue; and when he came on a young hind he tore her in pieces without even asking for her opinion of virtue, since he felt so sure she had no regard for it.

Towards evening he found himself among his old haunts, and presently heard familiar sounds: the running brook and the calm tenor voice of Avadavanda singing an *Ode to Annihilation*. Leaping out from the thicket, he confronted the holy man.

'Tremble, Avadavanda! Your hour has come. Tremble, heartless hypocrite! Down on your knees, blasphemer! You feign to be virtuous, but what is virtue to you? A nothing, a toy, a worthless thing to be thrown away on tigers.'

So saying he launched himself at the hermit. Quick as thought Avadavanda reckoned up the amount of virtue he had acquired since parting with the tiger, and decided it would be adequate.

'Receive my virtue!' he cried.

In mid-spring the tiger crumpled, and fell at Avadavanda's feet.

'No more,' he whimpered, 'I can't bear any more.' His body was shaken with a fit of hysterical weeping. Then, with a heavy sigh, he folded his paws, and lay dead.

Pondering on the inexorable harmonies of the universe, Avadavanda buried the tiger under a may tree, thus beginning his third accumulation of virtue.

11 The Magpie Charity

A magpie, by thrift and diligence, had made a fortune. Now he was dying, and called to his deathbed his two brothers, his heir, a crow, and a rook.

'I am dying,' he said in a feeble voice. 'Are you sure that we are safely private? No one about? No cats?'

They assured him that there was no one about.

'Good. Now I will make my will. After my death I wish you to carry my collection of silver spoons and all my other treasures to the bank and have them changed into money. The bank will make no difficulty, I am sure of that. The diamond is of the finest water, the spoons are solid silver, everything is hallmarked. Such objects are always honoured at a bank, whoever deposits them. I have frequented banks; I know all about it. Once I stole a half-sovereign from the Bank of England, so cleverly that a clerk was dismissed the same evening. Hark! Did I not hear a noise? Something soft-footed? Pray look about, and make sure we are safe from interruption.'

'Only a caterpillar,' said the crow. 'And I have swallowed it.'

'May it do you good! Now I can go on. After my fortune has been turned into money I wish it to be divided thus. Two-thirds to go to my son and heir. But as he is inclined to be rash and spendthrift, I appoint you, my dear brothers, to act as his guardians. You will be recompensed for your trouble.'

The brothers said it would be a pleasure.

'The remaining third,' said the magpie, 'is to be divided into one hundred equal parts.'

'Good gracious, Papa!' said the heir. 'Have you really one hundred friends?'

'God forbid! One hundred enemies, more likely. Nasty sly

animals, greedy-guts, rapacious caterwauling harpies, as bad by night as by day. It is they who have worn me down with nerve trouble and heart failure. If it were not for them, I should not now be lying here. However, since I am, we had best get on with business. Now pray take notice, for this is complicated. Out of those hundred equal parts I bequeath twenty-five parts apiece to my two brothers. Of the remaining fifty parts I bequeath twenty-four parts to you, Master Rook, and the same, Master Crow, to you. On this condition: that you will become trustees and sole administrators of the charitable fund which I propose to endow with the two parts left over. What was that noise I heard just then?'

'Only a bough creaking in the wind,' said the rook.

'I thought it was something worse. The interest (they will explain all that at the bank; I have not time to go into it now) on this charitable fund is to be devoted to relieving the necessities of wholly indigent cats.'

'Lawks!' they exclaimed in chorus. 'Relieving cats? Why, are not cats the very creatures you hate most?'

'I hate all cats,' said the magpie. 'I would like to peck out their staring eyes. But of all cats the cats I most hate, dread, and abominate are starving cats. A starving cat is a menace to society. It is to make the world safe for magpies (or at any rate safer) that I have devised this philanthropic scheme. Now listen! The interest is to be used to buy mice. Buy them wholesale, of course. A genuinely indigent cat will not mind if a mouse is not perfectly fresh. Thus supplied with a mouse weekly one indigent menace at any rate will be kept quiet.

'But observe,' said the magpie impressively, 'the cats must be wholly indigent. I cannot have my mice distributed among horrid healthy cats who will hunt the harder for being well fed. Now let us say no more of it, for I detest the subject. But remember! The cats must be wholly indigent.'

He died. His executors carried out his wishes to the letter; the bank, too, was most helpful and understanding. After allowing a year or so for the interest to accumulate, and waiting for an advantageous moment to buy mice wholesale, the rook and the crow let it be known that they were ready to look into the claims of any indigent cats who applied for relief.

For some while there was no response. The rook and the crow sat waiting in vain, agreeing that the magpie had been terribly taken in, that there was no distress among cats, that they were luxurious animals who turned up their noses at wholesome wholesale mice, and that even a distressed cat was too proud and too lazy to go a step to ask for help. But after a long spell of rain and floods a few cats came to the office, walking stiffly and looking ashamed of themselves.

Mindful of the magpie's parting words, the rook and the crow made careful inquiries. It was as they expected: not one of these cats could be considered adequately indigent. Some were young and strong, and could look out for themselves. Others were old, and so had many descendants whose sacred duty it was to support them. Others were pretty cats and might reasonably expect to be adopted by some human household. Others again had fishbones put away.

Sighing over the deceitfulness of catkind the rook and the crow sat on the box which held the wholesale mice and wished they had not bought so many.

At last, stumbling and limping and blundering, an old black cat came in and asked to be granted relief. It really looked quite like a genuine case. He was blind, lame, and almost stone-deaf. He was old, yet he had no descendants, for he was a neutered cat. He was so very ugly that no one would ever adopt him. He had no fishbones and scarcely a tooth in his head.

'I really think we might let him have a mouse — a moderate-sized mouse — weekly.' said the crow.

'He is so completely destitute that I should have no hesitation in classing him as a menace to society; and that, you know, was what the Benefactor had in mind.'

'Softly, softly,' said the rook. 'Let me question him a little more.'

'What would you do with a mouse?' he inquired. There was no answer, and remembering that the applicant was deaf he hopped closer and screamed into the jagged ear:

'WHAT WOULD YOU DO WITH A MOUSE?'

After a pause the cat said in a low flat voice:

'Eat it.'

'What would you do with its bones?'

This time the cat answered immediately, and said:

'Scraunch them!'

The rook flew back rather hastily, and remarked:

'There is no doubt that we can class him as a menace. How right our dear friend was! How discerning!'

Yet even now they had scruples, and hesitated. They felt a certain impiety in diminishing the fair total of the wholesale mice which had been so long intact, spoiling the cream-laid ledger page by such a poor vulgar entry as: **NAME:** *Nigger.* **PATRONYMIC:** *None.* **SEX:** *None.* **AGE:** *17.* **ADDRESS:** *None.* **CONDITION:** *Destitute.* **GRANT:** *One Mouse.*

While they were fidgeting round the inkpot, taking one pen and then changing it for another, brushing a cobweb off the blotter, and at the same time keeping a wary eye on the cat, the rook exclaimed:

'Merciful heavens! We have been on the brink of a frightful error. Fortunately I thought of it in time. My dear Crow, this cat is no more indigent than I am.'

'I suspected it, I thought so all along,' said the crow. 'Indigent, indeed! But — er —?'

'Do you know that catskins fetch a very high price in the market? This old imposter is walking about with a good sixpennyworth on his back.'

'Outrageous!' cried the crow. 'Tell him so at once. And don't mince it, either.'

Hearing the two birds squawking and fluttering their wings, the cat turned his blinded head towards them. He supposed they were bringing him the mouse. He began to quiver and growl, and the tip of his tail beat on the floor.

'Ahem!' said the rook. 'We are sorry, Mr Nigger, but it is not possible for us to grant you a relief mouse. You do not comply with the regulations of the Fund. Until you have sold your skin we can do nothing for you.'

12 The Fox-Pope

A fox who had been reading the *Lives of the Saints* was so delighted with the style of the book that he decided to become a saint himself. It seemed to him that he would be happiest as a hermit; so he retired to the Transylvanian Alps, taking with him a great bundle of lettuces, and a cold chicken to eat on Sundays and saints' days.

There he lived contentedly, modelling his deportment upon the best examples. St Jerome kept a skull to meditate on: when the fox had eaten all the chicken and crunched the bones he preserved the head, and meditated upon that. St Jerome kept a lion too, and St Anthony was tempted by nymphs: the fox procured a female rabbit, who supplied him with both totem and temptation; and as solitude is essential to hermits, when his rabbit had a litter of young ones he ate them. St Mary of Egypt slept in a den, and never changed her hair-shirt: the fox found a nice dry den; and by day he sat in the sun, meditating on the skull, resisting the female rabbit, and occasionally scratching out one two of the fleas which he kept about him as a mortification.

One day he saw two cardinals approaching. They looked hot and earnest. 'O Fox,' said the first cardinal, 'your blameless retired life is celebrated throughout Christendom.'

'Do not flatter me,' said the fox austerely. 'But rather, since you look hot, let me offer you a few lettuces.'

Waving away the lettuces they said:

'We have come to summon you to the chair of St Peter.'

'*Nolo episcopari*,' said the fox.

'Nonsense!' retorted the second Cardinal. 'No man in his senses would refuse such an invitation.'

'I am a fox,' said the fox.

'Gently, Pippo! That's not the way to handle him,' whispered the first cardinal. He continued in a louder tone:

'We know that we are inviting you to no easy life. The banqueting alone would wear out the toughest animal. The artfulness required to steer the Ark of the Church through the troubled waters of this world demands incessant caution and the sprightliest cunning. Moreover, you would be the Prisoner of the Vatican. And though the gardens are extensive and full of bushes, no dogs are allowed, only turkeys, swans, geese (the Bird of the Capitol), chickens, quails, and pigeons.'

'*Nolo episcopari*,' repeated the fox, adding: 'Why don't you find some man for this supreme honour? There used to be plenty about.'

'Out of the question!' exclaimed the second cardinal. 'The times are grown so bad that they need an unparalleled remedy. Men now are so headstrong they will not listen to a man. We did think of a giant panda; but they are Confucians and, anyhow, all the available giant pandas are females. A white raven? Mockers would say it was bleached. A unicorn? ...'

The first cardinal cut him short.

'Fables and trumpery! Every zoological garden has its panda. But in you, fair fox, we see the true Nonpareil. A Fox of Blameless Life! Nothing else could arrest the gadding wits of this century.'

The second cardinal broke in.

'Consider the frightful state of society! Consider the rampings of the powers of evil! Consider to what a desperate pitch we —'

'Enough, Pippo! No doubt these considerations have already occurred to him.'

'And are things really so bad?' inquired the fox. 'How terrible! But of course I, being a hermit, know nothing of the world.' And he smiled in a manner which both the cardinals found galling.

'Come, lovely Fox!' said the first cardinal. 'Adapting the profane lines of Waller, you are wasting our time. The desert is no place for you. Come forth. Suffer yourself to be attired, and don't be missish. You are such a personable animal that I would suggest you revive the title of Formosus.'

'I won't be Pope!' cried the fox. 'I dare not. I am only a poor frail mammal, and distressingly subject to temptation. Suppose I fell? Think of the scandal!'

'God tempers the wind to the shorn lamb. You have lived so long in this cranny that you have lost your sense of proportion. What are a few temptations compared to the great task you can perform for a world hastening towards damnation? Fie, Fox! Shun this fugitive and cloistered virtue.'

'But it is my dearest possession.'

'Aren't you being a *little* selfish?'

'But my immortal soul? Would you have me hazard my immortal soul?'

'Stuff and nonsense!' interjected the second cardinal. 'Why, you're only a fox. I never heard so much fuss about nothing.' And with a dexterous movement he dropped his cape over the fox, picked him up, and made a bundle of him, observing to the first cardinal:

'There! You'd have been a week doing it.'

'Well, well. Don't suffocate him,' was the mild reply.

Transferred to a strong crate, the fox was jolted across south-eastern Europe, bewailing his lost quietude and thinking bitterly that by now the sherabbit would have devoured every one of his young lettuces. At intervals he heard the cardinals planning the details of his pontification, and twice a day he was given a chunk of horseflesh. At night he was chained securely to the foot of a bedstead. But on the sixth night of their journey the wife of the innkeeper at Nagy Kanizsa utterly refused to have a fox brought indoors, saying that there had never been fleas in her beds and never should be while she had a say in the matter. As there was no other inn within miles the cardinals gave way. The crate was put in the stable under lock and key, and a large tag threatened with excommunication anyone who should tamper with its fastening.

It was a cold night, the stable was draughty, and they had forgotten to feed him. The fox, sorrowing to himself, and counting up his misfortunes, lost his self-control and began to curse and swear. To his surprise his stream of filthy language was answered by a stream of Hail Marys.

'Who the hell are you?' he inquired snappishly.

He learned it was a stable-boy, a simple youth who had got tipsy, fallen asleep in the straw, and was now locked in with him.

The fox redoubled his blasphemies, and the crate shook as he scratched and bit. The boy redoubled his Hail Marys.

The sound of these innocent devotions reminded the fox of how happy he had been as a hermit. He exclaimed:

'Don't go on so! Every word causes me agonies.'

'In that case you must be the devil,' replied the stable-boy.

'Let me out, let me out!' shrieked the fox.

'Let out the devil?' said the stable-boy. 'God forbid!'

'Let me out, I say!' howled the fox. 'They're taking me to Rome to make me Pope!'

The accents of truth are unmistakable. The stableboy fell on his knees, trembling at the news that the devil was going to be made Pope.

'If you have a shred of Christian feeling,' bewailed the fox, 'you'll let me out.'

The stable-boy had a great deal of Christian feeling. He saw in a painful flash that it must depend on him whether or no the devil became the head of the Church.

'Do you solemnly promise that if I let you out you will not go to Rome?'

'I solemnly promise,' said the fox in a voice broken by sobs.

'And that you will do no harm, but go away at once? And quietly?'

'I swear I will not harm a hair of your head. On the contrary, I will be gone before you've had time to see the tag at the end of my tail.'

It's true, then, thought the boy. He's got a tail. He said: 'Well, look out, then.'

First he pried open a little window. Then he crossed himself. Then, taking a hatchet, he struck a great blow on the corner of the crate and broke it open. Something hot, furry, and smelling of geraniums flashed past him. The devil was gone, the papacy was saved from the dominion of the evil one.

As for the fox, once out in the stable yard, he gave himself a shake and a twitch, and snuffed the air. It smelled strange to him, and for a moment he felt rather sorrowful.

'Back again,' he said, 'where I started from. Back again in the workaday world. I don't suppose I shall ever find my wilderness any more. I'm not sure that I want to. My vocation has been torn from me.'

He snuffed once more.

'But at any rate I have resisted the temptation to spiritual pride.'

Saying this, he trotted quietly towards the henhouse.

13 The Phoenix

Lord Strawberry, a nobleman, collected birds. He had the finest aviary in Europe, so large that eagles did not find it uncomfortable, so well laid out that both humming-birds and snow-buntings had a climate that suited them perfectly. But for many years the finest set of apartments remained empty, with just a label saying: '*PHŒNIX. Habitat: Arabia.*'

Many authorities on bird life had assured Lord Strawberry that the phœnix is a fabulous bird, or that the breed was long extinct. Lord Strawberry was unconvinced: his family had always believed in phœnixes. At intervals he received from his agents (together with statements of their expenses) birds which they declared were the phœnix but which turned out to be orioles, macaws, turkey buzzards dyed orange, etc, or stuffed cross-breeds, ingeniously assembled from various plumages. Finally Lord Strawberry went himself to Arabia, where, after some months, he found a phœnix, won its confidence, caught it, and brought it home in perfect condition.

It was a remarkably fine phœnix, with a charming character — affable to the other birds in the aviary and much attached to Lord Strawberry. On its arrival in England it made a great stir among ornithologists, journalists, poets, and milliners, and was constantly visited. But it was not puffed up by these attentions, and when it was no longer in the news, and the visits fell off, it showed no pique or rancour. It ate well, and seemed perfectly contented.

It costs a great deal of money to keep up an aviary. When Lord Strawberry died he died penniless. The aviary came on the market. In normal times the rarer birds, and certainly the phœnix, would have been bid for by the trustees of Europe's great zoological societies, or by private persons in the USA; but as it happened Lord Strawberry died just after a world war, when both money and bird-seed were hard to come by (indeed the cost of bird-seed was one of the things which had ruined Lord Strawberry). The London *Times* urged in a leader that the phœnix be bought for the Zoo, saying that a nation of birdlovers had a moral right to own such a rarity; and a fund, called the Strawberry Phœnix Fund, was opened. Students, naturalists, and schoolchildren contributed according to their means; but their means were small, and there were no large donations. So Lord Strawberry's executors (who had the death duties to consider) closed with the higher offer of Mr Tancred Poldero, owner and proprietor of Poldero's Wizard Wonderworld.

For quite a while Mr Poldero considered his phœnix a bargain. It was a civil and obliging bird, and adapted itself readily to its new surroundings. It did not cost much to feed, it did not mind children; and though it had no tricks, Mr Poldero supposed it would soon pick up some. The publicity of the Strawberry Phœnix Fund was now most helpful. Almost every contributor now saved up another half-crown in order to see the phœnix. Others, who had not contributed to the fund, even paid double to look at it on the five-shilling days.

But then business slackened. The phœnix was as handsome as ever, and as amiable; but, as Mr Poldero said, it hadn't got Allure. Even at popular prices the phœnix was not really popular. It was too quiet, too classical. So people went instead to watch the antics of the baboons, or to admire the crocodile who had eaten the woman.

One day Mr Poldero said to his manager, Mr Ramkin: 'How long since any fool paid to look at the phœnix?'

'Matter of three weeks,' replied Mr Ramkin.

'Eating his head off,' said Mr Poldero. 'Let alone the insurance. Seven shillings a week it costs me to insure that bird, and I might as well insure the Archbishop of Canterbury.'

'The public don't like him. He's too quiet for them, that's the trouble. Won't mate nor nothing. And I've tried him with no end of pretty pollies, ospreys, and Cochin-Chinas, and the Lord knows what. But he won't look at them.'

'Wonder if we could swap him for a livelier one,' said Mr Poldero.

'Impossible. There's only one of him at a time.'

'Go on!'

'I mean it. Haven't you ever read what it says on the label?'

They went to the phœnix's cage. It flapped its wings politely, but they paid no attention. They read:

'PANSY. *Phœnix phœnixisima formosissima arabiana*. This rare and fabulous bird is UNIQUE. The World's Old Bachelor. Has no mate and doesn't want one. When old, sets fire to itself and emerges miraculously reborn. Specially imported from the East.'

'I've got an idea,' said Mr Poldero. 'How old do you suppose that bird is?'

'Looks in its prime to me,' said Mr Ramkin.

'Suppose,' continued Mr Poldero, 'we could somehow get him alight? We'd advertise it beforehand, of course, work up interest. Then we'd have a new bird, and a bird with some romance about it, a bird with a life-story. We could sell a bird like that.'

Mr Ramkin nodded. 'I've read about it in a book,' he said. 'You've got to give them scented woods and what not, and they build a nest and sit down on it and catch fire spontaneous. But they won't do it till they're old. That's the snag.'

'Leave that to me,' said Mr Poldero. 'You get those scented woods, and I'll do the ageing.'

It was not easy to age the phœnix. Its allowance of food was halved, and halved again, but though it grew thinner its eyes were undimmed and its plumage glossy as ever. The heating was turned off; but it puffed out its feathers against the cold, and seemed none the worse. Other birds were put into its cage, birds of a peevish and quarrelsome nature. They pecked and chivied it; but the phœnix was so civil and amiable that after a day or two they lost their animosity. Then Mr Poldero tried alley cats. These could not be won by good manners, but the phœnix darted above their heads and flapped its golden wings in their faces, and daunted them.

Mr Poldero turned to a book on Arabia, and read that the climate was dry. 'Aha!' said he. The phœnix was moved to a small cage that had a sprinkler in the ceiling. Every night the sprinkler was turned on. The phœnix began to cough. Mr Poldero had another good idea. Daily he stationed himself in front of the cage to jeer at the bird and abuse it.

When spring was come, Mr Poldero felt justified in beginning a publicity campaign about the ageing phœnix. The old public favourite, he said, was nearing its end. Meanwhile he tested the bird's reactions every few days by putting a little dirty straw into the cage, to see if it were interested in nesting yet. One day the phœnix began turning over the straw. Mr Poldero signed a contract for the film rights. At last the hour seemed ripe. It was a fine Saturday evening in May. For some weeks the public interest in the ageing phœnix had been working up, and the admission charge had risen to five shillings. The enclosure was thronged. The lights and the cameras were trained on the cage, and a loudspeaker proclaimed to the audience the rarity of what was about to take place.

'The phœnix,' said the loud-speaker, 'is the aristocrat of bird-life. Only the rarest and most expensive specimens of oriental woods, drenched in exotic perfumes, will tempt him to construct his strange love-nest.'

Now a neat assortment of twigs and shavings, strongly scented, was shoved into the cage.

'The phœnix,' the loud-speaker continued, 'is as capricious as Cleopatra, as luxurious as the du Barry, as heady as a strain of wild gipsy music. All the fantastic pomp and passion of the ancient East, its languorous magic, its subtle cruelties —'

'Lawks!' cried a woman in the crowd. 'He's at it!'

A quiver stirred the dulled plumage. The phœnix turned its head from side to side. It descended, staggering, from its perch. Then wearily it began to pull about the twigs and shavings.

The cameras clicked, the lights blazed full on the cage. Rushing to the loud-speaker Mr Poldero exclaimed:

'Ladies and gentlemen, this is the thrilling moment the world has breathlessly awaited. The legend of centuries is materializing before our modern eyes. The phœnix ...'

The phœnix settled on its pyre and appeared to fall asleep.

The film director said:

'Well, if it doesn't evaluate more than this, mark it instructional.'

At that moment the phœnix and the pyre burst into flames. The flames streamed upwards, leaped out on every side. In a minute or two everything was burned to ashes, and some thousand people, including Mr Poldero, perished in the blaze.

14 Apollo and the Mice

For some weeks Apollo had been pestered by the prayers of a husbandman, who said that mice were snatching the bread from his children's mouths and making his life a misery.

Stupid prayers are often the soonest answered, for no deity can stand them. So it was in this case. And being slightly ashamed of giving way to the importunities of a fool while the requests of so many wise men were still unanswered, the god decided that he might as well be hanged for a sheep as a lamb, and so would look into the matter personally.

It was hot harvest weather. Apollo put on a broadbrimmed hat of plaited straw. As he fastened the ribbons under his chin he thought how elaborate a universe it is, in which a sun-god must shelter himself against his own arrows.

So he set out, in the cool of the morning, and left the cork trees and olive groves of Delphi, and went to the husbandman's farm. It lay in a wide valley. Much of the harvest was already cut, heaped in stooks or lying in heavy-headed sheaves on the stubble. It was very hot, and thousands of small points of light winked from the stubble and the flints.

Apollo sat down in the shade. He thought he would repose himself a little before meeting that talkative husbandman. The only shade he could find was a piece of standing corn.

Presently he heard two small voices beside his ear. 'I dare say he will reap this tomorrow. Then what shall we do?'

'Perhaps if he takes the two stalks in one swath the nest will hold together.'

'Perhaps, perhaps! You are always hopeful, dear friend, but I feel catastrophe in my bones. Now the nest will be broken and all those lovely little ones spilled.'

'If only they were a day or two older! You should not have had this last clutch.'

'Whose fault was that?'

The words were severe but followed by a titter.

Apollo saw that two stalks of corn were bound together by a small knot of grass, which was indeed a nest. Two little animals whose very long tails were twined around the cornstalks sat beside it. They had bright eyes and sharp innocent faces.

'That's a man.'

'Yes. But he hasn't a reaping-hook. Dear me, how painful to be such a size! Just think of the amount of grain he must find in order to keep himself alive. I suppose the poor large creature runs about after it from morning till night.'

'He's not running now.'

'And not a vestige of tail. Well, we have to work hard for a living, and we lose ever so many children, and the owls are a perpetual nuisance — but I thank the gods I am not a man.'

'They say the gods are even larger.'

'Impossible!'

'I don't suppose,' thought Apollo, 'that either of these estimable animals has ever uttered a prayer in its life.'

He retied his hat ribbons, shook the grit out of his sandals, and went on to find the husbandman. The husbandman saw him coming and ran towards him, bobbing his head and crying out:

'Welcome, welcome, my golden one! What a pleasure! How unexpected! And just in the nick of time! Now you can see for yourself my splendid harvest. Look at these sheaves, examine this ear of corn. Every kernel plumped out. Bite one, I pray, taste how sweet it is. Ah, what a crop! Well ripened, and cut just in the moment of perfection.'

'I am glad the mice have not done as much harm as you anticipated.'

'Mice? Mice? No such thing, I assure you. Scarcely a mouse in the place. It has been a wonderful year for owls, you see, and then I keep some fine cats. No, no! You need not be afraid of the mice. You won't find a nibbled ear to the acre, I assure you.'

He peeped up under the broad brim. His face which had been so open and smirking became overcast with doubt.

'You're *not* the corn-merchant!'

'I am Apollo.'

The husbandman cast himself down and worshipped, apologizing for his error, due, he said, to bad sight brought on by so much labour and anxiety. He worshipped for a good fifteen minutes, throwing in a mention of Apollo occasionally, but for the most part giving an account of himself and his affairs. At length he got to the mice.

'Oh, they're something terrible! Bold as lions they are, run up your legs and eat the corn out of your wallet. And plentiful! Now if there were a market for mice, what a crop I'd have this year — only you can't catch them. They multiply like fleas in a mattress. It's this blazing, scorching summer we've had, encourages the mice and takes the heart out of the owls. Yes, what a wonderful summer! Phœbus in his majesty, as I've said all along to my children ... but it brings the mice, dirty little longtailed reptiles! But you have heard my prayers, gracious one ... now I shall be saved, and what's left of the harvest. The mice have had half of it. You may have noticed that I made light of them, in a manner of speaking, while I thought you were the corn-merchant. But what else is an honest man to do when it's rogues he's dealing with? And to think I mistook you, glorious Apollo, for a corn-merchant! Ah, my poor eyes!'

'These mice you complain of,' said Apollo, 'are those long-tailed mice, I think?'

'Yes, lord. Harvest mice, and rightly called so. Thousands of them. Very prolific, O life-giving one!'

'So I gather.'

'Worse than cats, and that's saying a good deal. Oh, dear, how my cats do carry on! What do they think they are — gods and goddesses? They don't seem to realize they're kept to be useful. But the mice, lord … fair son of Latona! To think you've come all this way to answer my prayer! I did pray, didn't I? And sacrifice, eh? I knew you were the one to pray to, I knew you'd do something for me.'

'I certainly will. It is a little late to do anything this year. It is no use shutting the stable door after the horse is stolen. But I can promise you that you will not be troubled by mice next harvest.'

'My golden one! How can I thank you? How will you manage it?'

'Quite simply. I will send a flood.'

'A flood!'

The husbandman stood aghast.

'That is my method with mice.'

The husbandman grovelled at Apollo's feet, praying him not to send a flood. It was by far the best prayer he had made.

'Your prayer is heard,' said Apollo.

He walked off before the husbandman could recover his speech.

'Really a very reasonable transaction,' he said to himself. 'I have acceded to a prayer not to do a thing which I had no intention of doing. A rare experience — as novel as being taken for a cornmerchant.'

Recollecting that he still had a purpose to carry out, Apollo turned aside to the piece of corn where he had found shade. The nest was still swinging between the cornstalks, and the two harvest mice were still engaged in conversation, their noses affably pressed together.

Apollo bent down and very carefully broke off the two cornstalks which supported the nest. As they began to shake, the mice fastened themselves even more securely by their tails, and began nibbling the corn in the ear.

He carried the nest on its long golden pillars (and in his hand they looked like a sceptre) to a cornstook. He settled it carefully in among the sheaves where no owl or cat was likely to notice it. Pleased with his handiwork, he stood back and examined it.

'Dear me, dear me! Here we are in quite a new place. A little sunless, do you think?'

'But much safer. We shan't be reaped here. Still, it's certainly rather odd. How did we get here, do you suppose?'

'My dear, I haven't the least notion. What's more, this reversal of natural laws would never have occurred to me. But it's very satisfactory.'

Perhaps a word of thanks would have been gratifying. But then, though they did not thank, equally they did not pray. And walking homeward towards the cool mountains and his holy temple Apollo reflected that he might do worse than to become the patron of mice.

15 The Widow's Portion

Alone, in a hovel near the edge of some cliffs, lived a widow. She was old, friendless, poor, and disagreeable. She had but one treasure, and that was her avarice.

Her avarice was so powerful that it made her rejoice in her poverty. 'If I had money,' she said, 'willy-nilly I should begin to spend it. If I had fifty pounds I should be tempted to buy a second-hand money-box. If I had investments I should buy a newspaper in order to read about them in the City column. If I had expectations from a rich uncle I should have to send him a Christmas card every year of his life. The card would be threepence and the postage would be twopence. Fivepence clean gone! If he lived for ten years — and what rich uncle lives for less — that would be four and twopence, besides the envelopes, which could not be less than fourpence a packet. Nor would it be any better to go and live in his neighbourhood. Far worse! He might want grapes.'

Having said this she placed three carrots in a string bag, put on galoshes and a mackintosh, and went out for a picnic. For it was a cold misty day, and if she stayed at home she might be led away into lighting the fire. Similarly, she was a strict vegetarian, as the only food she enjoyed was meat.

She walked on the cliff's edge, peering through the mist and remembering how once she had found a number of damaged oranges cast up on the beach. Far below, she saw a man seated disconsolately on a rock round which the tide was fast rising. He looked upward, as though imploring the face of the precipice to show him a way to safety. Seeing her, he began to shout and wave a handkerchief.

'What a nuisance,' she thought. 'Some shipwrecked sailor, I suppose. Shall I tell the coastguards? If I do, there may be no end to it.' And her imagination presented her with scenes each more horrid than the last: the rescued sailor coming to express his gratitude, and herself obliged to put more tea into the pot; the sailor then remarking that the rocks had torn his clothes, and herself impelled to give him a pair of her husband's old trousers; the clergyman getting up a fund for him, and expecting her to head the subscription list. The man continued to signal and halloo. Pulling herself together, she remarked in a calm voice:

'Why it's a monkey, I do declare! Poor creature.'

Obeying an impulse to make the man seem more like a monkey, she threw down a carrot. Then she walked on.

Three days later she was annoyed to hear music. She was even more annoyed to see a number of brightly dressed figures approaching her hovel. Dancing girls scattered roses and camellias, turbaned musicians played drums and trumpets, acrobats turned somersaults, grave bearded men, some leading tigers, walked with a stately gait, slaves staggered under bales and baskets, and in the midst of the throng moved an elephant hung with jewels and Persian rugs. On the elephant was a howdah, and in the howdah was a handsome dark-skinned man wearing a lounge suit and some orders of the British Empire.

All these stopped before her door. One of the grave bearded men leaned a golden ladder against the elephant and the gentleman in the lounge suit descended.

'I tell you this!' shouted the widow. 'I can't and won't undertake refreshments.'

Another of the grave bearded men replied:

'Madam, refreshments will be provided.'

At a waft of his hand the slaves undid their bales and baskets, and spread out a lavish and delicate feast, while the dancing girls tripped among the raised pies and the epergnes scattering *marrons glacés*.

Meanwhile the gentleman from the elephant was bowing courteously to the poor widow.

'Excuse this suddenness,' said he. 'But I cannot leave this place without offering you my thanks for preserving me from an ineligibly watery grave. That carrot which you so benevolently cast down gave me renewed strength, so that I was able to scale the cliff, walk to the hamlet, and telephone to the India Office and the Bank of England. Perhaps I should add that I am the Rajah of Golconda, and that I was yachting at Cowes when a storm drove my yacht from its anchorage and shipwrecked it in the Channel, whence I swam ashore. It is true that you believed me to be a monkey. But to the eyes of heaven an act of benevolence is beautiful, upon whatever species it be bestowed. I have brought you a few flowers.'

He handed her a bouquet. Concealed among the roses were ten Bank of England one-hundred-pound notes.

The widow turned pale and uttered a hoarse shriek.

'My tigers are quite harmless,' said the Rajah soothingly.

It was sunset before she could get rid of them, and even when they were gone the heath where they had picnicked reminded her only too instantly of their visit, being strewn with camellias, roses, *marrons glacés*, uncut rubies, mango-stones, crumbs, tufts of tiger fur, and cigar bands. In the hovel the widow sat trembling with nervous exhaustion, clasping a broken teapot which contained the Bank of England notes.

'All those rubies to pick up!' she lamented. 'And it's getting too dark to see them; I shall have to use my electric torch, sheer waste of a battery. It's just throwing money away. But I can afford it now, ha ha!'

With a maniac laugh she brandished the torch and rushed out. She had barely picked up a dozen rubies before she remembered the teapot, and rushed back with a maniac yell. Thus passed a miserable night.

The days that followed were fully as miserable. Nothing but cares and expenses confronted her. The seagulls had arrived and were devouring the crumbs and the *marrons glacés*. Such waste was intolerable, and she felt she must buy a couple of hens that could be fattened for nothing; but first she must pick up the *marrons glacés*, for they could be made into jam. Yet to do this she must light a fire and buy jampots. Something must be done, too, about those wretched roses and camellias. If there had happened to be a death in the village she could have sold them for the funeral, but only the flowers showed signs of dying, so she would have to walk to the market, where she could sell them in threepenny bunches; yet this might well be so exhausting that she would be lured into a teashop, where she would spend sixpence on a cup of tea and a bun. The tiger fur would knit up into a scarf; but to knit it she must needs buy a distaff and knitting needles. And so on. Thus she suffered agonies of indecision, and her mind was in such a tumult that she could not think of even the simplest and most obvious economies, such as stealing jampots from the vestry, where they were kept for Easter decorations.

Moreover, even if she overcame these problems she would still be burdened with forty-three uncut rubies and a thousand pounds. Sometimes she thought she would bury them. But how could she bury them where no thief would find them? Sometimes she thought of banking them. But even from a bank the odour of her riches would assail her, seducing her to write cheques and be extravagant. Sometimes she thought she would drop them over the cliff. But that would be wasteful.

Life had no more joys for her. She no longer dared to take her favourite walk along the cliffs, in case she inadvertently rescued another benefactor. The thought that she was rich poisoned all her little economies; it was no longer a pleasure to find that raw turnips gave her heartburn. Worst of all, reckless fancies tormented her, blinding her to the charms of thrift. Often she rolled on the floor, struggling against the temptation to light a fire or purchase a fireproof safe.

She was thus employed when a figure darkened her doorway. It was a woman with a collecting-box, who said:

'Good morning. Would you like to give something to Foreign Missions?' Gloomily from the floor the widow replied:

'I can't afford to. Good morning.'

Those beautiful words, *I can't afford to*, mocked her with the remembrance of past serenity. Springing up in a rage, she seized a handful of rubies and hurled them at the woman's back. Some hit and bounced off. The woman turned, and gave her a reproachful Christian glance. Howling with mortification, the widow crept out and picked up the rubies. Counting them over, she found that one was missing.

Strangely enough, she did not mind. Forty-two rubies, forty-three rubies, what was the odds? She called to mind the day she lost a bone button off her mackintosh, how zealously she had sought it, how rapturously she had found it.

'Drat and drabbit those rubies!' she exclaimed. 'Drat and drabbit that Rajah! I wish his elephant would eat him.'

So she sat cursing and bemoaning till evening.

Evening fell early. A storm was getting up. The clouds lowered, the wind whistled over the heath. It seemed to her that she heard voices in the wind. Creeping to her window, she looked out, and saw in the gathering dusk a sight that chilled her blood. A few yards from her door, grovelling on hands and knees, was the dark form of a curate. Hither and thither he crawled, combing the grass, and his hat was slouched over his face as though to conceal his identity. Presently another form, also on all fours, emerged from a gorse brake. It was the woman who had come with the collecting-box.

'Have you found any more?' whispered the curate.

'Nothing but broken glass and fruit-stones,' she replied.

They continued to crawl around. At last, after a murmured colloquy, they parted. The curate arose, dusted his knees, sucked the gorse prickles out of his hands, and advanced towards the hovel. The widow hurried herself and her treasure under the bedclothes. The curate stood at the door and knocked.

The widow said nothing. Presently she saw the curate's face pressed to the window-pane. After a while he returned to the door and knocked louder. Then the handle rattled. Then the door slowly opened, and he came in.

'Good evening, Mrs Simpson. As I was passing this way I thought I'd look in on you.'

The widow groaned.

'I fear you are unwell,' said the curate.

'Never better in my life,' said the widow.

'But perhaps you are troubled in mind. Is there anything you would like to say to me, Mrs Simpson?'

'Not that I know of,' said the widow.

'You are very snug in here, Mrs Simpson. But don't you sometimes feel lonely? Are you not afraid of thieves?'

'Too poor for that,' said the widow.

'Others, you know, are even poorer. You are rich, Mrs Simpson —'

She shook her head vehemently.

'— rich in faith. Do you ever think of the poor heathen?'

'Can't say I do,' said the widow.

The curate sighed and withdrew.

Under the bedclothes the bank-notes rustled, the rubies clinked, as the widow tossed to and fro.

First she thought she would buy a padlock. Then she thought again of the bank. But probably the bank would boggle at receiving rubies, she would have to sell them, and would certainly be cheated. Then she thought of digging a hole. Then she thought of throwing herself over the cliff. Then she thought she heard thieves. But at last she fell asleep, and dreamed she had exactly three and ninepence halfpenny in the house, and was putting sand into her tea to save sugar.

Waking, she instantly remembered her riches. But she remembered the dream too. She seemed to hear a voice saying: *Belle Simpson, it's now or never.*

'It's now,' she said. 'Heathen or no heathen, curate or no curate, it's now.'

She found an old cardboard box which she had long ago picked off a rubbish heap and put by, knowing that such things come in useful sooner or later. She packed the rubies, wadding them with the notes so that they should not rattle. Then she turned an old envelope inside out, and wrote:

Kindly convert the Rajah of Golconda, and Oblige.

Then she addressed the parcel to *The Society for the Heathen, London.*

Then she walked to the village and dropped the parcel into the letter-box, unstamped.

Returning home, she spent the rest of the day thinking what a fool she had been, and searching for more rubies. But at intervals, like a flickering sunlight, a quiet contentment enlightened her and seemed to promise happy days in store. Also she found several pennies and a buttonhook, which must have dropped out of the curate.

She was fondling these when something struck her a blow, and a rough voice said:

'Come on! You've got more than that. Fork out!'

It was a tramp, and in his hand he had a blackthorn cudgel.

'I've got nothing.' she said. 'I'm a poor widow.'

'You've got something put away, widow or no widow. Poor widows don't throw jewellery into collecting-boxes. Come on, hand it over, or it will be the worse for you.'

'I have nothing,' she repeated.

'A likely story! And all these cigar bands lying around. Where do you keep it?'

For the third time she told him she had nothing. He said no more, but began to hit her with the blackthorn, to kick her and drag her hither and thither. He dragged her to the hovel.

'Show me where it is, or I'll finish you,' he said.

She was too near dying to speak again. He began to search, ripping open the mattress, poking among the rafters, coming back sooty from the chimney, and whimpering like a dog as he hunted and did not find.

Her eyes were full of blood, but she watched him. Her mind was going, but she thought: 'He'll get nothing from me, and that's a comfort.'

Thinking thus, she died happy.

As for the parcel, since there is no Society for the Heathen, the postman took it from one missionary society to another. As it was unstamped and postage dues would have to be paid on it, each society in turn thriftily refused it. In the end it was put in the Lost Parcels Office, where it is to this day.

16 The Two Mothers

In a lair under a fallen pine tree a wild cat was crooning to her young. Though they were only five days old she had already named them.

'You, Alistair,' said she, 'will be the pride of Scotland, for your head is large and round, and already when I lick your face the coming whiskers prick my tongue. And you, Donald, though you are now rather weak in the hindquarters, will not lag far behind your brother; I can tell by the way you tug at my teats that you are full of ambition and strategies. And you, Flora, my flower, what hearts you will break! I prophesy that you will have ten wooers for every ring on your tail. And you, Mairget, the woods will echo with your cries, and every bird on the bough will fear you. As for you, my little Archibald, my sly one, what bright eyes you will have when your eyes have opened! Never have I borne a finer litter. Never have there been more creditable kittens. In four days more your eyes will open; for another six weeks I shall suckle you. Day by day you will grow more sprightly and savage, until I can no longer endure your stabbing teeth, and begin to wean you. O joys of motherhood! How delightful it will be when I bring a maimed rabbit alive into the nest for you to tear!'

These words put her in mind that she was hungry herself, and shoving the kittens further under the fallen tree she trotted off to find a meal. A brace of young grouse afforded a quick lunch, and licking her lips she returned. But as she neared the lair a stinking odour met her. With a shriek of rage and alarm she rushed forward — only to find every one of the kittens lying draggled and dead. For the polecat had found them, and sucked their blood.

Sneezing and furiously lashing her tail she walked off, and sat herself down at a distance, and began to sing the coronach. While she sat howling and lamenting a ewe came stepping through the wood and said:

'I fear, Madam Cat, you are labouring under a bereavement.'

'Get out from here!' replied the wild cat.

'You should try to moderate your feelings,' said the ewe, moving a pace backward, 'and show more resignation.'

'I'll show that polecat,' said the wild cat. 'That's what I'll show.'

'Poor thing! It must be doubly painful to be robbed of your young by an animal rightly classed as vermin. There, indeed, you are to be pitied,' said the ewe. There was ill-nature in her voice, and the wild cat left off yowling and gave her a look, which made the ewe add hastily, and in a woolier tone:

'We mothers are doomed to suffering, and, believe me, I feel much sympathy for you. But do try to rise above your sorrow, and not howl so disturbingly. It quite rends my heart to hear you. Be comforted, I pray. Very likely you'll have another litter in the autumn.'

'They won't be the same kittens!' cried the wild cat. 'Ochone, my Alistair, and my little Archibald!'

'They'll be pretty much the same,' said the ewe with gentle firmness. And spying a little hillock of green grass, she began to nibble at it.

After the wild cat had finished her coronach she began to look more attentively at the ewe. 'Did you not lose a lamb this season?' she inquired.

'I did, I did! He was carried off by an eagle. The third I have lost in this manner.'

'His twin is left you, I believe?' continued the wild cat.

'Heaven be thanked for it!' cried the ewe. 'A lovely child, the apple of my eye. Ah, how glad I am he was spared to me!

All through the summer he will gambol at my side. I shall teach him to eat grass, to drink only from the purest brooks, and to lie down in the shade at noon. When he is a little older he will learn his catechism, and grow up to love nature, respect women, honour the king, and do his duty. So happily the sweet summer will go by.'

'And then?' said the wild cat.

'Then it will be time for him to go to the butcher,' replied the ewe with mournful dignity. 'Alas, it is the price one must pay for Southdown blood. The butcher always thinks highly of my lambs.'

'Vegetarian!' exclaimed the wild cat. 'Have you no energy in your blood? Are you incapable of resentment? Catch me saying: The polecat always thinks highly of my kittens!'

The ewe coughed.

'Excuse me,' she said. 'But there is a certain difference, though you, perhaps, may not be sensible of it. A polecat is not quite the same as an eagle, is it? Or quite the same as the butcher?'

'The polecat kills my young ones,' said the wild cat. 'And the eagle and the butcher kill yours. I see no difference.'

The ewe drew herself up.

'Your children are killed by a common low polecat. Mine are taken by the eagle, who is the King of Birds, or the butcher, who is a man and Lord of Creation. Such deaths are splendid and honourable. *Dulce et decorum est*.'

17 The Donkey's Providence

A certain donkey, born of humble parents, belonged to a fishmonger in East Lothian. He was a sober, good-hearted animal, and with a better fortune in life he might have been even good-looking and intelligent; but from the day he was old enough to carry a load he had been the fishmonger's donkey, and that was not a calling to foster beauty or intellect.

On weekdays early he was put to the cart and went the round of his master's customers. The fishmonger had worked up a considerable trade, especially among the local gentry. As their houses lay scattered far and wide, the donkey covered many miles each morning; and as gentry like to get their fish delivered early, he was obliged to keep at a brisk trot, and was thumped whenever he slacked his pace.

When the delivery round was over, the fishmonger drove him to the coast. There on the sand-dunes he would stand for many hours, enduring the winter rain or the summer horse-flies, and listening to the scatter-brained song of the wind among the marram grass, while his master waited for the boats, examined the catches, and bargained with the fishermen. When the fishmonger had made his purchase the donkey drew him home with it. But his day seldom ended here; ten to one there would be some other errand — oysters, maybe, to be delivered for a grand dinner, a load of kelp to be carted for a neighbour, or a cheerful party going to a wake or a lying-in who hired the fishmonger's cart to carry them there and home again.

On the Sabbath the donkey did no work. His only duty that day was to carry the fishmonger and his wife to kirk. But the fishmonger's wife was a delicate theologian; she had assayed every minister between North Berwick and the Lammer

Law before she found the doctrine adequately delivered by the Reverend Mr MacWrath; and Mr MacWrath's kirk was nine miles distant. Luckily for the donkey she thought an evening worship flighty; so for the rest of the day the donkey had nothing to do but browse around and think forward to Monday. During the summer season visitors from Edinburgh took lodgings in the neighbourhood, some to enjoy the sea-bathing, some to shoot partridges. One day while the donkey was waiting outside a house called Dumpie Castle he overheard an Edinburgh gentleman conversing with a little boy as they strolled to and fro on a shady lawn.

'Everything in nature,' said the Edinburgh gentleman, 'teaches us the same lesson. Squirrels lay up nuts against the winter. The ant and the bee have their storehouses. The beaver in his lodge is mindful of the days when he can no longer supply himself with nourishment. Bears and marmots deliberately put on flesh in autumn. The camel has five stomachs."

'And lions too?' asked the little boy.

'Assuredly. Have you not seen our good dog burying bones? No doubt the same provident instinct is implanted in the king of beasts. And if so with the beasts, how much more so with man? This poor fishmonger — do you suppose he labours only that he may eat? In that case he would not labour so much. He is putting something by, my child, he is putting by for his old age.'

'And does that make him happy?'

'He is happy in any case, William. Labour makes men happy. But he is doubly happy because not only does he labour, but he labours enough to store up against the day when old age will overtake him, *the day when the keepers of the house shall tremble, and the strong men shall bow themselves, and the grinders cease because they are few, and those that look out of the windows be darkened, and the doors —*'

Just then the fishmonger returned, jumped up on the cart, touched his hat to the gentleman, whacked the donkey, and drove off.

The donkey was greatly impressed by what he had heard. Not only did it explain much that had puzzled him in the fishmonger; he felt the personal application too. He had seen old donkeys, and knew that their last years were seldom happy. Yes, thought he, one ought to put by something against one's old age. At the moment he could not see plainly what he could put by; but no doubt that too would become clear to him later.

Time went on. The young donkey grew to a middle-aged donkey. The fishmonger grew rich enough to retire. The donkey heard him saying that he had something put by, very little but enough to keep a roof over his head. He heard other people saying that the fishmonger had put by something considerable, and now had nothing but pleasure before him.

The fishmonger sold the donkey to a huckster. The donkey had new roads to go, and a different cart to draw. Otherwise his life was much the same, and no easier. The huckster swapped him to a chimneysweep, and the chimneysweep to a rag-and-bone man. The rag-and-bone man died of typhus, and the parish authorities, who buried him, sold the donkey to defray the cost of the funeral. The donkey was bought by another fishmonger, and went back to the old life.

When he reappeared on the beach his former acquaintances recognized him — though now he was much changed for the worse — and set up a braying.

'Come away, Neddy! Here's Neddy back again. Are you still putting by, Neddy?'

And many of them tittered. For he was both old and shabby.

'Yes,' said he. 'I'm still putting by.'

They jeered the more. Every day when he came stumbling

over the links they asked him the same question and he gave them back the same answer.

One afternoon, when the March wind was blowing in over the sea, keen as a knife and salt as a herring, and the fishwives were quarrelling, with the tears running down their cheeks for cold, and the sun was shining like an insult, the donkey came dragging along, limping and twitching his coat. And they greeted him with the old question.

'Aye,' said he. 'But I've about made my fortune now.'

They laughed loud at this.

He raised his head.

'All these years, day by day, I've been putting by against my old age, so that I should not come to it unprovided. Some days I put by an ache, and some days I put by a blow. I've put by sprains, and sores, and cudgellings, hunger and neglect and weariness. Out of the winters I stored up cold nights and rheumatism. Out of the summers I stored up thirst and the stings of insects. Some days have been more profitable than others, but never a day has passed when I haven't found something to put by. All my life long I've been mindful of my old age, and now I needn't give it another thought. I've put by so much hardship and ill-usage that I'll never be older than I am at this hour.' So saying, he leaned hard against the right-hand shaft, and fell over. And after a groan or two, and a kick, he died.

18 The Trumpeter's Daughter

The Court Trumpeter's daughter did not know till her thirteenth birthday that she was a changeling. On that day her godmother said to her:

'You are the prettiest girl in the town, and the cleverest, and the best-mannered. But for all that, the sight of you turns my stomach.'

'Why, Godmother?' asked the girl in astonishment.

'Because you are not of mortal kind. In all these years you have not had the measles, nor fever, nor whooping-cough, nor smallpox, chickenpox, St Anthony's fire, St Vitus' dance, mumps, itch, or ringworm. Your legs are straight and you have not a decayed tooth in your head. Never once in all your life has the Lord's hand condescended to smite you. Away with you, you give me the creeps!'

The girl was frightened and ran home to her father. To him she said:

'Father, is it true I am not of mortal kind?'

He looked at her sadly, and said:

'So you have found it out? Now I must tell you the whole story. As you know, for twenty years I have been Court Trumpeter, and it is my duty to stand on the palace steps so that whenever His Electoral Highness goes in or out I may play a flourishing blast. Our Elector, God be praised for it, is a very healthy and energetic man, and goes in and out a hundred times a day. Child, have you ever seen a cock crowing? And how, as he crows, his legs strain and tremble, the blood rushes to his comb, his eyes turn up like those of a dying man? So it is with me. At the end of a day's trumpeting I am totally exhausted. And so it was that I never had the strength to beget a child on your dear mother, though often she besought me. One day she went walking on the heath, where a little green man started up before her, holding in his arms what looked like a chrysalis. 'Take this home,' said he, 'and keep it in a covered vessel near the stove, as though it were bread set to rise. And when the new moon is full, take off the cover, and you will find a child. Her skin will be green, and for a while you must feed her on the juice of flowers and grasses, but when she is six months old she will be able to eat mortal food and will assume mortal colour.' And with this he put the chrysalis in her arms, and vanished. Woe is me, you are that child!'

'Then I have no place in this world?' said the girl.

'I fear not,' he answered. And picking up his trumpet he went off to his daily work.

The girl sat down in dejection. Presently the flourishing strains of the trumpet rang out, and she said to herself: 'The Elector has gone out to see his hounds fed in the kennels; my father's legs are trembling and his eyes turn up like those of a dying man. What a strange world this is in which I have no part!' After a while the church bells began to ring and the people walked by carrying their prayerbooks.

'Now,' said the girl, 'the pastor will stand up in the pulpit and declare the comings and goings of God. The blood will rush to his ears, he too will tremble and turn up his eyes. But the pastor has many children, and they certainly are not changelings, for at this very hour five of them have the measles. This, too, is very odd!'

Words and notes came into her head, and she made a song comparing God and the Elector, and saying that the Elector was the better served of the two. Presently all the townspeople were singing it.

The girl was delighted, and said:

'As a song-maker I may yet find a place in this world.'

But while she was devising another song two officers appeared, one dressed in scarlet and the other in black.

The black officer said:

'I arrest you for blasphemy.'

At the same moment the scarlet officer said:

'I arrest you for high treason.'

'Goodness!' said the girl. 'You must fight it out between you. There's not enough of me to serve both God and Mammon.'

'*Scandalum magnum*! She is no better than a Manichee!' exclaimed the black officer; and the scarlet officer, not to be outdone, exclaimed: '*Scandalum magnissimum*! She says our Elector is the devil!'

Each fastened a chain on her, and she was taken to prison, singing as she went that, though the poor man may not go to court nor the rich man hardly enter into heaven, the prison doors are open to one and all, even to those who otherwise have no place in this world. This song, too, was taken up by all who heard it, and spread like wildfire through the town.

In the ecclesiastical court she was tried for blasphemy, and in the secular court she was tried for high treason; and in both she got the death sentence. In neither court had she a sensible word to say for herself, only saying, when they told her that singing had brought her to ruin:

'My father is Court Trumpeter. There is music in the family, and I can do no otherwise.'

Taken back to prison, she was cast into the condemned hold. But even there she made up her songs, and the jailers heard them and hummed them, and presently these songs too were in everyone's mouth. One evening the door was unbarred, and in stepped the Lord Chamberlain.

'My girl,' said he, 'as your father's daughter you must know that our gracious Elector is a most discerning patron of the arts, especially of the art of music. You will not have the happiness of being his subject much longer. Would it not be befitting that you should dedicate the remainder of your simple talent to a song in his praise? Something really popular, with a catchy tune.'

'Certainly,' said the girl. 'I will teach it to the youngest turnkey. He has a quick ear.'

An hour later the door opened again, and in stepped the Bishop.

'My daughter,' said he, 'as one of the Christian flock you must know that the arts are the handmaidens of the Church, none more so than the art of music. Your days in this world are numbered. Is it not your duty to devote your last hours to a sacred strain? I would suggest a hymn, something fervent, yet quite simple, with a melody suitable for congregational use.'

'By all means,' replied the girl. 'Send round the organist, and he can note it down.'

The song in praise of the Elector and the song in praise of God were published on the next day. Some preferred one and some the other; and by nightfall the townspeople were divided into two bands, and marched to and fro all night, each band trying to bawl down the other. Nothing was heard but singing and disputing, and on the morrow the tumult grew worse. The merchants closed their shops. The country people left their husbandry. The soldiers neglected their drill and formed rival choirs, and in the law-courts the opposing advocates forgot their pleas and argued before the judge which song should be given the verdict. Even the beggars forsook their trade, and turned to singing and musical criticism.

On the third day the girl was led out to be executed. The headsman stood waiting on the scaffold, and the chaplain accompanied her up the scaffold steps. Meanwhile in the market-place all the citizens were singing and disputing, so taken up with debating which was the better song that they could spare no attention for the execution of the song-maker.

The girl laid her head on the block. The headsman began to whistle.

'What!' cried the chaplain. 'Would you foul my ears with that trumpery tune? Sing the hymn, fellow!'

'Fellow to you!' replied the headsman. 'I'll sing what I like. And the Elector's song is the song for my money.'

In an instant the chaplain and the headsman were at each other's ears.

The girl got up and stood on the scaffold. Never had she seen such a turmoil, never had she heard such a shindy. The church-organ was thundering and her father was trumpeting out the Elector's song with the full power of his lungs.

'Hush, all of you! For now I will sing you my latest song, which is also my best.'

Words and music rushed into her head. At the top of her voice she sang a song in praise of art, peaceful happiness, and the midnight sky. It was by far her finest song. No one heard a note of it.

After a while, seeing that no one would attend to her, and that the headsman and the chaplain were still scuffling, she stepped down from the scaffold and made her way through the crowd. She walked on, past the church, and past the palace, and past the municipal slaughter-house, and out through the gates of the city, and so came to the heath. And since at this moment she could think of no more songs herself, she hummed as she went the chorale:

> Vexatious false world,
> Farewell will I give you.

When she had been walking for an hour or two a tall brown man started up before her. Remembering the story of her mother, she thought: 'Though he is not green, perhaps he will give me a baby.'

So she stopped, looking at him. And he stood looking at her. At last she said:

'Who are you? Have you a place in this world?'

'I have a hundred places,' he replied. 'I am a gipsy, and go where I please. Last week I was in Denmark, and tomorrow I am going to Wales.'

'That sounds a life to suit me,' said the girl. And she went with him.

19 Death in the Mouth

A publican was walking through a wood, telling himself that he was the most henpecked man in Ireland, when he heard a billy-goat bawling. Looking about he saw the animal. Its chain had become entangled in a hazel-stump, and the goat was held fast and could not stir a step.

'There's some worse off than you,' said the publican bitterly. The goat gave him a glance, as much as to say: 'Poor honest man, I know it.'

'I myself,' continued the publican, 'may seem to you as free as air. But in half an hour's time I must be back to tea, or she'll be after me for neglect and loose living.'

'My heart bleeds for you,' replied the goat. 'The worst of it is, you must abide it, for you are married to the woman. I, however, am not married to this hazel-stump.'

Struck by the truth of this reasoning, the publican disentangled the goat; and as the ground was spoiled and trampled he hauled up the stake and replanted it where the goat could find fresh pasture.

'I'll show you something,' said the goat. He searched among the grasses till he found a plant with spotted leaves. He cropped a leaf, and instantly fell down dead.

'Well, he's out of his miseries,' said the publican. 'A fine goat too. But I must be getting home.'

The goat spat out the leaf and jumped up lively as before.

'Thank you,' said the publican. 'It was as good as a theatre, I'm sure.'

'You might try the same trick,' said the goat. 'Many a married man would like to be dead if it were not for the discommodity of dying. While you hold a leaf of this plant under your tongue you can be dead for as long as you please and no longer. What's more, you can hear every word the mourners say of you, if that's any pleasure.'

The publican thanked the goat, put a leaf or two in his pocket-book, and went home.

Now that he had a remedy to end his sorrows he found it easier to endure them. Not till the third Wednesday in Lent, when the chimney was smoking and his wife reminded him of how he had stood by and allowed her to be insulted by his cousin Matilda, did he feel that the hour for death had come. Knocking out his pipe he put a leaf under his tongue, and in an instant lay like a corpse, stretched peacefully on the horsehair couch.

After a while his wife noticed that he breathed no longer, and was stiffening. She called a neighbour. The neighbour agreed that if he were not dead he was dying. The wife threw her apron over her head, and exclaimed:

'Oh, my poor devoted husband, how could you have the heart to leave me? Run, Mrs Flanagan, and fetch the priest. And, Mrs Flanagan, dear, will you lend me a hand in the taproom? For when the news gets round there'll be more trade than one poor widow woman can deal with.'

Then she began to search through all the drawers, chests, and boxes, to find what money he had put away, and if there was a will. The publican lay there, full of grateful thoughts of the goat. There had not been such a pleasant feeling in the house for years.

Presently he heard the priest's boots, and his wife saying what a shock it was, and that there was a tidy piece of money put away but no will; and that as husbands go she couldn't complain of him. But the priest said it would go ill with the best man in the world who died without the rites of the Church — and that the publican had fallen short of that. But maybe, he added, something might yet be done. Then bending over the couch he said:

'James O'Farrell, do you repent of your sins, namely, pride, envy, wrath, sloth, avarice, gluttony, and fornication — and especially neglect of your religious duties? And do you, in this your last hour, purpose to make atonement by mending the chapel roof and installing a heating system in the vestry where it's badly needed?'

No word came from the publican.

'He's past speech,' said the priest. 'But he rolled his eye at me, and I've never seen a more penitent roll of the eye. Cheer up, Mrs O'Farrell! We'll have him in purgatory yet.'

For three days the publican lay dead, hearing nothing but praises. The taproom was full of people drinking rest to his soul. His wife had not a word against him. The laying-out woman said she had never handled finer legs, and the priest declared he had seldom seen a more edifying departure.

'It's as good as a week-end at a seaside hotel,' thought the publican. 'I wish it were not so nearly over.'

However, there was nothing else for it. He was happy dead, but he did not wish to be buried. So just as they were carrying him to the grave he spat out the leaf, and knocked on the coffin-lid till they were obliged to interrupt the funeral and unscrew him.

Scarcely had he finished giving an interview to the *Ballina Guardian and Advertiser* when his troubles began again. Those who knew him thought poorly of him for coming back to life, saying that he was never a man who could keep his mind made up, and regretting the flowers and kind words they had lavished on what was not even a corpse to be worthy of them. The priest called to remind him of his dying wish to repair the chapel roof and heat the vestry. The undertaker sent in a bill. An inspector came from the distillery. And for all these things his wife reproached him, and also for the anguish he had given her, and for the careless way he left money about, and for the upstart behaviour of his relations at the funeral.

The publican thought more and more tenderly of the billy-goat, who had been such a friend to him. Death had been delightful; but not perfect, for burial and resurrection came after it. Perhaps the goat might know of some other leaf with all the merits of the spotted one but without its defect of driving a man from the horsehair couch to the graveyard and thence back into life again.

On the afternoon of Palm Sunday he walked in the wood. There was the goat. It looked thinner than ever, but its eyes were as bright as gin in a bottle.

'How did you like it!' he inquired.

'Very pleasant indeed,' replied the publican. 'But it's not perfect.' Then he explained to the goat what a quandary he was in, and his troubles with the chapel roof and the vestry heater.

'For whichever I do, I'm bound to suffer for it. Here's Easter hot upon us, and if I don't give him his desire the priest will denounce me from the altar. And if I do, I shall never hear the end of it from my wife, who will tell me that I'm snatching the bread from her mouth, and all because I've lived such a sinner that I can't be sure of heaven without a twenty-pound bill from T Callaghan, Builder, Plumber, and Decorator.'

'Terrible,' agreed the goat. 'But you don't mean to part from all that money, surely?'

'I'll boil in hell first,' said the publican. 'And that brings me to another question. Shouldn't I rather ask you for a herb that will make me immortal, at any rate till after my wife is gone? For if I should die before her, she'd have the roof and the heater done as my memorial. There's nothing that woman wouldn't do to thwart me.'

'Make a will,' said the goat, 'and leave your money tied up on some dear friend or deserving object.'

'In that case,' said the publican, 'you must find me a better herb than the spotted one, for if she discovers I've willed it away from her (and how will she not discover it? The woman's got a nose like a bronchitis kettle) I shall have neither peace nor rest.'

The goat sniffed about thoughtfully. At last he indicated some small brown mushrooms growing from the bark of a yew tree.

'Take one of these in a double whisky,' he said. 'I think that's best suited to your case.'

Next morning the publican rode into the market town, and had his will drawn up by the solicitor, signed and witnessed, and put into a sealed envelope marked *Last Will and Testament of James O' Farrell, Esq.* And he carried it home with him. When he had taken off his boots he lay down on the couch, put the mushroom in his mouth, washed it down with a double whisky, and soon lay looking quite as dead as before. But this time he heard no praises. There were none to hear. No one would waste a good word on a fellow who might be alive again within the week; and it was a question, the priest said, whether Christian burial should be allowed to such a heathen. The publican had left the whole of his fortune to the West of Ireland Goat-Keepers' Association.

In the end he was buried in the north side of the graveyard, among the stillborns and the low characters. Surmising that he was not properly dead this time either, the mourners stood around the graveside saying what they thought of him in loud clear voices for an hour and a half by the clock. But they wasted their breath. He was dead, and did not hear a syllable.

20 The Traveller from the West and the Traveller from the East

It was autumn. Harvest was over and along every road and riverway people were coming to the great fair.

Every harvest was over but the harvest of the innkeepers. Now was their season, for which they laid in wine and beer and spirits, prepared cakes and spiced meat, and beat the bugs out of the bedding.

The innkeeper's wife put another armful of peat on the fire, for it was evening, and chilly. To do so she had to lean over the English traveller's knee. Her bosom in its gold-starred handkerchief brushed his thigh. But he neither stirred nor smiled. It was a mystery what he was doing on the road, for he was not going to the fair.

When she turned round, another traveller was entering the room, a traveller who entered quietly, saluting the company with a quick glance, and then seated himself modestly under a bench near the door.

'Hey, look at that! Even the cats are going to the fair.'

'What has a cat by way of merchandise?'

'Mouseskins, to make babies' mittens.'

'Partridge feathers, to stuff a pillow.'

The cat smiled politely but did not answer these repartees. Presently it began to clean the dust of travel off its fur.

The next to come in was a zither-player, and after him a rich merchant, and after him two Jews from Minsk, and a fat woman who was a priest's housekeeper. The innkeeper's wife bustled round bringing food and drink, and there was great hospitality and good manners.

All of a sudden the cat leaped out from under the bench and caught a mouse.

'A good deed is worth paying for,' said the innkeeper's wife. And she poured milk in a saucer and gave it to the cat. The priest's housekeeper pulled her by the sleeve.

'Look at the gentleman in the chimney-nook. What's come over him?'

Sure enough, the Englishman was leaning back with closed eyes, pale as death and holding his hand to his heart.

'Leave this to me,' said the priest's housekeeper. And pulling a handful of feathers from her bundle she set fire to them, and held them smouldering under the Englishman's nose. The merchant chafed his hands, the zither-player stroked his head, the innkeeper poured vodka between his teeth. So they brought him round. When he ailed no longer, they asked him what ailed him.

'Nothing, nothing, good people.'

'It must have been something, surely,' ventured the elder Jew. 'For but a moment ago you were like one who feels the tooth of the angel Shalmaneser.'

'It upset me to see the cat catch a mouse. To me that is a most painful spectacle.'

It was the longest sentence he had yet spoken and they listened respectfully. After a while the merchant said:

'Still, you know, that's what cats are for.'

'Not everyone can afford a mousetrap,' said the zither-player.

'And even a mousetrap calls for cheese,' added the younger Jew.

The Englishman pulled out his pipe and his tobacco pouch, and filled the pipe very carefully, and drew a puff or two, and replaced the tobacco pouch, and leaned back, stretching out his toes to the fire. And all the time his face wore an expression of immovable melancholy.

'Perhaps I had better explain,' said he. 'Three years ago I fell in love with a very beautiful girl. She was amiable, gentle, accomplished, witty, and well bred. Her skin was white as milk, her hair the palest flaxen. She had large pale-green eyes. I have never seen a woman move so gracefully, and her footstep was as noiseless as the falling snow. She seemed to be made of snow and swansdown; one would say a breath would melt her, a breath blow her away. But she was perfectly healthy, indeed her constitution was remarkably tough. It was wonderful to see her play tennis. She leaped in the air like blown spray, she darted about the court like a dragon-fly. I loved her, and I married her.'

The zither-player would have said: What a woman! but the Englishman's expression was so mournful that it forbade any such exclamation.

'I married her. And on our wedding night I sat down on the bed and began to caress her, to stroke her white shoulders and kiss her hair. She lay on the pillows, full of languishing pleasure, and pinched my ear. Then, suddenly, her whole demeanour changed. Her face grew sharp, her eyes gleamed with excitement and even squinted, and the hand that had been pinching my ear now swept over my cheek and ripped it open with a finger-nail. She quivered, she drew her limbs together. And in a flash she leaped out of bed and began to spring madly about the room. She was chasing a little mouse.

'I sat on the bed imploring her to desist. All the grace, all the lightness and agility I had admired became horrible to me as I watched her prancing about the room, casting herself hither and thither, catching the mouse and letting it go again, catching it again, and tossing it in the air and catching it in her jaws as it fell. At last she settled down in a corner and ate it. And when she had finished this frightful meal she came towards the bed, walking a little unsteadily as though she were drunk, with her eyes serenely clear and her brow as bland and pure as a lily.

'You must forgive me,' she said. 'My grandfather married a white Angora, and so my blood is one-quarter Cat. All the fur is inside, thank heaven! But when I see a mouse I cannot resist it.'

'But how could I forgive her? It was not even her fault. There is no injury so impossible to forgive as an impersonal injury. That very night I left her, and I have not seen her since. My lawyers pay her a handsome allowance, and, as for me, I am making the Grand Tour in the hope of forgetting her. So far it has been quite unsuccessful.'

Murmurs of awed sympathy arose. It was difficult to know what to say after so strange and tragic a story. The zither-player, feeling he must express his condolences somehow, spat out a plum-stone towards the wayfaring cat, and said:

'Shoo, deceiving animal!'

The merchant was the first to recover, and he told how vilely he had been tricked by a girl in Lubeck. The priest's housekeeper followed him with a story about a cat who was, in truth, an evil spirit that sucked the cows. The rest chimed in, some telling of the treachery of cats and others of the falsity of women. By degrees the stories became humorous, and even the Englishman smiled once or twice.

All this time the wayfaring cat sat by the empty saucer, looking at the fire and sometimes giving another polish to his whiskers. Now he spoke, addressing himself to the Englishman.

'You have suffered by a mixed marriage. I too have proved to myself that bitterness lies at the bottom of a mixed cup. For many years I loved a woman, loved her with my whole being. She was not so beautiful as your woman, her movements were often clumsy, and her footsteps quite painfully audible;

but she had no trace of feline blood — one should not expect figs from thistles. Nevertheless, she charmed me. She was married, and I might have been jealous if she had not shown me so plainly that she preferred me to her husband. When he got up in the morning she would call me to her bed. And then she would tell me I was her comfort and her solace, and we would lie there caressing each other and praising each other's eyes.

'He drank too much, and died. And she wept bitterly, for he had left her nothing but debts. There was no food in the house except a few rats — and she could not eat these. She wept and bewailed, and said that now she must go out into the world and earn her bread. She said, too, that I should leave her because there was no more milk.

'It wounded me that she should think so poorly of my devotion, and so poorly of my capacities. That night I went out and killed five chickens. And when she woke in the morning they were on her bed. I said to her that she should become a poulterer, and live comfortably, supported by my industry. She laughed, and kissed me under the chin, and said I was indeed her true cat and kinder than any man.

'She wrote on a piece of paper: *Game and Poultry for Sale*, and put it in the window; and wearing a pretty apron and her long earrings she sat down in the window herself with a pot of flowers beside her. I played for a little with the earrings, then I went out to work.

'Hard work it was, too. I was out in all weathers, and as time went on I had to go further afield, and into the forest and the moors. I killed hens and ducks and pigeons, wild fowl, rabbits and hares. Killing was the least of it. When they were killed I had to drag them home. A hare is a heavy burden for a cat. Also I had to watch out for my life. For she would tell me, laughing, how farmers were complaining of their lost poultry, were setting traps and sitting up with guns to catch the thief.

'For a while trade went well, but not for long. Finding how agreeable it is to make money she began to set her prices higher and higher, till no one would buy. The house was full of maggoty birds and stinking hares. And there she would sit in the midst of them, holding a handkerchief to her nose and biting it with her big white teeth. And so, except that we could eat pheasant, we were as poor as the poorest.

'I was out of health and out of spirits. My system was poisoned by regular industry, for there is nothing so alien to a cat. My love was poisoned too and no longer a pleasure. How could it be a pleasure to love a person so obviously lazy, greedy, dirty, and inefficient? I was forced to admit it: she was no more than human. Yet I still clove to her, and though I could not imagine how we could live I could not imagine living without her. Then one day she washed herself all over with scented soap and went to the brothel.

'To a cat there is no place so frightful — for it is all shouting and screaming, tobacco smoke and drunkenness, trampling feet and snoring concertinas. Yet I followed her. And when she saw me she screamed out: 'Oh, drive away that odious cat! He's brought me nothing but ill-luck.' I gave her a look and came away.'

No murmurs of sympathy followed this narrative. Such a tale, a tale of unnatural affection, brothels, and poultry-stealing, outraged the whole assembly.

After looking at the fire a little longer the cat said:

'You see, my lord, you are not the only sad traveller along these roads. But because you and I have both chanced to come to grief by loving astray, do not be misled. Quite ordinary normal loves may be just as distressing. And now I must be getting on.'

After his departure they began to tell stories again. But now, as the wind was rising and the lightning flickered behind the forest, they told stories of ghosts, famines, and the pestilence.

21 Bread for the Castle

In the department of Lot there lived a baker, who was a widower. He had one daughter, and baked twice a week. For his customers were people of the village, who preferred their bread stale, since stale bread goes further.

One day his daughter came back from the butcher's, and said:

'Here's a fine piece of news! You know the castle up on the mountain with the cut hedges around it, and the iron gates that are always locked, and the gardens that have not a soul walking in them except the statues of gods and goddesses? Well, there's a great family coming to live there, lords and ladies, sons and daughters, fiddlers and pipers, men-servants and maid-servants. Think of that!'

'Why should I?' said he. 'Families of that sort bring their baker with them.'

Then he began to preach to her on his favourite subject: that a small trade, but regular, is the surest in the end, and that the huckster who sold tape through the provinces made a bigger fortune than his cousin who sold lace in Paris.

The girl sat listening, rolling and unrolling the ends of her apron-strings. And as she listened she grew pensive. It was not for anything her father was saying; she had heard all that many times before. But when she came back from the butcher's the news of the great family arriving had seemed good news, since it promised sights and wonders, new fashions to observe, new stories to hear; and now it seemed only that their coming must mean that she could no longer walk up the mountain on Sunday evenings with her young man, to stare through the iron gate at the garden, and the statues rising out of the long grass.

By the time her father had reached the end of his discourse and was assuring her that she would have a comfortable little dowry she was as sober as the church clock.

The great family came; and just as the baker foretold, they brought their baker with them, and a confectioner too. Very little trade came into the village through them.

Then one afternoon a footman from the castle appeared in the village, running as though the devil were after him. And he knocked on the baker's door. The girl let him in. He was so out of breath he could not speak, but she guessed his errand, and said:

'Do you want bread? This is all we have till Thursday, when my father bakes again.'

He looked at it scornfully, and said: 'This is maslin stuff. We don't chump such bread at the castle. Have you no rolls, no crescents?'

'Only for weddings,' said the girl. 'My father can bake them, but only to order.'

'Then in God's name,' said the footman, 'let him bake to order.'

The girl said that must be as her father chose.

Just then the baker came in from the garden, where he had been thinning his artichokes. By this time the footman had recovered his breath, and he explained that the castle's own baker, a townsman, had mistaken the hooting of the owls in the castle garden for the howling of wolves; and so he had run away, taking the confectioner with him as a protection.

'And now,' said the footman, 'we shall have no bread for tomorrow's breakfast unless you bake for us.'

The baker sucked in his lips as though he were sampling a brandy.

'Have you pure white flour up at the castle?'

'Naturally. What else should we have?'

'Then bring it me, and tomorrow you shall have bread."

No sooner was the footman gone than he began to skip round the room, slapping his thighs and singing the *Carmagnole*.

That night he baked rolls and crescents, buns and long rolls; and as the work was heavy his daughter stayed up to lend him a hand. At six in the morning the bread came out of the oven, smelling like a wheat-field in the sun. By seven it was at the castle. The girl accompanied her father and the donkey up the mountain, though she was very sleepy. She had said to herself: 'Now I shall get into that garden.' But on the contrary she did not even catch sight of the garden, for they went to the back door.

The baker ordered sacks of pure white flour from the miller, and now every night he baked the castle bread; and now every night the girl must needs sit up along with him, to help him knead the dough and afterwards to sing; for he was afraid that otherwise he might fall asleep and let the bread scorch in the oven. She sang love-songs mostly, for they were the songs she liked best; and between one song and another the baker would talk to her of the fortune he was gaining, and of his intention to have a board placed above the door, saying: *Baker to the Castle*, and that the words should be painted in gold leaf on a blue ground. And sometimes he would pat her cheek with a floury hand, and tell her what a magnificent dowry she would have. So he baked, and so she sang, with the tears of weariness running down her face. And when the cocks crowed at midnight she would think: 'Now my love lies sleeping on his right side.' And when they crowed again she would think: 'Now he has turned over and lies on his left side.' And sometimes she would say to her father:

'Father, when shall I be married?'

And he would answer:

'When your fortune is made. But it is a pity your betrothed is no more than a farmer's son.'

So all through the summer they baked the castle bread and into the autumn. And the nights began to grow cold, and the wind to blow from the mountain, and the fallen leaves to patter against the bakehouse door. And the walls of the bakehouse that had been limewashed as white as arrowroot were now chequered all over with the sums in addition and compound interest that the baker scrawled in charcoal.

These sums became ever more interesting to him. And that was a good thing, for lately his daughter's singing had become so harsh and droning that there was no encouragement in it. There she sat, perched on the edge of the kneading-trough, humped up with sleepiness, and wrapped in a brown hooded cloak; for in spite of the heat from the oven she complained incessantly of feeling cold. There she sat, with her staring great eyes, ringed around with sleeplessness. There she sat, singing:

'*Où donc sont mes amours? Où, où? Hou-hou-hou!*'

'Surely she has grown smaller,' thought the baker. 'Or do my eyes deceive me?' Looking at her more attentively he saw that his daughter had changed into an owl.

'But this is frightful,' thought the baker. 'My poor girl, with such brilliant prospects, and such a good daughter into the bargain, so handy and willing! What shall I do without her?'

He opened the oven-door and turned the bread. The bread was all right: nothing untoward had happened to the bread.

'It must be an illusion,' said the baker. 'Probably I have strained my eyes doing so much arithmetic.'

But when he looked at her again he saw that she was quite unmistakably an owl.

'She will change back at sunrise,' he told himself. 'After all, if she chooses to be an owl at night … It is inconvenient, of course. An owl is a depressing companion. Many people say that owls are unpropitious. I can't look for an owl to help me knead the dough. Still, if she chooses to be an owl at night, that is her affair. Girls get queer notions. No doubt it will pass over when she is married! Ah, how I shall miss her help when she is married! Though of course an owl is not much help to a man.'

So he talked to himself till the time came to take the bread from the oven, wrap it in baize cloths, saddle the donkey, and carry the bread to the castle. The sun had not risen when he set out.

'I shall find her her usual self when I get back,' he thought. When he reached home the sun had risen, the day was bright and clear. He hurried into the bakehouse. No owl was there.

'God be praised!' said the baker. 'No doubt she is in the kitchen making coffee.'

But there was no sign of the girl in the kitchen, or in her bedroom, or anywhere in the house or anywhere in the garden. But at last, searching in the woodshed, he glanced up, and there sat an owl on the rafter.

Now came sad days for the baker. He had to do everything for himself, cook and sweep and wash the linen and mend his own clothes. And all this he had to do in secret, lest people should say to him:

'Why, what has become of your daughter, that you are keeping house?'

And on Sunday when he went to mass he was obliged to say:

'My poor girl was sleeping so soundly that I had not the heart to wake her.'

But every night when he went to the bakehouse the owl came silently flying in, and perched on the kneading-trough, and sang: 'Hou–hou–hou!'

One night he became angry. He went up to her and shook his fist before her staring eyes.

'Name of God!' said he. 'Can you do nothing but hoot and hoo? At least, can't you catch mice?'

She fluttered her feathers. She spread her wings and rose into the air, and flew into a dark corner of the bakehouse, and came back with a mouse in her claws, and ate it.

The winter drew on. Now it was Christmas Eve. There was nothing for it, the baker must go to the midnight mass, and go alone. In the church porch he saw his daughter's young man.

'Why, where is Celestine? Is she not well?'

'Yes, yes, she is well. She is blooming. She will be here presently, no doubt. She delayed a little because she was busy.'

'What busied her, then?'

'Catching mice,' said the baker.

He hurried into church and fell on his knees.

Presently he heard all around him a whispering and a skirmishing.

'Look, what's that? How did it get in? Ah, horrible creature, there is nothing more unlucky. Shoo it out!'

The baker shut his eyes. The priest came from the vestry and began the mass. The baker opened one eye. There, perched on the sounding-board of the pulpit, sat the owl. The instant that mass was ended, people began to hurry out of church, not even waiting to let the castle people pass out first. As they went they whispered among themselves that it would be an unlucky year and a bad harvest.

With the new year came snow. The baker could scarcely make his way up to the castle. When the snow melted there were disastrous floods. After the floods came high winds, hail, and thunderstorms. One melancholy April morning the footman came to the baker's house and said:

'You need not bake for us any more.'

'And why not? Does not my baking give satisfaction?'

'As for the baking,' said the footman, 'it's well enough, I suppose, for a place like this. But the truth of it is that we are going back to Paris. Life here is barbarous, and we can't be expected to endure it a day longer.'

That night at the accustomed hour the baker went into the bakehouse. Presently the owl flew in and perched on the kneading-trough.

'We're not baking tonight,' he said. 'The people at the castle have gone back to Paris.'

She stared at him with her round eyes, and he repeated:

'They have gone back. The castle is empty once more. There will be no more baking.'

The owl rose in the air. She flew to the door and battered against it with her wings, and hooted wildly. Her father opened the door, for he was afraid of her. It was a clear starlight night. She spread her wings and flew straight off towards the castle. As she neared it she saw the shapes of the cut hedges, and the pattern of the iron gates against the sky. She flew over the gates, and swooped low to the lawns and terraces, and circled round the statues that were cold with dew. There in the castle garden she stayed.

As for the baker, his life fell all to pieces. He baked but twice a week and slept at night. The fine white flour he took back to the miller, for it was too good to be mixed into maslin loaves; and the charcoal figures on the bakehouse wall blurred and faded, and at last he washed them over with a new coat of whitewash and forgot them. For now that he could not add to his riches, his riches were no longer a pleasure to him. Not till he died would the world know of them, and then he would not be there.

On the morning of the first of May his daughter's young man came to the house and said:

'Where is Celestine? For today is a holiday, and I would like to walk with her to the castle, where we can look in through the gates at the lilacs and the syringas.'

'Alas!' said the baker. 'Celestine is not here. She went away with the people from the castle, and now, I suppose, she is in Paris.'

The young man sank down on the threshold. The baker patted his arm, and said:

'It is very sad, is it not? Naturally, I do not care to speak of it. It is no pleasure to tell of a daughter's ruin. But there it is, she is gone, and I do not suppose we shall see her again. She would have had a good dowry, too. It is a great loss, and I feel for you most sincerely.'

22 Popularity

Once upon a time there was a young wolf who yearned for popularity. But though he did his best to please, no one, except a few other wolves, thought much of him; and even they said he would be better if he did not fool around but attended to business.

One day he went to the dog, and said:

'Excuse me —'

'Go away!' said the dog. 'Bow-wow!'

The wolf smiled and looked propitiating.

'Excuse me,' he repeated, 'dear dog. But I am young, and yearn for popularity. How is it to be won? You must certainly know the secret, for you are exceedingly popular.'

'You must learn to wag your tail,' said the dog, 'eat starchy foods, and never attack mankind unless a man bids you.'

The wolf went off and studied this. He wagged his tail, he got dog-biscuit and ate it till he had severe indigestion. And when he met a man he wagged his tail and stood with one paw raised, waiting to be bidden to attack mankind. But men threw stones at him and he was still unpopular.

So he went to the cat, and said:

'Excuse me —'

The cat hissed and arched her back.

'Excuse me,' he repeated, 'dear cat. But I am young, and yearn for popularity.' Then he said what he had said to the dog.

'You must learn to purr,' said the cat, 'wash your face, and rub against women's legs except when they throw the saucepan lid at you.'

The wolf went off and studied this. He purred, and washed his face, and approached women in order to rub against their legs; but he never got near enough to carry out this intention, for they screamed and threw saucepan lids at him. So he was still unpopular.

So he went to the sheep, and said:

'Excuse me —'

The sheep took to her heels; but he ran after her, rubbed against her legs, and asked her the secret of popularity.

Trembling and gasping for breath, she replied:

'You must eat grass, allow men to shear off your fur, and run away if anyone speaks to you. Now get off, you nasty creature!'

He learned to eat grass — which disagreed with him even more than dog-biscuit — he ran away if any spoke to him, and he hung about hoping that someone would shear off his fur. But no one attempted to do so, and so he was still unpopular.

So he went to the blackbird, and said:

'Excuse me —'

'Tirrup-tirree, tirrup-tirree!' said the blackbird angrily.

The wolf explained his yearning for popularity.

'You must eat grubs and learn to sing,' answered the blackbird.

The wolf went off, ate grubs, and practised singing. He sat in orchards in the early morning and sang. People opened their windows and catapulted him. So he was still unpopular.

So he went to the lion, and said:

'Excuse me —'

He paused; he was used by now to being interrupted. The lion said nothing.

'Excuse me, dear lion. But I am young and yearn for popularity.'

'Pooh!' exclaimed the lion. 'Popularity is base and vulgar. You should desire to be esteemed.'

'There is nothing I would like better. How is it to be managed?'

'You must be swift, strong, and ruthless,' replied the lion. 'You must be dignified, and you must wear a mane.'

The wolf went off. He massaged his neck to make his hair grow. He practised gymnastics by the hour, and when he was out of breath he practised dignity. And to show his ruthlessness he fell on the dog, the sheep, and the cat, and devoured them. The man, the woman, and the shepherds all let off guns at him. So he was still unpopular.

So he went to the owl, and said:

'Look here! —'

'Excuse me,' said the owl. She flew down from her branch, seized a field-mouse and began to eat it. The wolf explained his yearning for popularity. He recounted how he had learned to wag his tail, wash his face, purr and sing; how he had eaten starchy foods, grass, and grubs; how he had waited for men to tell him to attack mankind, tried to rub against women's legs, and grown a mane; how he had been swift, strong, ruthless, and dignified, hung about waiting to have his fur sheared off, and run away when anyone spoke to him.

'All this,' said the owl, speaking with her mouth full, 'is just waste of time. Wolf you are, and wolf you will remain. The only thing you can do is to be as wolfish as possible.'

So he went away and was as wolfish as possible.

Having sharpened his wits by learning such difficult arts as purring and singing; having hardened himself by so many austerities like eating grass and dog-biscuit; having strengthened himself by all those gymnastics and grown a great mane, he became the most wolfish and redoubtable wolf that had been known since the Wolf of Gévaudan.

So one day all the men of the village went out with clubs and guns, and finished him off.

23 Bluebeard's Daughter

Every child can tell of his ominous pigmentation, of his ruthless temper, of the fate of his wives and of his own fate, no less bloody than theirs; but — unless it be here and there a Director of Oriental Studies — no one now remembers that Bluebeard had a daughter. Amid so much that is wild and shocking this gentler trait of his character has been overlooked. Perhaps, rather than spoil the symmetry of a bad husband by an admission that he was a good father, historians have suppressed her. I have heard her very existence denied, on the grounds that none of Bluebeard's wives lived long enough to bear him a child. This shows what it is to give a dog a bad name. To his third wife, the mother of Djamileh, Bluebeard was most tenderly devoted, and no shadow of suspicion rested upon her quite natural death in childbed.

From the moment of her birth Djamileh became the apple of Bluebeard's eye. His messengers ransacked Georgia and Circassia to find wet-nurses of unimpeachable health, beauty, and virtue; her infant limbs were washed in nothing but rosewater, and swaddled in Chinese silks. She cut her teeth upon a cabochon emerald engraved with propitious mottoes, and all the nursery vessels, mugs, platters, ewers, basins, and chamber-pots were of white jade. Never was there a more adoring and conscientious father than Bluebeard, and I have sometimes thought that the career of this often-widowered man was inevitably determined by his anxiety to find the ideal stepmother.

Djamileh's childhood was happy, for none of the stepmothers lasted long enough to outwear their good intentions, and every evening, whatever his occupations during the day, Bluebeard came to the nursery for an hour's romp. But three days before her ninth birthday Djamileh was told that her father was dead; and while she was still weeping for her loss she was made to weep even more bitterly by the statement that he was a bad man and that she must not cry for him. Dressed in crape, with the Bluebeard diamonds sparkling like angry tears beneath her veils, and wearing a bandage on her wrist, Fatima came to Djamileh's pavilion and paid off the nurses and governesses. With her came Aunt Ann, and a strange young man whom she was told to call Uncle Selim; and while the nurses lamented and packed and the governesses sulked, swooned, and clapped their hands for sherbet, Djamileh listened to this trio disputing as to what should be done with her.

'For she can't stay here alone,' said Fatima. 'And nothing will induce me to spend another night under this odious roof.'

'Why not send her to school?'

'Or to the Christians?' suggested Selim.

'Perhaps there is some provision for her in the will?'

'Will! Don't tell me that such a monster could make a will, a valid will. Besides, he never made one.'

Fatima stamped her foot, and the diamond necklace sidled on her stormy bosom. Still disputing, they left the room.

That afternoon, all the silk carpets and embroidered hangings, all the golden dishes and rock-crystal wine-coolers, together with the family jewels and Bluebeard's unique collection of the Persian erotic poets, were packed up and sent by camel to Selim's residence in Teheran. Thither also travelled Fatima, Ann, Selim, and Djamileh, together with a few selected slaves, Fatima in one litter with Selim riding at her side, doing his best to look stately but not altogether succeeding, since his mount was too big for him, Ann and Djamileh in the other. During the journey Ann said little, for she was engaged in ticking off entries in a large scroll. But once or twice she told Djamileh not to fidget, and to thank her stars that she had kind friends who would provide for her.

As it happened, Djamileh was perfectly well provided for. Bluebeard had made an exemplary and flawless will by which he left all his property to his only daughter and named his solicitor as her guardian until she should marry. No will can please everybody; and there was considerable heartburning when Badruddin removed Djamileh and her belongings from the care of Fatima, Ann, and Selim, persisting to the last filigree egg-cup in his thanks for their kind offices towards the heiress and her inheritance.

Badruddin was a bachelor, and grew remarkably fine jasmines. Every evening when he came home from his office he filled a green watering-pot and went to see how they had passed the day. In the latticed garden the jasmine bushes awaited him like a dumb and exceptionally charming seraglio. Now he often found Djamileh sitting among them, pale and silent, as though, in response to being watered so carefully, a jasmine had borne him a daughter.

It would have been well for Djamileh if she had owed her being to such an innocent parentage. But she was Bluebeard's daughter, and all the girl-babies of the neighbourhood cried in terror at her father's name. What was more, the poor girl could not look at herself in the mirror without being reminded of her disgrace. For she had inherited her father's colouring. Her hair was a deep butcher's blue, her eyebrows and eyelashes were blue also. Her complexion was clear and pale, and if some sally of laughter brought a glow to her cheek it was of the usual pink, but the sinister parental pigmentation reasserted itself on her lips which were deep purple, as though stained with eating mulberries; and the inside of her mouth and her tongue were dusky blue like a well-bred chow-dog's. For the rest she was like any other woman, and when she pricked her finger the blood ran scarlet.

Looks so much out of the common, if carried off with sufficient assurance, might be an asset to a modern miss. In Djamileh's time taste was more classical. Blue hair and purple lips, however come by, would have been a serious handicap for any young woman—how much more so, then, for her, in whom they were not only regrettable but scandalous. It was impossible for Bluebeard's badged daughter to be like other girls of her age. The purple mouth seldom smiled; the blue hair, severely braided by day, was often at night wetted with her tears. She might, indeed, have dyed it. But filial devotion forbade. Whatever his faults, Bluebeard had been a good father.

Djamileh had a great deal of proper feeling; it grieved her to think of her father's crimes. But she had also a good deal of natural partiality, and disliked Fatima; and this led her to try to find excuses for his behaviour. No doubt it was wrong, very wrong, to murder so many wives; but Badruddin seemed to think that it was almost as wrong to have married them, at any rate to have married so many of them. Experience, he said, should have taught the deceased that female curiosity is insatiable; it was foolish to go on hoping to find a woman without curiosity. Speaking with gravity, he conjured his ward to struggle, so far as in her lay, with this failing, so natural in her own sex, so displeasing to the other.

Djamileh fastened upon his words. To mark her reprobation of curiosity, the fault which had teased on her father to his ruin, she resolved never to be in the least curious herself. And for three weeks she did not ask a single question. At the end of the third week she fell into a violent fever, and Badruddin, who had been growing more and more disquieted by what appeared to him to be a protracted fit of sulks, sent for a doctoress. The doctoress was baffled by the fever, but did not admit it. What the patient needed, she said, was light but distracting conversation. Mentioning in the course of her chat that she had discovered from the eunuch that the packing-case in the lobby contained a new garden hose, the doctoress had the pleasure of seeing Djamileh make an instant recovery from her fever. Congratulating herself on her skill and on her fee, the old dame went off, leaving Djamileh to realize that it was not enough to refrain from asking questions, some more radical method of combating curiosity must be found. And so when Badruddin, shortly after her recovery, asked her in a laughing way how she would like a husband, she replied seriously that she would prefer a public-school education.

This was not possible. But the indulgent solicitor did what he could to satisfy this odd whim, and Djamileh made such good use of her opportunities that by the time she was fifteen she had spoilt her handwriting, forgotten how to speak French, lost all her former interest in botany, and asked only the most unspeculative questions. Badruddin was displeased. He sighed to think that the intellectual Bluebeard's child should have grown up a dullard, and spent more and more time in the company of his jasmines. Possibly, even, he consulted them, for though they were silent they could be expressive. In any case, after a month or so of inquiries, interviews, and drawing up treaties, he told Djamileh that, acting under her father's will, he had made arrangements for her marriage.

Djamileh was sufficiently startled to ask quite a number of questions, and Badruddin congratulated himself on the aptness of his prescription. His choice had fallen upon Prince Kayel Oumarah, a young man of good birth, good looks, and pleasant character, but not very well-to-do. The prince's relations were prepared to overlook Djamileh's origin in consideration of her fortune, which was enormous, and Kayel, who was of a rather sentimental turn of mind, felt that it was an act of chivalry to marry a girl whom other young men might scorn for what was no fault of hers, loved her already for being so much obliged to him, and wrote several ghazals expressing a preference for blue hair.

> *'What wouldn't I do, what wouldn't I do,*
> *To get at that hair of heavenly blue?'*

(the original Persian is, of course, more elegant) sang Kayel under her window. Djamileh thought this harping on her hair not in the best of taste, more especially since Kayel had a robust voice and the whole street might hear him. But it was flattering to have poems written about her (she herself had no turn for poetry), and when she peeped through the lattice she thought that he had a good figure and swayed to and fro with a great deal of feeling. Passion and a good figure can atone for much; and perhaps when they were man and wife he would leave off making personal remarks.

After a formal introduction, during which Djamileh offered Kayel symbolical sweetmeats and in her confusion ate most of them herself, the young couple were married. And shortly afterwards, they left town for the Castle of Shady Transports, the late Bluebeard's country house.

Djamileh had not set eyes on Shady Transports since she was carried away from it in the same litter as Aunt Ann and the inventory. It had been in the charge of a caretaker ever since. But before the wedding Badruddin had spent a few days at the village inn, and under his superintendence the roof had been mended, the gardens trimmed up, all the floors very carefully scrubbed, and a considerable quantity of female attire burned in the stable yard. There was no look of former tragedy about the place when Djamileh and Kayel arrived. The fountain splashed innocently in the forecourt, all the most appropriate flowers in the language of love were bedded out in the parterre, a troop of new slaves, very young and handsomely dressed, stood bowing on either side of the door, and seated on cushions in stiff attitudes of expectation

Maya and Moghreb, Djamileh's favourite dolls, held out their jointed arms in welcome.

Tears came into her eyes at this token of Badruddin's understanding heart. She picked up her old friends and kissed first one and then the other, begging their pardon for the long years in which they had suffered neglect. She thought they must have pined, for certainly they weighed much less than of old. Then she recollected that she was grown up, and had a husband.

At the moment he was not to be seen. Still clasping Maya and Moghreb, she went in search of him, and found him in the armoury, standing lost in admiration before a display of swords, daggers, and cutlasses. Djamileh remembered how, as a child, she had been held up to admire, and warned not to touch.

'That one comes from Turkestan,' she said. 'My father could cut off a man's head with it at a single blow.'

Kayel pulled the blade a little way from the sheath. It was speckled with rust, and the edge was blunted.

'We must have them cleaned up,' he said. 'It's a pity to let them get like this, for I've never seen a finer collection.'

'He had a splendid collection of poets, too,' said Djamileh. 'I was too young to read them then, of course, but now that I am married to a poet myself I shall read them all."

'What a various-minded man!' exclaimed Kayel as he followed her to the library.

It is always a pleasure to explore a fine old rambling country house. Many people whose immediate thoughts would keep them tediously awake slide into a dream by fancying that such a house has — no exact matter how — come into their possession. In fancy they visit it for the first time, they wander from room to room, trying each bed in turn, pulling out the books, opening Indian boxes, meeting themselves in mirrors ...

All is new to them, and all is theirs.

For Kayel and Djamileh this charming delusion was a matter of fact. Djamileh indeed declared that she remembered Shady Transports from the days of her childhood, and was always sure that she knew what was round the next corner; but really her recollections were so fragmentary that except for the sentiment of the thing she might have been exploring her old home for the first time. As for Kayel, who had spent most of his life in furnished lodgings, the comfort and spaciousness of his wife's palace impressed him even more than he was prepared to admit. Exclaiming with delight, the young couple ransacked the house, or wandered arm in arm through the grounds, discovering fishponds, icehouses, classical grottoes, and rustic bridges. The gardeners heard their laughter among the blossoming thickets, or traced where they had sat by the quantity of cherrystones.

At last a day came when it seemed that Shady Transports had yielded up all its secrets. A sharp thunderstorm had broken up the fine weather. The rain was still falling, and Kayel and Djamileh sat in the western parlour playing chess like an old married couple. The rain had cooled the air, indeed it was quite chilly; and Kayel, who was getting the worst of the game, complained of a draught that blew on his back and distracted him.

'There can't really be a draught, my falcon,' objected Djamileh, 'for draughts don't blow out of solid walls, and there is only a wall behind you.'

'There is a draught,' he persisted. 'I take your pawn. No, wait a moment, I'm not sure that I do. How can I possibly play chess in a whirlwind?'

'Change places,' said his wife, 'and I'll turn the board.'

They did so and continued the game. It was now Djamileh's move; and as she sat gazing at the pieces Kayel fell to studying her intent and unobservant countenance. She was certainly quite pretty, very pretty even, in spite of her colouring.

Marriage had improved her, he thought. A large portrait of Bluebeard hung on the wall behind her. Kayel's glance went from living daughter to painted sire, comparing the two physiognomies. Was there a likeness — apart, of course, from the blue hair? Djamileh was said to be the image of her mother; certainly the rather foxlike mask before him, the narrow eyes and pointed chin, bore no resemblance to the prominent eyes and heavy jowl of the portrait. Yet there was a something … the pouting lower lip, perhaps, emphasized now by her considering expression. Kayel had another look at the portrait.

'Djamileh! There is a draught! I saw the hangings move.' He jumped up and pulled them aside. 'What did I say?' he inquired triumphantly.

'Oh! Another surprise! Oh, haven't I a lovely Jack-in-the-Box house?'

The silken hangings had concealed a massive stone archway, closed by a green baize door.

Kayel nipped his wife's ear affectionately. 'You who remember everything so perfectly — what's behind that door?'

'Rose-petal conserve,' she replied. 'I have just remembered how it used to be brought out from the cupboard when I was good.'

'I don't believe it. I don't believe there's a cupboard, I don't believe you were ever good.'

'Open it and see.'

Beyond the baize door a winding stair led into a small gallery or corridor, on one side of which were windows looking into the park, on the other, doors. It was filled with a green and moving light reflected from the wet foliage outside. They turned to each other with rapture. A secret passage — five doors in a row, five new rooms waiting to be explored! With a dramatic gesture Kayel threw open the first door.

A small dark closet was revealed, perfectly empty. A trifle dashed, they opened the next door. Another closet, small, dark, and empty. The third door revealed a third closet, the exact replica of the first and second.

Djamileh began to laugh at her husband's crestfallen air.

'In my day,' she said, 'all these cupboards were full of rose-petal conserve. So now you see how good I was.'

Kayel opened the fourth door.

He was a solemn young man, but now he began to laugh also. Four empty closets, one after another, seemed to these amiable young people the height of humour. They laughed so loudly that they did not hear a low peal of thunder, the last word of the retreating storm. A dove who had her nest in the lime tree outside the window was startled by their laughter or by the thunder; she flew away, looking pale and unreal against the slate-coloured sky. Her flight stirred the branches, which shook off their raindrops, spattering them against the casement.

'Now for the fifth door.' said Kayel.

But the fifth door was locked.

'Djamileh, dear, run and ask the steward for the keys. But don't mention which door we want unfastened. Slaves talk so, they are always imagining mysteries.'

'I am rather tired of empty cupboards, darling. Shall we leave this one for the present? At any rate till after tea? So much emptiness has made me very hungry, I really need my tea.'

'Djamileh, fetch the keys.'

Djamileh was an obedient wife, but she was also a prudent one. When she had found the bunch of keys she looked carefully over those which were unlabelled. They were many, and of all shapes and sizes; but at last she found the key she had been looking for and which she had dreaded to find. It was a small key, made of gold and finely arabesqued; and on it there was a small dark stain that might have been a bloodstain.

She slipped it off the ring and hid it in her dress.

Returning to the gallery, she was rather unpleasantly struck by Kayel's expression. She could never have believed that his open countenance could wear such a look of cupidity or that his eyes could become so beady ... Hearing her step, he started violently, as though roused from profound absorption.

'There you are! What an age you have been — darling! Let's see, now. Icehouse, Stillroom, Butler's Pantry, Wine-cellar, Family Vault ... I wonder if this is it?'

He tried key after key, but none of them fitted. He tried them all over again, upside-down or widdershins. But still they did not fit. So then he took out his pocket-knife, and tried to pick the lock. This also was useless.

'Eblis take this lock!' he exclaimed. And suddenly losing his temper, he began to kick and batter at the door. As he did so there was a little click; and one of the panels of the door fell open upon a hinge, and disclosed a piece of parchment, framed and glazed, on which was an inscription in ancient Sanskrit characters.

'What the ... Here, I can't make this out.'

Djamileh, who was better educated than her husband in such useless studies as calligraphy, examined the parchment, and read aloud: 'CURIOSITY KILLED THE CAT.'

Against her bosom she felt the little gold key sidle, and she had the unpleasant sensation which country language calls: *The grey goose walking over your grave.*

'I think,' she said gently,' I think, dear husband, we had better leave this door alone.' Kayel scratched his head and looked at the door. 'Are you sure that's what it means? Perhaps you didn't read it right.'

'I am quite sure that is what it means.'

'But, Djamileh, I do want to open the door.'

'So do I, dear. But under the circumstances we had better not do anything of the sort. My poor father … my poor stepmothers …'

'I wonder,' mused Kayel, 'if we could train a cat to turn the lock and go in first.'

'Even if we could, which I doubt, I don't think that would be at all fair to the cat. No, Kayel, I am sure we should agree to leave this door alone.'

'It's not that I am in the least inquisitive,' said Kayel, 'for I am not. But as master of the house I really think it my duty to know what's inside this cupboard. It might be firearms, for instance, or poison, which might get into the wrong hands. One has a certain responsibility, hang it.'

'Yes, of course. But all the same I feel sure we should leave the door alone.'

'Besides, I have you to consider, Djamileh. As a husband, you must be my first consideration. Now you may not want to open the door just now; but suppose, later on, when you were going to have a baby, you developed one of those strange yearnings that women at such times are subject to; and suppose it took the form of longing to know what was behind this door. It might be very bad for you, Djamileh, it might imperil your health, besides birth-marking the baby. No! It's too grave a risk. We had much better open the door immediately.'

And he began to worry the lock again with his pen-knife.

'Kayel, please don't. *Please* don't. I implore you, I have a feeling —'

'Nonsense. Women always have feelings.'

'— as though I were going to be sick. In fact, I am sure I am going to be sick.'

'Well, run off and be sick, then. No doubt it was the thunderstorm, and all those strawberries.'

'I can't run off, Kayel. I don't feel well enough to walk, you must carry me. Kayel!' — she laid her head insistently on his chest — 'Kayel! I felt sick this morning, too.'

And she laid her limp weight against him so firmly that with a sigh he picked her up and carried her down the corridor.

Laid on the sofa, she still kept a firm hold on his wrist, and groaned whenever he tried to detach himself At last, making the best of a bad job, he resigned himself, and spent the rest of the day reading aloud to her from the Persian erotic poets. But he did not read with his usual fervour; the lyrics, as he rendered them, might as well have been genealogies. And Djamileh, listening with closed eyes, debated within herself why Kayel should be so cross. Was it just the locked closet? Was it, could it be, that he was displeased by the idea of a baby with Bluebeard blood? This second possibility was highly distressing to her, and she wished, more and more fervently, as she lay on the sofa keeping up a pretence of delicate health and disciplining her healthy appetite to a little bouillon and some plain sherbet, that she had hit upon a pretext with fewer consequences entailed.

It seemed to her that they were probably estranged for ever. So it was a great relief to be awakened in the middle of the night by Kayel's usual affable tones, even though the words were:

'Djamileh, I believe I've got it! All we have to do is to get a stonemason, and a ladder, and knock a hole in the wall. Then we can look in from outside. No possible harm in that.'

All the next day and the day after, Kayel perambulated the west wing of Shady Transports with his stonemasons, directing them where to knock holes in the walls; for it had been explained to the slaves that he intended to bring the house up to date by throwing out a few bow-windows. But not one of these perspectives (the walls of Shady Transports were exceedingly massy) afforded a view into the locked closet. While these operations were going on he insisted that Djamileh should remain at his side. It was essential, he said, that she should appear interested in the improvements, because of the slaves. All this time, she was carrying about that key on her person, and debating whether she should throw it away, in case Kayel by getting possession of it should endanger his life, or whether she should keep it and use it herself the moment he was safely out of the way.

Jaded in nerves and body, at the close of the second day they had a violent quarrel. It purported to be about the best method of pruning acacias, but while they were hurrying from sarcasm to acrimony, from acrimony to abuse, from abuse to fisticuffs, they were perfectly aware that in truth they were quarrelling as to which of them should first get at that closet.

'Laterals! Laterals!' exclaimed Djamileh. 'You know no more of pruning than you know of dressmaking. That's right! Tear out my hair, do!'

'No, thank you.' Kayel folded his arms across his chest. 'I have no use for *blue hair.*'

Pierced by this taunt, Djamileh burst into tears. The soft-hearted Kayel felt that he had gone too far, and made several handsome apologies for the remark; but it seemed his apologies would be in vain, for Djamileh only came out of her tears to ride off on a high horse.

'No, Kayel,' she said, putting aside his hand, and speaking with exasperating nobility and gentleness. 'No, no, it is useless, do not let us deceive ourselves any longer. I do not blame you; your feeling is natural and one should never blame people for natural feelings.'

'Then why have you been blaming me all this time for a little natural curiosity?'

Djamileh swept on.

'And how could you possibly have felt anything but aversion for one in whose veins so blatantly runs the blood of the

Bluebeards, for one whose hair, whose lips, stigmatize her as the child of an unfortunate monster? I do not blame you, Kayel. I blame myself, for fancying you could ever love me. But I will make you the only amends in my power. I will leave you.'

A light quickened in Kayel's eye.

So he thought she would leave him at Shady Transports, did he?

'Tomorrow we will go *together* to Badruddin. He arranged our marriage, he had better see about our divorce."

Flushed with temper, glittering with tears, she threw herself into his willing arms. They were still in all the raptures of sentiment and first love, and in the even more enthralling raptures of sentiment and first grief, when they set out for Teheran.

Absorbed in gazing into each other's eyes and wiping away each other's tears with pink silk handkerchiefs, they did not notice that a drove of stampeding camels was approaching their palanquin; and it was with the greatest surprise and bewilderment that they found themselves tossed over a precipice.

When Djamileh recovered her senses she was lying in a narrow green pasture beside a watercourse. Some fine broad-tailed sheep were cropping the herbage, and an aged shepherdess was bathing her forehead and slapping her hands.

'How did I come here?' she inquired.

'I really cannot tell you,' answered the shepherdess. 'All I know is that about half an hour ago you, and a handsome young man, and a coachman, and a quantity of silk cushions and chicken sandwiches appeared, as it were from heaven, and fell amongst us and our sheep. Perhaps as you are feeling better you would like one of the sandwiches?'

'Where is that young man? He is not dead?'

'Not at all. A little bruised, but nothing worse. He recovered before you, and feeling rather shaken he went off with the shepherds to have a drink at the inn. The coachman went with them.'

Djamileh ate another sandwich, brooding on Kayal's heartlessness.

'Listen,' she said, raising herself on one elbow. 'I have not time to tell you the whole of my history, which is long, and complicated with unheard-of misfortunes. Suffice it to say that I am young, beautiful, wealthy, well born, and accomplished, and the child of doting and distinguished parents. At their death I fell into the hands of an unscrupulous solicitor who, entirely against my will, married me to that young man you have seen. We had not been married for a day before he showed himself a monster of jealousy; and though my conduct has been unspotted as the snow he has continually belaboured me with threats and reproaches, and now has determined to shut me up, for ever, in a hermitage on the Caucasus mountains, inherited from a womanhating uncle (the whole family is very queer). We were on our way thither when, by the interposition of my good genius, the palanquin overturned, and we arrived among your flocks as we did.'

'Indeed,' replied the aged shepherdess. 'He said nothing of all that. But I do not doubt it. Men are a cruel and fantastic race. I too have lived a life chequered with many strange adventures and unmerited misfortunes. I was born in India, the child of a virtuous Brahmin and of a mother who had, before my birth, graced the world with eleven daughters, each lovelier than the last. In the opinion of many well-qualified persons, I, the youngest of her children, was even fairer —'

'I can well believe it,' said Djamileh. 'But, venerable Aunt, my misfortunes compel me to postpone the pleasure of hearing your story until a more suitable moment. It is, as you will see, essential that I should seize this chance of escaping from my tyrant. Here is a purse. I shall be everlastingly obliged if you will conduct me to the nearest livery-stables where I can hire a small chariot and swift horses.'

Though bruised and scratched, Djamileh was not much the worse for her sudden descent into the valley, and following the old shepherdess, who was as nimble as a goat, she scrambled up the precipice, and soon found herself in a hired chariot, driving at full speed towards the Castle of Shady Transports, clutching in her hot hand the key of the locked closet. Her impatience was indescribable, and as for her scruples and her good principles, they had vanished as though they had never been. Whether it was a slight concussion, or pique at hearing that Kayel had left her in order to go off and drink with vulgar shepherds, I do not pretend to say. But in any case, Djamileh had now but one thought, and that was to gratify her curiosity as soon as possible.

Botching up a pretext of having forgotten her jewellery, she hurried past the house steward and the slaves, refusing refreshment and not listening to a word they said. She ran to the west parlour, threw aside the embroidered hangings, opened the green baize door, flew up the winding stair and along the gallery.

But the door of the fifth closet had been burst open. It gave upon a sumptuous but dusky vacancy, an underground saloon of great size, walled with mosaics and inadequately lit by seven vast rubies hanging from the ceiling. A flight of marble steps led down to this apartment, and at the foot of the steps lay Kayel, groaning piteously.

'Thank heaven you've come! I've been here for the last half-hour, shouting at the top of my voice, and not one of these accursed slaves has come near me.'

'Oh, Kayel, are you badly hurt?'

'Hurt? I should think I've broken every bone in my body, and I know I've broken my collar-bone. I had to smash that door in, and it gave suddenly, and I pitched all the way down these steps. My second fall today — Oh!'

As she leaned over him the little golden key, forgotten and useless now, slid from her hand.

'My God, Djamileh! You've had that key all this time. And so *that* was why you came back?'

'Yes, Kayel. I came back to open the door. But you got here before me.'

And while that parry still held him she hastened to add:

'We have both behaved so shockingly that I don't think either of us had better reproach the other. So now let us see about your fracture.'

Not till the collar-bone was mending nicely; not till the coverlet which Djamileh had begun to knit as she sat by her husband's bedside, since knitting is always so soothing to invalids, was nearly finished; not till they had solved the last of the acrostics sent to them by a sympathizing Badruddin, did they mention the affair of the closet.

'How could I have the heart to leave you — you, looking so pale, and so appealing?' said Kayel suddenly.

'And the lies I told about you, Kayel, the moment I came to ... the things I said, the way I took away your character!'

'We must have been mad.'

'We were suffering from curiosity. That was all, but it was quite enough.'

'How terrible curiosity is, Djamileh ! Fiercer than lust, more ruthless than avarice —'

'Insatiable as man-eating tigers —'

'Insistent as that itching-powder one buys at low French fairs ... O Djamileh, let us vow never to feel curiosity again!'

'I made that vow long ago. You have seen what good it was.'

They meditated, gazing into each other's eyes.

'It seems to me, my husband, that we should be less

inquisitive if we had more to do. I think we should give up all our money, live in a village, and work all day in the fields.'

'That only shows, my dearest, that you have always lived in a town. The people who work all day in the fields will sit up all night in the hopes of discovering if their neighbour's cat has littered brindled or tortoiseshell kittens.'

They continued to interrogate each other's eyes.

'A man through whose garden flowed a violent water-course,' said Djamileh, 'complained one day to the stream: "O Stream, you have washed away my hollyhocks, swept off my artichokes, undermined my banks, flooded my bowling-green, and drowned my youngest son, the garland of my grey head. I wish, O Stream, that you would have the kindness to flow elsewhere." "That cannot be," replied the stream, "since Allah has bidden me to flow where I do. But if you were to erect a mill on your property, perhaps you would admit that I have my uses." In other words, Kayel, it seems to me that since we cannot do away with our curiosity, we had best sublimate it, and take up the study of a science.'

'Let it be astronomy,' answered Kayel. 'Of all sciences, it is the one least likely to intervene in our private life.'

To this day, though Bluebeard's daughter is forgotten, the wife of Kayel the Astronomer is held in remembrance. It was she whose sympathetic collaboration supported him through his researches into the Saturnian rings, it was she who worked out the mathematical calculations which enabled him to prove that the lost Pleiad would reappear in the year 1963. As time went on, and her grandchildren came clustering round the telescope, Djamileh's blue hair became silver; but to the day of her death her arched blue brows gave an appearance of alertness to her wrinkled countenance, and her teeth, glistening and perfect as in her girlhood, were shown off to the best advantage by the lining of her mouth, duskily blue as that of a well-bred chow-dog's.

Notes on the stories

BY KATE MACDONALD

1 The Kingdom of Elfin

This essay was first published in *Eve: The Lady's Pictorial*, 5 October 1927, 14–15.

Blake: presumably the poet and visionary William Blake (1757–1827).

the Brownies: Puck, according to Shakespeare, would hobnob with anyone; house fairies with an urge to complete unfinished domestic tasks overnight.

mess of pottage: in Genesis 25, verses 29–34, Esau sold his inheritance to his brother Jacob in return for a bowl of lentil stew. A fifteenth-century English interpretation referred to the lentils as 'a mess of pottage', and this has become a standard metaphor for an unequal and possibly foolish exchange.

vervain and dill: Warner was interested in herblore, corresponding with Elizabeth Wade White and others on American and English variations. Vervain and dill, however, do not appear to have any particular properties against witches.

Robert Wace: a Norman poet (c.1110–1174) and later Canon of Bayeux, most well-known now for his Arthurian poem the *Roman de Brut*.

Broceliande: a forest in Brittany, held to be a former fairy domain.

eke: also.

Robert Kirk: (1644–92) minister of the Church of Scotland in Aberfoyle, Perthshire, and a noted folklorist. He was the author of *The Secret Commonwealth* (collected 1691–92, published 1815), the first treatise on the lives and habits of fairies, witches and other supernatural manifestations.

Jonet Morisoune: quotation from *The Witch-Cult in Western Europe*, by Margaret Murray (1921) in Appendix I. The *Journal of the Sylvia Townsend Warner Society* (16:1, 2015) notes that Warner makes an error with the date: Jonet was accused in 1662.

Peeping Tom: a voyeur, a man who spies secretly on people for prurient pleasure.

ayah, amah, Coal-black Mammy: the latter term is undeniably racist but it is so out of kilter with Warner's tone here that the phrase could be read as an ironic quotation. In grouping a enslaved nurse with colonial nurse-servants she makes the point that the 'less sophisticated races' are those which have been colonised and enslaved by white westerners. It also makes an original ethnographic point that humans need to consider that they may be seen by fairies as no more than an enslaved race.

bovine: like a cow, obedient and unthinking, essentially food on legs.

lying-in woman: a lactating woman hired to breastfeed the infant child of a noblewoman in the mother's stead. This function was often combined with being the child's nurse.

Waldron: George Waldron (c. 1690–1730), poet, commissioner of excise and author of, among other works, *A Description of the Isle of Man* (1731), which contains a lengthy chapter on fairies. His Works were published by his widow in the year of his death.

Pomponius Mela: (died c. 45 CE), wrote the only Classical discussion of geography in Latin.

Bertrand du Guesclin: (c.1320–80) A Breton nobleman, and Constable of France under Charles V.

'Laquelle avoit ... d'astronomie': '[She] was about four-and-twenty, had never once married, and was good and docile, and much gifted in the art of astronomy'.

Guy de Lusignan: (1150–94), a knight of Poitou, a Crusader, and briefly King of both Jerusalem and Cyprus. He led a colourful life. Sir Walter Scott's *Minstrelsy of the Scottish Border* (1802–03) made Guy's connection to Melusine widely known.

2 Narrative of Events Preceding the Death of Queen Ermine

Yule log: an unburned piece of the last year's Yule log, which was to be used to start the fire for this season's Yule.

Snapdragon: a sixteenth-century party game for winter which involved placing raisins on the surface of a bowl of brandy, setting the brandy alight, and then retrieving the raisins with the lights out.

wassailed: it is still an English West Country tradition to serenade orchards of cider-producing apple trees with songs and rhymes on Twelfth Night (6 January) to encourage a good harvest in the year to come.

to exhibit his profile: to put his nose in the air.

pace: Latin for 'with respect to', 'referring to'.

the bag: hunting term meaning the number of creatures killed during the sport.

naked women: until the 1842 Miners and Collieries Act British women worked in coal mines pulling carts, and were notoriously liable to do this work semi-naked due to the intense heat underground.

scamped: did the work poorly, partially, or failed to do any at all.

dues: their tithe, or their rent.

rheumatism: a painful condition of the joints that could be relieved with a warmer climate or hot conditions, presumably by reducing the inflammation.

pepper-castor: a shaker for ground pepper, ie the unfamiliar sight of a bell tower on a church.

Hungary water: a medicinal distillation made of rosemary in wine or brandy, used as a cure-all.

Jefferson: Thomas Jefferson (1743-1826), one of the Founding Fathers of the United States of America, had a palatial estate called Monticello.

3 Queen Mousie

pasquinade: a satirical attack in writing on a particular person, displayed in public.

whaup: Scots for a curlew.

the Killing Times: during the 1680s in Scotland fierce persecution of the Covenanters and other Presbyterians led to deaths and martyrdoms, over the rule of Scotland by the Calvinist Church of Scotland (Calvinism derived from the writing of John Calvin of Geneva), or by the Crown and the Established Church (Oxford had been Charles I's base during the English Civil Wars and represented the heartland of Anglicanism).

perukes: powdered curled wigs for men.

sotto voce: a lowered voice.

4 An Improbable Story

Styria: now south-eastern Austria, and parts of former Yugoslavia and Slovenia.

Tamarind: a leading character in 'The Power of Cookery', in Warner's *Kingdoms of Elfin*. He claimed to come from the Kingdom of Tishk, and thus gained admittance to the Drieviertelstein court.

le phlegme anglais: English phlegm, or *sang-froid* and coolness.

surtout: French for 'above all' or 'over all', used to name an eighteenth-century man's overcoat or frock-coat, first worn over a uniform.

spittoon: a vessel to receive the results of spitting, which was a necessity when chewing tobacco.

bowdlerise: Thomas Bowdler famously published a censored edition of Shakespeare's plays, in 1807, and has given his name to the process of unnecessary artistic sanitisation or expurgation.

bolster: a long cyclindrical pillow the width of a bed, used to prop oneself up while sleeping, in addition to or in place of a pillow. Usually more hard than yielding.

mutes: hired professional mourners, wearing black and looking severely sad. They say nothing.

5 The Duke of Orkney's Leonardo

born with a caul: born with a membrane covering his face, an uncommon occurrence.

Sir Glamie: a protagonist in 'The Late Sir Glamie' in *Kingdoms of Elfin*.

Ossian: a fabled poet of the third century CE whose works were published in 1760 by James Macpherson. He turned out to have been their author and the inventor of the revived Ossian myth.

bitch: in the sense that she is behaving like a mother dog, constantly on the look out for her charges' welfare and comfort, whether they want it or not.

blowflies: a particularly horrible kind of parasite, that lays its eggs in an open wound.

Jew's-ears: a common edible bracket-shaped fruiting fungus commonly found on elder, the tree from which Judas Iscariot was supposed to have hung himself.

despatched: killed.

wimple: a cloth scarf worn to cover the head and neck, leaving the face clear.

6 Stay, Corydon, Thou Swain

puggy: stumpy.

vicar-choral: a vicar appointed specifically to sing parts of the church service where choral worship is characteristic for that congregation, eg in a cathedral.

Wesley: 'Ascribe Unto the Lord', using words from Psalm 96.

Dissenter: as Mr Mulready worships in a Bethel Chapel, he is a Nonconformist and a Dissenter from the rulings of the Church of England. While these terms are from the seventeenth century, theological arguments still ran wild through the Established and Nonconformist variants of Protestantism in the United Kingdom in the nineteenth century, when this story is set.

dipped: Baptists are welcomed into the Baptist congregation by full immersion in a specially built bath in the church.

Stay, Corydon, Thou Swain: a madrigal by Wilbye from the very late sixteenth century.

> Stay, Corydon, thou swain,
> Talk not so soon of dying:
> What though thy heart be slain,
> What though thy love be flying?
> She threatens thee, but dares not strike,
> Thy nymph is light and shadow-like;
> For if thou follow her, she'll fly from thee;
> But if thou fly from her, she'll follow thee.

high-flier: lives a fast and exciting life, and is likely to come to a slightly disgraceful end.

almanac: an annual book of useful household knowledge, facts and wisdom, sometimes also with prophecies and puzzles, depending on its quality. Formerly very popular among the barely literate as a principal source of knowledge.

flannel and sarcenet: fabrics used for home dress-making.

stay-laces: the hard-wearing laces that held corsets and stays in place around the body.

tarnished snow: old white blackthorn blossom.

7 Introduction

This house is based on Frankfort Manor in Norfolk, where Warner and Valentine Ackland lived from 1933 to 1934. There they gardened and nurtured their cats, until the arrival of an inexplicable plague which killed many local animals and all but one of their cats.

mullions and transoms: mullions are the stone uprights separating the panes of glass in the windows of old stone houses, transoms are the horizontal pieces separating the window from the wall.

cobbily: like a cob horse, sturdy with short legs.

loose-boxes: formerly occupied by horses, unharnessed.

Aesop: slave and storyteller in classical Greece, purported to be the author of the Fables.

The Cat on the Dovrefell: a traditional Norwegian fairytale, also known as 'The Cat on the Dovre Mountain' and 'The Trolls and the Pussycat'.

Perrault: Charles Perrault (1628–1703), French author and adapter of traditional tales, most famous for his retelling of Cinderella, and an important source for modern western fairy tales.

declassé: reduced in social status.

teased: nagged, pestered.

shanachie: from the Gaelic for a traditional storyteller, a seanchaidh or seanchaí.

Marshak: Samuil Yakovlevik Marshak (1887–1964), a Russian and Soviet author and translator of children's literature.

The History of Little Henry and His Bearer: a much-translated children's story by Mary Martha Sherwood, first published in 1814, notable for its imperialist and evangelising themes.

urtext: an unknown text that is deduced to have existed from the later texts that are held to have descended from it.

Havelock Ellis: (1859–1939), a leading English authority in the study of human sexuality. In 1936 Warner wrote in a letter that she was looking for a copy of his *Studies in the Psychology of Sex* for a present, 'that I enjoyed a great deal when I was young' (quoted in Peter Haring Judd, *The Akeing Heart. Letters between Sylvia Townsend Warner, Valentine Ackland and Elizabeth Wade White*, 2018, 218). At that date it was unavailable in the UK.

pother: archaic form of 'bother'.

Extra judice: outside the jurisdiction of the law.

Joanna Southcott: (1750–1814) an eighteenth-century visionary and prophet with a large following, who left instructions that after her death her sealed box of prophecies should not be opened except during a national crisis in the presence of twenty-four bishops. There has been dispute over the whereabouts of the box for over a century.

murrain: a medieval term for, variously, an epidemic, death itself, and a range of infectious diseases liable to attack animals, humans and crops.

Eothen: *Eothen, or, Traces of travel brought home from the East* (1844) by Alexander William Kinglake (1809–91) was a work of Eastern travel describing a journey had had made with a friend through Syria, Palestine and Egypt.

8 Odin's Birds

leman: medieval Scots for mistress or bed-partner.

9 The Castle of Carabas

rampings: its fierce upright struttings, undoubtedly with claws out and a big grin.

motive: motif.

hatchment: a large black-bordered lozenge- or square-shaped wooden plaque bearing the heraldric device and motto of the family. Seventeenth- and eighteenth-century examples may be found on display in older estate churches.

gato: Spanish for cat.

Mon amie ... l'enfant: My dear, not in front of the child. French was conventionally used in western (but not French, obviously) upper-class families to say things that the children and servants were not to understand.

el combatidor: the warrior.

the Albigenses, the Cathari, and the Manichees: adherents to three of the principal Roman Catholic heresies.

holds the pyx: as the priest holds the vessel containing the Eucharist or consecrated Host during the Mass.

Roncesvalles: in Navarre, the site of the famous battle of 778 when Roland was killed as part of Charlemagne's rearguard.

el traidor: the traitor.

10 Virtue and the Tiger

strophe: a structural part of a poem, for instance a stanza.

11 The Magpie Charity

of the finest water: of the highest quality and value.

indigent: poor, in want.

Nigger: now considered offensive, this term was in common use in the 1940s when Warner was writing these stories. Its use in this story, to name a black cat, may also be seen as a commentary on the state's reluctance to give relief to those who most deserve it.

12 The Fox-Pope

Nolo episcopari: the formal refusal by a candidate when offered a bishopric. Three refusals indicated that he, or she, was serious.

Nonpareil: an Incomparable.

Waller: Edmund Waller (1606–87), an English poet, who wrote the song which begins 'Go, lovely Rose / Tell her that wastes her time and me'.

missish: tiresomely coy, playing at refusal.

Formosus: (c. 816–896), Pope from 891 to 896 with a peculiarly tumultuous reign. His exhumed body was put on trial for his political misjudgements.

13 The Phoenix

Cochin-China: a large feather-legged chicken reared for display and exhibitions, with striking bronze and black plumage.

du Barry: Madame du Barry (1743–93), a great French courtesan of the pre-Revolutionary period and *maitresse-en-titre* of Louis XV.

She was notorious for her personal extravagance and love of excess in clothes and lifestyle.

14 Apollo and the Mice

husbandman: farmer, smallholder.

Latona: or Leto, a Titan and the mother of Apollo and of Artemis.

16 The Two Mothers

coronach: Gaelic for the improvised singing at a funeral.

Dulce et decorum est: part of a now famous line by the Roman poet Horace, 'Dulce et decorum est pro patria mori', translated as 'It is sweet and proper to die for one's country'. Its use in the First World War poem by Wilfred Owen reframed the line as a sardonic commentary on the sacrifice of the young by the decisions of the old.

17 The Donkey's Providence

the grinders cease because they are few: from Ecclesiastes 12.3.

21 Bread for the Castle

department of Lot: the regional division in the mid-south-west of France.

maslin: country bread made of mixed grains, whereas the Castle would only have white bread, and patisserie.

Carmagnole: a song, and dance, of the French Revolution, triumphing over the deposed King and Queen.

Où donc sont mes amours? Où, où? Hou-hou-hou!: Where now are my loves? Where, oh where? To whit, tu whoo.

22 Popularity

Wolf of Gévaudan: the Beast of Gévaudan was a wolf that terrorised the population of Gévaudan in the south of France in the eighteenth century.

23 Bluebeard's Daughter

ghazal: a type of love poem in the Arabic tradition.

laterals: branches growing perpendicular to the ground.